THE

Playmaker

J. B. CHEANEY

A Dell Yearling Book

With thanks to Mary Flower for her expert advice.

Published by
Dell Yearling
an imprint of
Random House Children's Books
a division of Random House, Inc.
1540 Broadway
New York, New York 10036

Visit us on the Web! www.randomhouse.com/kids

Educators and librarians, for a variety of teaching tools, visit us at www.randomhouse.com/teachers

ISBN: 0-440-41710-4

Reprinted by arrangement with Alfred A. Knopf

Printed in the United States of America

First Yearling edition February 2002

10 9 8 7 6 5 4 3 2

To Mama, who always knew I could do it.

Contents

It has been said that the past is like a foreign country—"they do things differently there." One of the most obvious differences between Elizabethan society and ours is the mixing of religion and politics. The 1500s was the century of the Protestant Reformation, which began in Germany and spread throughout the continent over the next fifty years. King Henry VIII made England a Protestant nation in 1534 simply by breaking away from Rome, confiscating papal lands and property, and establishing the Church of England with himself as the head. That did not quite settle the issue, however. A few years after Henry died, his oldest daughter, Mary, made a violent attempt to restore Catholicism by closing Protestant churches and executing Protestant leaders. But when Mary died and her half sister Elizabeth became Queen in 1558, England swung back to Protestantism.

There was no such thing as "separation of church and state" at this time. Every citizen belonged to the Church of England at birth and was expected to attend all worship services. To be a Catholic was to be a suspected traitor. At the time our story begins, Elizabeth is sixty-four (quite elderly, for that time) and has no children or close relatives. Nor has she chosen anyone to rule England after her death, and this is a matter of grave concern. Many Protestants fear that if the Queen dies before naming a successor, unscrupulous Catholics might maneuver some "closet papist" to the throne. That fear, in some circles, borders on paranoia.

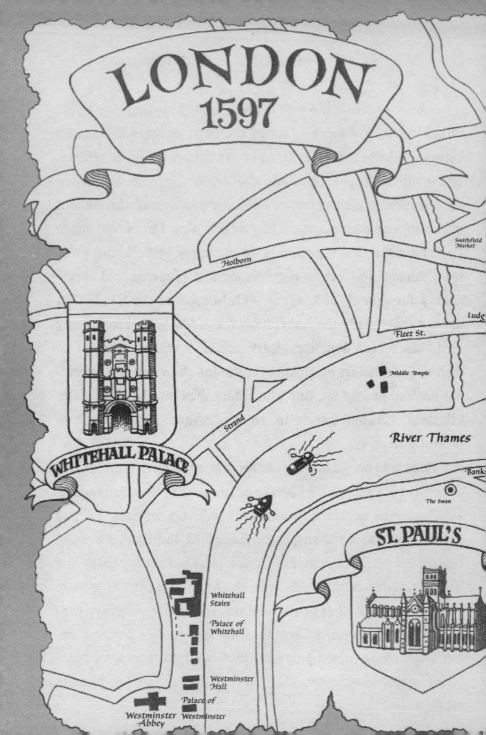

THE CITY

❖

Smithfield once blazed with burning martyrs.
An English boy of any education whatever knows that.
During the days of Bloody Queen Mary, who hoped to
restore a Catholic kingdom on our island, Protestants
were burned by the dozens on stakes erected in
Smithfield market, just outside the walls of London.
Of course, Mary had been dead these forty years and
England was safely delivered from the Pope's clutches
by our gracious Queen, Elizabeth. But Smithfield
surprised me nonetheless. From childhood I had
devoured Foxe's *Book of Martyrs,* with its bloody
tales of the tortures inflicted on Protestants in this
very place—I expected it to be grim or solemn. But
when I topped the rise near the Red Bull tavern, a
lively scene leapt into view—a clash of color and

sound that appeared to jump up and down and wave like a flag under the clear April sky. It took my breath away. For a moment I stared, my heart pounding in my ears. Then I shifted my pack from one weary shoulder to the other and pressed on, with the sensation of plunging into turbulent waves.

My progress slowed as the crowd thickened and vendors pushed their wares at me: goodwives offering apples and sausages, noisy apprentices hawking every sort of useless trinket, a fish-monger who all but hit me over the head with a flounder. I hesi-tated before a pastry seller, moved on a few steps, drifted back, and finally laid out a half-pence from my carefully guarded hoard for a small meat pie. The seller would swear only that it was meat, and would not say what kind, but my hunger was such that I gobbled half of it straightaway, then wrapped the rest in my handkerchief. I had learned to stretch food as long as possible and besides, half was all I could hold. Five days of eating catch-as-catch-can on the road had shrunk my stomach to the size of a fist.

"The mighty Benjamin! A farthing will make him dance, good folk, only a farthing!" A lean man in leather made this cry in a hoarse voice as he twirled a red stick over his head. Looming shadow-like behind him stood the biggest bear I had ever seen, tied to a stout pole set in the ground. I stopped to gawk at him as a nursemaid with two squealing children in tow handed a farthing to his keeper. Then the beast turned his head my way.

His eyes caught and held me. A bear's eyes are black and tiny as beads, or so they appear in the vastness of a round, furry face.

With his frayed leather collar attached to the chain that secured him, this one appeared more comical than dangerous: a grandfather of bears with dark brown fur silvered at the tips. As his keeper tapped the ground with the red stick, Benjamin shuffled through a lumbering dance, drawing a circle of onlookers. Once the performance ended, he took the nuts and crusts thrown to him with lordly indifference. But to me, he smiled.

Or perhaps the smile was only a fancy, for the moment I imagined seeing it, it was gone. But one thing sure: in the commotion of Smithfield market, in the shrill of vendors and din of penned-up livestock, it was me the beast sought out. The glint in those buttony eyes drew me in, and I was hardly aware of my own feet until I stood scarcely a yard from him. Then, quickly and without malice, he lifted a heavy paw and raked the knitted cap off my head. I felt the force behind that blow, and knew that only a slight shift in aim could have taken off my face. A rude laugh went up from the onlookers roundabout.

"Nah, nah, young master," said the keeper, easing me back with his stick, "Mind ye no' step too close. 'E's fiercer than 'e looks, aye, Benjamin? Give yon lad his covering back."

The bear had set my cap on his own head, to the vast amusement of the crowd. My face burned, for I realized I had been cozened into the show.

"Here, Benjamin." The laughter died as my voice rang out, steady as nerves alone could make it. A quarter of the meat pie trembled in my outstretched palm; his nose twitched as the smell

3

reached it. "Swap my cap for what's of more use to you, and let us be friends."

The offer met with approval, both from the bear and the onlookers. "There's a bold lad," ran the general refrain, while Benjamin gently cadged the morsel in his cracked yellow claws and suffered the cap to be lifted off his head by his keeper's stick. The man renewed his cries in praise of "The mighty Benjamin! A farthing will make him dance. . . ." I adjusted my pack again and gave the bear a last look. But his eyes were restless, already seeking out another cap to lift from an unwary head.

Directly before me loomed the thick gray walls of the city and the towering arch of Newgate. A stony chill fell upon me as I passed through the gate, trailing its long finger down my back as I moved out of its shadow. Then I stepped into a broad swathe of sunlight and blinked with amazement, overcome for the moment. I had arrived: this color, this clamor, this dust, stink, and roar, was London.

As I gazed around me like an idiot, a hard object struck the side of my head and bounced on the cobbled street. It was a piece of biscuit, as hard as any stone. "Ahoy, green lad!" called a coarse voice above my head. I glanced up to a row of narrow, barred windows, where a hand on a hairy forearm was waving. I could scarcely make out a face in the shadows. "You want a job?" Immediately the neighboring windows thronged with the thieves and ruffians of Newgate Prison, beseeching me to fetch them nuts and cheese and pints of ale, jeering when I shook my head and backed away.

"Watch your feet, boy," shouted one, "or we'll look to see you here with us!"

Such warnings were wasted on me. Though poor, I was well brought up and incorrigibly honest. Or so I thought at the time.

I was scarcely out of earshot from the gaol when a shop girl danced up to me, slender and graceful at a distance but riddled with pockmarks close up. Braying through horsy teeth, she shook a crosstree before my face, its branches rattling. "Beads! Wooden beads! Brass beads! Did you ever see the like? Beads for your lady-love!"

"I have no lady-love," I said, my head spinning with all the new sights packed into it. Otherwise I would have realized that she knew that already. I was not much to look at—never tall, and now underfed, with wide staring eyes that made me seem younger than my fourteen years.

"No lady-love? A likely fellow such as you?" Even I caught the mockery in this; as I moved to pass her, she added quickly, "Your mother, then. Your mother would want to know you've not forgot her."

I spun around. My mouth opened but no sound emerged— exactly as if an invisible hand had closed over my throat and squeezed hard. This was an affliction that had beset me since childhood: in moments of extreme feeling, I literally could not speak. Mother used to say that my eyes spoke for me at such times, but if they talked now, it was not in a language the bead seller understood. Her pitted forehead wrinkled in bewilderment as I labored to spit out two words. "H-how m-m-much?"

"Ha'penny for the wood, twopence for the brass."

I groped in the leather pouch at my belt and came up with a penny, which I offered to her. She looked at it with suspicion, as though I'd shaved it. "But it's two for the—"

I pointed to a string of painted wooden beads whose colors—blue and white with a soft, pearly luster—pleased me most.

"But I can't change a penny," she whined.

"K-k-keep it." I plucked the string of beads from their hook and turned away. My mother was barely a week in her grave.

I gripped the beads so hard they touched bone, thinking, I'll not forget you, ever. Nor desert you. Ever.

Not like *he* did.

My mother's illness was short, which may have been a blessing. One day she was queasy, the next faint; the third she took to her bed, and four days later departed this life for the next. Sir John Hawthorne, whom she had served as housekeeper, was not generous with the time he allowed his servants to be off work; he seemed to begrudge even the week she took to die, to say nothing of the labor lost by my sister, Susanna, and me while we tended her. Mother fretted over burdening us. Poor lady—I would have traded a year in purgatory for each additional day that I could sit by the bed, to hold her hand and spoon broth between her lips and sing back the Psalms she had taught me.

Rebekah Malory was her name. Rebekah Malory, Rebekah Malory—oft on my journey to London I caught myself saying it aloud, as if the sound alone could keep some part of her living still.

Sir John offered the position of housekeeper to Susanna at half the pay plus board. But there was no place for me, who had served him as a stable boy since I was old enough to shovel dung. All of England was suffering hard times after three years of bad harvests, and Sir John had no choice but to let me go. Not a tender man, but fair in his way, he'd slipped a silver sixpence into my palm with a furtive, sideways motion, as if his right hand truly did not know what the left was doing. "No hard feelin's, Richard, and I'm sorry about yer mother, God rest her soul, but the truth is you've been a burden for the last twelvemonth. I'd give you a hoe and set you in the field, but there's three lads had to be uprooted even there, you see. London's the place; I've been there twice meself. A word to the wise: don't ever eat with a fork. It's a fiendish device brought on us by the French, to make honest Englishmen poke out their eyes." Then he sent me off with an encouraging slap on the back that rattled my shoulder blades.

So I had turned my face toward London, only to be knocked off my course, moments after arriving, by a few chance words about my mother. For at least an hour after the encounter with the bead seller I wandered aimlessly, seeing much, understanding little, too confounded even to get my bearings and ask directions to Abbot Lane. Somewhere in the neighborhood of St. Paul's, two passing boys spotted the beads dangling from my hand.

"Yah!" piped one, a lad no older than twelve. "A murdering papist, then!"

"He's some gall, ha'nt he?" remarked his companion, "Waving a rosary about as if he'd a right to."

I hastily tucked the beads between the buttons of my doublet. "'Tis no rosary," was my protest. "I just bought them—"

But my explanation landed on deaf ears; these lads were in search of adventure, not enlightenment. Hearing in my voice the broad accents of the country, they fell upon me with a cry, not reckoning on the pack that held all my possessions. I swung the same, and caught the larger of the two square on his ear with all the force of its contents, which included a New Testament, a copy of Horace, and a Lyly's Latin grammar. I dealt the other boy a blow to the stomach with my stable-hand fist, and when he doubled over, I dodged away and sprinted down the busy cobbled street. I was not quite so puny as I looked, and necessity lent me speed.

After three or four turns down side streets I had shaken their pursuit and got myself winded as well as lost. A narrow alley beside an eel-seller's stall offered a place of rest and concealment while I took another look at those beads. Four blues alternated with two whites all the way around the string. It was not the proper sequence for a rosary, and the thought that anyone would take me for a Catholic stunned me. But then, I had never been a stranger before. Everyone in my home town knew me; in London, no one did. For all that anyone knew, I might be a Spanish agent, a cutpurse, a conspirator, a grave-robber, a rowdy, or any sort of public nuisance. Some might find it exhilarating, to start over and cast themselves anew in any mold they chose. But the very thought frightened me.

When I could breathe easier, I took out my wallet—nothing

more than a strip of soft leather folded once lengthwise and then in thirds across. In it were some personal papers, including a testimony from the rector of our village, which began, "To the reader: Be it known that Richard Malory, late of Alford in Lincolnshire, is of honest disposition and industrious habits . . ." I read the entire letter in that stinking London alley, as though to reassure myself that I was indeed the boy who could read Caesar and write a fair hand and quote scripture like a divinity student. Thus affirmed, I replaced the letter in my wallet, added the beads, folded it all up carefully, and tucked it away in my doublet. I finished off the last of the meat pie, washing it down with a half-pennyworth of ale, and set forth at last on my business.

On the day before she died, my mother had given me some words of counsel. Her hot hand seemed to weigh even now on my sleeve, gripping with unexpected force as she whispered, "When you get to London"—I leaned close, for her voice was failing and she had to rest after every phrase—"you must find . . . Martin Feather. On Abbot Lane, in Cheapside. Whether he's still there. . . I know not. But he was there . . . four years ago."

Four years ago was when she heard last from my father, who abandoned us when Susanna and I were very small. To say that she had heard from *him* may be overstating the case—we heard only from ten shillings sent by the hand of one Martin Feather, attorney. The money was not talkative; it merely muttered that my father, Robert Malory, was in London, at least at that time, and had come by a fair sum, which he entrusted to a lawyer to pass on to

9

his family. These tokens of support came to us now and again in the years following his departure, prompted either by a generous nature or a guilty conscience. But after the ten shillings sent by way of Martin Feather, the trickle had dried up altogether.

We knew nothing of this Martin Feather beyond his occupation and address, and could not guess his relation to my father. If I could not find him, there was one other possible source of aid. "If all else fails . . . ," Mother had whispered, "you may seek out your aunt."

"Anne Billings?" I asked, hesitantly.

"Aye," she said. "Anne Billings of Southwark. But do not apply to her unless you are starving, or—" Here she broke off in a coughing fit, and when she was quiet again I feared to pursue the subject. There was no love between her and my father's sister, though the meat of their quarrel was a mystery to me. Martin Feather sounded more promising: if nothing else, an attorney would be a useful man to know in London. Mother hoped for more—she hoped that the attorney would take me on as a clerk of some sort. I suppose she shared in the fond hopes of mothers everywhere that her boy should become a man of some account; a lawyer would do. Her family had respectable roots and she had seen to it that I received the best education our little village in Lincolnshire could supply. As a result I shined up well against the country oafs, but Lincolnshire is not London. This became plain to me once I began asking directions of Londoners and received, from all manner of folk down to the lowliest apprentice, that unmistakable look that a superior being bestows upon a . . . country oaf.

I turned east under the shadow of St. Paul's Cathedral, with its towering walls and buttresses. Just beyond St. Paul's, the narrow cobbled lane widens into Cheapside—the backbone of London, with counting houses, taverns, and shops of every description. The businesses are located at street level, with living quarters in the second or third storeys that jut out over the street and cut off great slices of sunlight.

Cheapside ends in three forks. Between two of these rises the Royal Exchange: a huge brick building with a lofty tower and wide doors where merchants and buyers pour in and out like ants, all day long. In this neighborhood I finally located Abbot Lane: one of the countless narrow, unpaved byways that make London a maze to rival the Minotaur's. The lane reeked with the slops of kitchen and sewer; I wondered how anyone could live in such a stench. Taking shallow breaths, I groped my way in the gloom to a half-timbered house with a red door and an outside staircase. The steps ended on a landing, where a small brass plate quietly announced that Martin Feather, Gentleman, dwelled within. Trembling with exhaustion and hunger and no little fear, I lifted the latch on the oak door and let myself into a cold, empty gallery with wide windows overlooking the street below.

Before knocking at the inner door, I took a moment to finger-brush my hair, which is reddish and springy and refuses to lie flat. Then I straightened my doublet and squared the threadbare elbows out of sight and looked to see that all the buttons held fast. It was my best item of clothing and made me look sober and industrious even though the seams were beginning to stretch. In the quiet, my ears picked up a rustling sound from the inner rooms. At my knock, the noise abruptly ceased. A pause stretched out before the rustling started again, louder this time. I heard the scrape of furniture being moved, then quick steps on a wooden floor, and felt an absurd impulse to run. The bolt shot back with a clang and the door creaked on its hinges. A sharp breath caught in my throat and lodged there.

But the face that gazed at me from the doorway was mild as milk: one of those faces that seems neither old nor young, with round blue eyes blinking behind round glass spectacles and a wide mouth opened in query; the furrowed brow of a sage and smooth cheeks of a baby. He looked every inch the lawyer, from the soles of his velvet slippers to the flat top of his cap with its silk tassel hanging down the right side of his face. One arm clutched a heavy book. Even at full height he stood only an inch or two taller than me. "Yes? What is it?"

I cleared my throat. "Are you—Am I addressing Martin Feather?"

"No, lad, you're not. You are addressing a lowly clerk in his employ." He stepped over the threshold, turned, and locked the door behind him with an iron key. "Master Feather is abroad for the month on business. If you will return around the first of May, and are prepared to wait for the better part of the day, I'm sure he can accommodate you—eventually. But you must apply to his chambers at Middle Temple, not his residence."

"Oh!"

The clerk, who had stopped to tie on a pair of wooden pattens to protect his slippers from road dust, must have heard the distress in my voice. He looked up. I saw enough interest in that look to blurt out, "But I'll starve before then! That is . . . I'm new in London, Your Honor. From the country. I was hoping for a position."

He studied me a moment longer and I began to feel a peculiar leaning toward him. This happens with the rare stranger— something in the look, or the tilt of the head, or even the set of the shoulders, that lets you know here's someone a bit like you. Someone whose spirit, in an inward place not immediately apparent, bears an uncommon resemblance to yours. Perhaps he felt it, too. One eyebrow rose. "Come along, lad. I'm in haste but you can walk with me."

By now dusk had fallen and the street population had thickened; we felt the force of it when we turned off Abbot Lane onto Cheapside. Since my clerk's business was taking him east, we found ourselves battling the tide that flowed from the Royal Exchange. Almost everyone traveled on foot, though here and there a great Lord or wealthy merchant glanced haughtily down from horseback. Sedan chairs carrying jeweled ladies appeared to float above the crowd, swaying gracefully—until I saw one tilt at a perilous angle when the foremost carrier stepped in a pothole, and its elegant cargo swore fit to blister my ears. My companion paid no heed to these amazing sights and sounds. "So," he remarked, in a quiet but carrying voice, "you wish to enter the law, hey? Do you value your life so little?"

"How is that, sir?"

"Why, in any London uprising the battle cry is, 'First, we kill the lawyers!'" At my puzzled look, he explained. "Just a line from a play, lad. My fellow clerks are not amused by it. I take it you read and write?"

"I do, sir. Our village rector credits me with a fairer hand than his."

"How's your Latin?"

"Passable, sir. The rector says I learned all he could teach me, and that readily."

"Where lives this admiring rector, then?" I heard the amusement in his voice and thought it best to trim my sails.

"Just a trifling place in Lincolnshire, sir. Village of Alford."

"Ah." He glanced my way. "Did you say your name, lad?"

"No, sir. 'Tis Richard Malory, sir."

My companion stumbled in his clumsy wooden pattens, striking the beefy arm of a leather-clad carter, which sent his book and papers flying. A bloody curse escaped him, and as we scrambled for the spilled papers his swearing continued, with some invention I thought: "By all the spiteful, sportive spirits—By the milk-white hands of the Virgin Mary—"

"Here, sir." I gathered all the loose papers I could reach and handed them over. He stuffed them into what I had thought was a book, but was actually a worn leather portfolio stamped with a rose.

"By the tortured Greek syntax of St. Paul!" He straightened, his

14

tassel bouncing with the emphatic shake of his head, clutching another sheaf of papers. I spied one more, which a cart had just run over, and picked it up. While glancing over the damage, I chanced to read some of the words on it: "By order of Philip Shackleford, Lord H—"

His hand came down on my wrist, gripping so hard I cried out. "Did your rector not teach you manners, then?"

"Yes, sir. F-forgive me, sir." He let go of my wrist to snatch the paper. Then he riffled through the contents of the portfolio with a distressed look and surveyed the area once more. Any loose papers would already have been trampled to shreds.

"No lasting harm done, then, just the usual dung and filth." His words rolled blandly, but he was nearly panting, as though he'd just come off a run. As for me, I kept my eyes on the ground, chafing my wrist. He was stronger than he looked. "Well—Richard, did you say? We must part soon, but let me offer a word of advice."

He continued his progress and I fell in beside him as before— unwilling to part company, but now rather wary of him, too.

"Is your heart set upon the law?" he asked.

"I . . . don't know, sir." Strangely, this was a question I had never pondered. "My mother thought it would suit me."

"Your mother. That's ofttimes the case. Well, would she be heartbroken if you chose another profession?"

I swallowed. "Not likely, sir. She's dead."

"I see." He stopped, and turned to me, and in one keen look seemed to grasp everything there was to know about that simple statement. Once again I felt that pull toward him, an inclination that defied reason. After a moment he nodded briefly, then walked on. I blessed him for saying no more. In my present condition, weak and weary and dispirited, any expression of sympathy might have reduced me to a puddle on the street. "You will wonder at what I'm going to tell you now, Richard, but trust me on it, as far as you can trust a stranger. It is this: do not attempt to join yourself to Martin Feather."

"Sir?"

We had reached the end of the lane, and my companion drew off a little from me, as if determined that here our ways should part. "I can tell you no more than this: he is a . . . precarious person to know. Even this much is in confidence—keep it close."

"What am I to do, then?" I blurted. "I must have a position!"

"Of course. Of course." He rubbed one side of his nose with an ink-stained finger, in the manner of certain scholarly men when they are thinking. I gazed upon that finger as though expecting my salvation to come from it. "Here is what you can do, and it may not suit you for the present, but times are hard. It will put bread in your mouth, and that's your chief concern, if I read you rightly. So tomorrow morning go down to Thames Street—hard by the river—and follow it east of the Bridge. Look amongst the wharves and warehouses there and you'll find the house of Motheby and Southern, Wine Merchants. I am aware that they could use a dock-hand. Yes, I can see you are too fine for that, but keep your wits about you and a better position will come your way."

He had misread the dismayed look on my face. It was not that I considered myself too fine for dock work, or not much—only too soft. "But sir—"

"Not that it matters overmuch to me." He hiked the furred collar of his black robe higher on one shoulder. "Do as you will, but if tomorrow finds you before Messieurs Motheby and Southern, tell them Peter Kenton sent you. I am not Peter Kenton, mind, only an acquaintance of his, but we'll consider you sent by proxy, hey?" He smiled then: a broad triangular smile marred only a little by his bad teeth. It went through me like a dart: a smile of naked collaboration, as though we two were snugged together in a plot. Yet my wrist was still throbbing. His humor was as unpredictable as Benjamin the bear's; as quickly as the smile appeared, it was gone. "Peace to you, Richard. Perhaps we will meet again."

"Wait!" In something of a panic, I grasped for another moment with him. He paused, yards away, his head tilted in a way that had already become familiar to me. "Might I have your name, too, sir?"

He shook his head. "My name would mean nothing to them. Just remember Peter Kenton's. And hold a moment—" He fumbled about in his robe for a coin. "Here's a half-groat. 'Twill get you lodging for the night, and a meal. The East Cheap taverns are a fair lot taken by and large, but hold on to your purse."

I caught the coin he tossed to me, and realized at once, by its feel and heft, that it was no groat. Indeed, it was an entire shilling, which would support me for a week if I took care of it. He must have known; it was as likely to mistake one for the other as to take a stone for bread. "Sir! Wait—"

But he had already turned his back and disappeared, and the populace closed like a door upon the most generous man in London. Your name would have meant something to *me*, I thought forlornly. And at that moment, I felt far more desolate than if we had never met.

A TOKEN

*M*otheby and Southern looked me over carefully. One was round and pale, the other thin and red, but in expression they were brothers. Both regarded me with the pursed-up, squinty look a housewife might bestow on a fish that was almost spoiled. "I didn't know Kenton was in the city," said Motheby to Southern.

"Nor I," said Southern to Motheby. "I've seen him not since March. He owes us five shillings."

"Five shillings? For what?"

"To be truthful," I offered, "I've never met Master Kenton, exactly. 'Twas a friend of his who sent me here."

"A friend?" said Motheby to Southern. "That waggish fop has friends?"

"He's right about the one thing," said Southern to Motheby. "We are short of dockers, by at least two."

"What mean you by two? I thought 'twas only one got his head knocked last week."

"There was another, drowned in a rain barrel Saturday last. Overindulged, I take it."

"Ah wine, wine." Southern, the stout one, shook his head. "How deceitful its charm."

"I can read and write," I put in desperately, "and cipher as well, if you need a clerk."

Motheby turned to Southern. "Do we need a clerk?"

"Our clerks keep their noggins in one piece and out of the water. We need hands, not heads."

"Here are two, then." I produced mine, hard enough after years of forking hay and shoveling dung, though I could see they were not overly taken with the rest of me.

"What do you think?" put Southern to Motheby.

"He's a fair-spoken lad."

"Much use we have for that!"

"Seems willing, though. Bright."

"Very well, boy." Master Southern addressed me for the first time since our interview began. "We shall put you on for board and lodging, and fourpence a week after trial. If it appears you will suit, we'll draw up the papers two weeks hence. Are we agreed?"

It seemed the best offer I could get. So we struck hands upon it, and I entered my term in hell.

In my brief years, I've noticed something about large business concerns that employ many laborers. When the masters are hard or deceitful, the workers unite against them. When the masters are fair, the workers—or apprentices, at least—turn upon each other. Motheby and Southern paid an honest wage for an honest day's labor, but they left the dockhands to look after themselves. Dockhands being of a rough cut generally, that put me in a bad way.

The first day, a Thursday, I was beaten under the pier at low tide by three of them. Then I was beaten above the pier at high tide by two. There was no malice in it, only contempt for my newness and rawness and a mistaken belief that I was ignorant of fighting. Not true; no boy growing up in your working-day English village is ignorant of fighting, and I had long ago learned to dodge the kicks aimed at me by James and Walter Hawthorne, my former master's pork-brained sons. Though not a strong boxer, I was naturally quick, and when forced to defend myself, I had been known to land a fortunate punch at a critical moment. But two or three bull-necked ruffians coming at me at once cast my small talent in self-defense to the wind.

Before, after, and in between beatings, I unloaded kegs of wine from the ships, trundled them into the warehouse, stacked them in ranks, and delivered them in barrows to nearby taverns. I slept on a rough sacking mattress nested among the other boys and awoke so sore that merely getting myself off the floor and into my clothes seemed labor enough for a Hercules. The beatings slacked off after the first day, but two fellows named Jack worked me over on Saturday afternoon, just to keep up their form.

I could not count on their taking Sunday off from this recreation, so after church that day I took a long walk to avoid them. The sky hovered dank and drizzly, as flat as my future looked. I crossed London Bridge, but mist hung so thick over the river I could make out little of it. On the other side lay Southwark, where my aunt supposedly lived, and as I warmed up in a tavern on the south bank my thoughts turned to her. I was just miserable enough to consider any fate preferable to another week at Motheby and Southern.

In the smudgy light of the tavern lamps I took out my wallet and removed two of its papers, which I had taken to pondering in forlorn moments because they made me feel less alone. Both had belonged to my mother. One was a sonnet written to her. The other was a rubbing, such as children make when they lay a paper on raised letters or figures and brush lightly over it with slate.

I remembered well the first time I saw it, on a cold dripping day like this one. I was eleven, and recovering from a spell of croup that kept me in bed for upwards of a week. My fever had broken and I was feeling better, but restless, and so had pulled a chest of my mother's belongings from under the bed and was rummaging through it. It was full of things we seldom saw: a lace tablecloth, a cap she wore at her wedding. Not much of interest to me, but at the bottom of the chest, under a pair of fine yarn stockings, was a thin packet of letters tied with a blue ribbon. Among them was this rubbing.

It showed two circles, which appeared to be both sides of a medal. On one circle were the words "Watch and Wait." The other displayed a cup in a disembodied hand, and over it arched the inscription *"Bibite ex hoc omnes."* These of course were the words of our Lord at His last supper: "Drink ye all of it."

I had stared long and hard at the image, wondering what such a strange device could signify. Then I looked at the packet of letters, which all seemed to be written in the same hand, small and neat. I turned over one of them and read the signature, Anne Billings—

Then my head jerked backward and my mother's voice above me cried, "Young mouse!" She had me by the hair, pulling so hard I thought my scalp might come off. "Nosing about in that which does not concern thee, hey?" She had a passionate nature, in spite of earnest efforts to keep control of it. She could skip like a child or scold like a fishwife. "Can I not keep some little thing to myself, without thy prying fingers seek it out?"

Directly she calmed down, and I tearfully begged her pardon, which she granted. But before going back to work, she pulled a chair up to our little fireplace and burned the letters one by one. I could still recall her face in the glow: her dark eyes and pert nose, and the soft girlish mouth that was made for smiling but seldom did, those days. After a while I asked, hesitantly, "Who is Anne Billings?"

I feared she would not answer, but after a long pause she did. "Your father's sister. She lives in Southwark, by London."

"He had a sister?" This was news; as my father had no kin nearby, I had supposed him to be kinless.

"Aye. And perchance he still does." Another silence followed.

"Where did you get the picture—of the hand with the cup—"

She held out an arm, with a sigh and a rueful smile. "Come hither, mouse." I went at once, and nestled beside her on the bench, which was barely wide enough for both of us. "I will strike thee a bargain, and tell this if thou'lt ask me no more. You children had just turned four when he first went to London, and was gone for a month. He said it was a family matter, some business his sister had to settle with him. He came back with a medal around his neck. I made the copy, one night while he slept. Two months after his return he left again, and this time for good. Whether that medal had aught to do with it, I know not. But it was of the devil, somehow." Tiny flames from the hearth fire danced in her dark eyes, bright with tears. "It was a devilish business."

With such an opinion, I supposed she had burned the rubbing along with the letters. But later I found it, in a box with her most prized possessions. I took it to keep, with the notion in mind that there might be someone in Southwark who could tell me what it meant.

The tavern keeper had never heard of Anne Billings; nor had the strolling musician I encountered on the street, nor the maid who sold honey cakes in a nearby stall. By then the sun was setting and a thick fog had rolled up from the river, throwing a blanket of gloom upon Southwark. Wads of torchlight flickered past, men and women brushed by me with muffled apologies or curses or no sound at all. I made my way along the bank, heading west. Anne Billings? Know you a lady hereabouts called Anne Billings? The name began to echo inside my own muddled head until it seemed I was asking the question of myself. Three brass helmets leapt out of the fog, so suddenly I made a little yelp, but they passed me by unseeing: members of the city watch patrolling the streets, as alike as mechanical men.

The evening chill seeped through my clothes. I wrapped my arms about me, shivering in my thin doublet and hugging the wallet that held those scraps of who I was. With heavy steps and a heavier heart, I turned and made my way back to the warehouse.

On Monday morning, after breakfast, I raised my eyes from a stack of empty kegs to see two apprentices approaching gleefully over the boards. The masters were nowhere in sight; I was trapped at the end of the pier and lacked the spirit to dodge them. My body quaked, a lump of flesh appealing to heaven for deliverance.

Deliverance came, and that swiftly. Into my head darted the words of Psalm 71. They lodged, they grew, and so filled my mouth that I had only to open swollen lips for the verses to roll out, on full-rounded syllables: "Deliver me, O God, out of the hand of the wicked, out of the hand of the unrighteous and cruel man!"

This stopped the cruel and unrighteous in their very tracks. Though it seemed a fair guess that scripture study did not take up their free hours, they knew their Psalms, as all Englishmen did. The dilemma showed in their faces: here before them was a sniveling shrimp, begging for a wallop, but it might be inviting wrath from heaven to punch a mouth filled with the word of God.

"Let them be confounded and consumed that are adversaries to my soul! Let them be covered with reproach and dishonor that seek my hurt!"

My voice is strong, especially for a lad of my size, with a carrying power that could shiver the rafters of our cottage in Alford. Mother often commended its pleasing melody when I declaimed scripture indoors, while Susanna put her hands to her ears in protest. On the pier in a fishy April breeze, the words mounted up on eagle's wings and dove straight at my tormentors. They paused, they considered—and in a moment they backed away.

I tried not to look too obviously relieved.

My whispered prayer of thanks was interrupted by the sound of vigorous applause, which changed in tone as soon as I looked that way. A girl was straddling two of the upright piles that supported the dock. Though rather plump, she balanced easily, a market basket dangling from one arm and a long shawl from the other, whipping in the breeze. Once she had my attention, the clapping slowed to a steady pound of one hand against another in mocking compliment. Deliberately, I turned my back.

Later that day, as Mistress Southern served dinner from a brick fireplace the size of a hut, one of the boys sidled up to me: a stocky, moon-faced lad with freckles. "Saw you face down those two on the dock. Ruffians, the lot of them. Clever work. Ralph Downing's my name."

"Richard's mine." I was devoting full attention to dinner. Indeed, I never devoted anything less than full attention to meals at Motheby and Southern, the best thing about working there. For the first time in months, I was getting enough to eat. I did take time to notice Ralph's ear, which had a chewed look, as though he had been on the wrong side of a sharp encounter. "'Twas God's work," I added, giving credit where it was due as I swallowed a mouthful of brown bread and cheese.

"Look you. I'm going over to Southwark on Saturday next. Would you come along?"

"For what?"

"Why—" He slid me a sideways look, appraising my wits. "A play, that's what. A play at the Rose. Only a penny gets you in."

"Plays are of the devil. I'll none of them."

Ralph jerked back, as though I had told him I bore the plague. "Call yourself a Londoner? But no, I hear the country in your voice. Full of pigs and cabbages, for all you talk like the Lord Mayor. Huh. I'll shug off, then." And he did, having discovered that I was not worth an honest Londoner's time.

I understood what he meant about talking like the Lord Mayor only later. It happens that His Honor is opposed to all forms of the theater and never misses an opportunity to shut it down. He sees it as a school for vice, a seedbed of rebellion, and a thief of the laborer's time, which could be better spent elsewhere. My mother shared this view, and it was her saying I quoted back to Ralph Downing with hardly a thought. My true opinion, however, was more complicated.

One of my first memories is of a play. I was only three years old, standing in the yard of the Royal Inn of Lincoln. It must have been a market day, for the inn yard was full, and all eyes turned upon a cleared space at one end. I clung to the hem of a man's brown wool cloak and caught the fever of anticipation in the crowd. Shut out of it, as all children are by their size, I whimpered and tugged at the cloak until two strong arms came to my aid. They swept me into the sky, settling me upon broad shoulders. From a paltry nothing, I was suddenly master of the inn yard, surveying the whole of the crowd as they gazed intently toward one spot.

This was a rude wooden platform holding a host of players, fantastically dressed: clowns and kings, demons and saints. I remember nothing of the play save that the devil was literally in it, capering about in red with fiery horns and forked tail and sent to hell in the end by means of a trapdoor. I remember being so startled at his disappearance that I cried out, and felt the shoulders beneath me shake with laughter. Such a laugh my father had—boisterous and catching, like a fever—bystanders turned to look at us and smiled.

I had seen no plays since then, for he was not there to take me. Yet though I agreed with the logic of my mother's arguments against the theater, I could never summon her passion. Despite my quick response to Ralph Downing, I found myself reconsidering his offer.

"I told you," said Motheby to Southern, "He's a bright lad. We can put him on the Châlons run."

"On the Châlons run?" said Southern to Motheby. "What's become of young Taylor, then?"

"Cut up in a dagger match with a lad from Coverdale's warehouse."

"Ah youth, youth," sighed Master Southern, shaking his head. "How lethal its folly." They had paused, in the course of their customary morning walk, to watch me sweep the dock. After one week on this job, I had mastered its few demands; my muscles had hardened up already and I could stack and toss my share of kegs and make nearby deliveries without getting lost.

"But the Châlons run," Southern continued. "That's a heavy charge. And he's not bound to us yet. Can we trust him?"

They studied me as I went on sweeping in a most trustworthy manner. I was eager for any chance to get off the docks. After a moment, Master Motheby raised his voice. "Look you, boy—"

I straightened to full height, even stretching a little as I held the broom upright. "Sir?"

"You see that ship." He pointed to a long double-masted vessel—a galleass, as I had learned to call it, rocking gently on the current. "'Tis loaded with a priceless cargo we receive once per fortnight: burgundy from the Châlons vineyards of France."

"Very choice," put in Southern.

"Very select," his partner agreed, and they both appeared to swell like a pair of roosters. "And who do you suppose has the sole right to import it to England's blessed shore?"

I appeared to ponder this question. "Could it be you, sirs?"

"The same. And, marry, 'twas your friend Peter Kenton who secured us that right." I thought to remind him that I had never met Master Kenton, but considered it better to look as delighted as they obviously felt.

They went on to explain that almost all the Châlons burgundy went to a tavern at Middle Temple, the school of law, where attorneys, clerks, and professors paid well for it. My ears pricked up at this, for the fellow I still remembered as "my" clerk had told me that Attorney Martin Feather kept chambers there. Though mindful of the clerk's warning not to attach myself to the man, surely it would do no harm to have a look at him some day. Thus, as Motheby and Southern spoke of the glories of their wine, I bowed and flattered at fitting moments, and won the job for my pains.

The wine from Châlons was "select" indeed—only a dozen kegs were shipped every fortnight, and they all went to the Lion and Lamb Tavern on Fleet Street. Ralph Downing and I delivered six kegs apiece on our one-wheeled barrows. He led the way, but as he could not read or write, it fell to me to manage the papers. The finical tavern steward took his time in settling accounts, carefully noting the Châlons seal on each keg: a little crossbow burned into the head. While waiting for him to satisfy himself, my eyes roved about the tavern seeking a slight fellow in legal robes, with a face neither old nor young, whose round blue eyes peered out from round glass spectacles. I wished to thank him for the shilling, but also to see his triangular smile as he recognized me, hear his warm voice saying, "Richard! So they have you delivering to Middle Temple already?" But my searching eyes did not discover him.

The tavern steward was at last signing a receipt for the twelve kegs when I asked him, "Sir, could you tell me where Master Martin Feather has his chambers?"

The quill pen in his hand skipped, leaving a dot of ink on the paper, which he blotted with a rag. "Who?" he asked sharply.

"Why . . ." The intensity of his gaze made me stammer. "M-m-master Feather?"

"I know him not. Take your receipt and be off!"

On the street Ralph eyed me curiously. "And what was that, then?" I merely shrugged, though the steward's response puzzled me also. "I'm bound for the Rose Theater tomorrow," he reminded me. "Will you come, or do you still fear the devil?"

"Another time. Come on, I'll race you to Ludgate." That cut short his questions, as we set off with our empty barrows, weaving amongst the traffic as quickly as possible without knocking down some eminent jurist who could haul us into court.

Saturday dawned clear, for the first time in a week. After knocking off work an hour after noon, I donned my tight doublet, straightened my hose, dusted off my cap, and joined the happy throng of Londoners pouring over the Bridge into Southwark.

London Bridge springs across the Thames on twenty stone arches, stout enough to support an entire village on their backs. Shops, stalls, and fine houses line both sides of the Bridge, yet leave enough width in the center for two carts to pass each other. The river itself is broad and deep and alive, clear enough to take its color from the sky. Looking east, one can catch the briny breath of the ocean in his face and feel the thundering current underfoot. The grim stone fortress of the Tower dominates the scene: home to the royal menagerie, the royal treasury, and prisoners of high rank. Beyond the Tower, as far as the eye can see, bare-masted ships line the bank. An old seaman taking the sun on a stone bench shuffled over to point out a vessel from the darks of Africa and a tobacco ship from the Caribbean. Sailors from these ships thronged the streets of London, men of fabulous colors: copper, ash, brown, or black as tar, jabbering in outlandish tongues. It was all I could do not to stare after them—did they eat and sleep, as I did? Were they all the way human, or some variation of mankind?

West of the Bridge, where the exuberant current piles up against the piers on its way seaward, the watermen ply their trade—hundreds of boats, all sizes and sorts, busily ferrying people from London to Southwark and back again, their oars blurring like dragonfly wings. Little one-seater wherries dart here and there, cleaving a path among the covered barks and cargo vessels, while jeweled barges of the nobility glide on the rise and dip of long oars.

The sight was so lively, so merry, I almost laughed out loud—

until the swoop of a raven's wing drew my eye to the memorial tower nearby. Spiked to the wall, about fifteen feet up, the heads of three traitors stared a grim warning to boats and foot travelers alike. Traffic passed unheeding below their eyeless gaze. One was no more than a skull; the others soon would be, once the ravens had done their work. Quickly sobered, I cut short my gawking.

West of the Bridge lay Bankside, where I had wandered the week earlier. This time I turned east, and began my search at the Anchor and Chain tavern, where a weather-beaten anchor swung rustily over the door. "My pardon, lady," I addressed the serving maid, who blushed at the compliment, "know you anything of one Anne Billings?"

About an hour later I was asking the same question of the innkeeper at the Sir Francis, who scratched his dirty scalp and shook his puzzled head. Then a raspy voice in the corner rumbled, "Not so fast, Jamie. The lad may be asking after Holy Nan." I turned to confront two little berry-black eyes in a face as wrinkled as a collapsed tent. "That who you mean, boy?"

"I know not, sir. All I know her by is Anne Billings."

He nodded. "That be her name, I do believe. What you do is, go back to the broad way—Southwark Street—and take it south, near half a mile I'm thinking, and when you get to St. Alban's church, turn east and start asking after the foundling hospital. There you'll find her."

My heart rose. "I'm right obliged to you, sir."

He waved a hand. "Tell her we miss her in these parts." The

innkeeper sniggered and the sailor grinned. Nodding to both of them, I hurried out of the inn, hearing Master Jamie's voice behind me: "A bit old to be a foundling, think you?" Overcome by his own wit, he wheezed out a laugh.

Southwark is built upon a marsh, crisscrossed by ditches that fill at high tide and make a small, muddy Venice of the town. I had to follow a tangle of these watery paths and bridges, losing my way and getting myself redirected a half-dozen times. The foundling hospital, when I finally came upon it, was a gray stone structure with the look of a convent or monastery, tucked between a fish market and a counting house and surrounded by a high wall with a wicket gate. A dull, whey-faced maid let me in and made me wait while she carried word of my arrival to her mistress. After no less than five minutes she returned and led me through the yard, where a small flock of goats grazed placidly. A smell of mildew, sour milk, and fish permeated the whole, and the whiff of anything close to it reminds me of my aunt to this day.

She was of medium height and age, with a thin nose and small, penetrating eyes and a wide, limber mouth. She dressed plainly in white and blue, her only ornament a string of beads tucked into her bodice. We met in a little room off the entrance hall, where soft footsteps sounded on the floor above and the plaintive bleating of goats drifted in through open windows. Those were the only noises I heard, though it did not occur to me until later that if this was a home for orphans, where were the children? My aunt seemed not the motherly sort, and when I addressed her as

Goodwife Billings, she corrected me sharply. "I am not married, young man. Now or ever."

"Forgive me, I only thought—as you're my father's sister . . . yet you bear not the same name—"

"Half sister. Our mother only we shared."

"I see." That left me with no notion what to call her. Since her reception of me had been as chilly as the old stone walls, "Aunt" seemed too familiar. Though I did not expect her to throw her arms about me and weep over my long-lost head, this seemed to go to the other extreme.

"My time is dear—Richard, is it? What would you ask?"

I took a breath. "Ah . . . do you know anything of my father?"

"I could not say."

"Why . . . Does that mean that you do not know?"

She fixed her eyes on a point above my head and her voice took on a curious, airy tone. "It means I could not say. We were never close, Robert Malory and I."

"Could you say where he lived, then, the last you saw him?"

"That I could not. He moved about. His feet were . . . restless."

I might have told her that. What disturbed me was that we were speaking in the past tense. "If—if you please, though, I would be most grateful for any knowledge of him."

"Why?"

My mouth opened, but no sound came out. In truth, I knew not how to answer. Resentment of my father ran deep. But still . . . but still, the sound of his laugh haunted my memory, as did the strong arms that once had lifted me to his shoulders. Perhaps there was more to him than his back, forever turned as he walked away.

"I wish to know him," I said, simply.

"Does your mother wish it?"

"She is dead."

"I am sorry to hear that."

Her voice did not sound especially sorrowful. With a peculiar tightness about my throat I asked, "Did you ever meet her?"

"I did. Once."

Here, with almost anyone else, some compliment regarding the deceased would follow—whether sincerely meant or no. My aunt's silence grew so prickly I made the compliment myself. "She was very beautiful, didn't you think?"

"Beauty has its perils."

"Why, what mean you by that, Mistress?"

She tightened her mouth and squinted her eyes to raisins; beauty would be no peril for *her,* I thought. "A pretty face can combine with a wandering eye to make a tempest in the household."

Her words made no sense to me at first, then blazed to sudden comprehension. "Do you mean—are you saying that she was unfaithful to my father?"

"I say only that jealousy of her drove him out—with good cause, he claimed."

"Th-that is a—That is—a lie!" I jumped to my feet, so angry I could barely see her pale, pinched-up face with its sharp accusing nose. My fist ached with a longing to flatten that nose. I had never felt anything like it, and to feel it toward a woman shocked me. I was not a quick-tempered lad—"Slow to flame, long to burn" was the way my mother put it—but here I stood with doubled fist, blazing. "She was—she was the m-most virtuous lady in England!"

My aunt showed no alarm, nor remorse. "I only know what my brother told me."

"Then—" I stopped for breath, and grip. "Then he was lying!"

"Sit down and collect yourself, boy. Or leave my house, else."

I would have followed her second suggestion but for knowing that it was exactly what she wanted. I would not give her the satisfaction, and besides, my business was not yet done. After cooling down a bit, I sat and fixed her with as steady a look as I could manage. If nothing else, I would show her good manners, taught by the same person she so ignorantly slandered.

"Begging your pardon, Mistress Billings. But I will hear no words against the lady I knew and loved better than anyone. You may believe what you will, but I pray you say no more against her." She only looked at me, her face impassive. I took another deep breath to calm myself. "But there is a thing I will ask yet; answer me this, and I'll trouble you no more."

I undid the middle buttons of my doublet and took out my leather wallet, unfolded it, and removed a slip of paper—all done quickly, to stop my hands from trembling. I showed the image of the medal to my aunt, and for the first time provoked a response in her.

She blinked, and pulled in a sharp breath through her nose. It was scarcely seen and heard, and she recovered herself in an instant. "How came you by this?" she asked, in a voice calm but quickened, I thought, by apprehension or outright fear.

"My father wore it, and my mother made the copy."

"Without his knowing?" When I nodded, wondering at the question, she sniffed. "Is that the act of an honest woman?"

I replaced the paper in my wallet while struggling to keep my anger in check. "She was his wife, lady. She feared it was of the devil."

"How could that be? With the very words of our Lord on it?"

"You read quickly—unless you already knew the writing?"

She waved a hand. "I have some Latin, and it's a common saying."

"But you *have* seen it before." My voice was rising again. "What does it signify?"

"You presume too much, boy. I can tell you nothing about it. And I have no more time to spare for young vagabonds who intrude upon their relations. Whatever you want from me, you may see for yourself I am a poor woman—"

I leapt to my feet again. "I am not a beggar, Mistress. I have work—on the docks—" I meant to tell her what I thought of her insinuations, but the only words that came to mind were insults.

"Do you?" she said, to that undefined spot beyond my head. "That is where you belong, then. I shall call Lydia to see you out."

Lydia saw me out, though I didn't need seeing. By then it was nearly dark, and Londoners were pouring back into the city after a merry afternoon of plays and bear fights. I made a gloomy contrast to them, feeling the need of an extra leg to kick myself. Of course she knew more than she said, and may have betrayed some hint if I had been more clever. I could have made more of the fact that she seemed to know already what the writing was, but instead I let myself be goaded into sputtering incoherence.

Her insinuations touching my mother had done it, of course. "Holy Nan" Billings herself must have made up such rubbish—I could not believe Robert Malory put the notion in her head. Only a madman could have doubted my mother's virtue, and from all I knew of him, my father was not mad.

Some years before I was born, he had come to Alford to be the schoolmaster, and remained one after he married. Though not native to Lincolnshire, he fit himself to its ways and was well liked by the children he taught. His disappearance was still whispered about in Alford, where everyone had guessed its cause: he was abducted by pirates; he had lost his heart to some London lady; he was robbed and murdered on the highway and his body thrown in a cave. None of these were any comfort to me. As a child, I imagined that he had embarked on some noble calling, greater than wife or family, and would someday return when his work was done. I may have outgrown such fancies, but still it was hard to give him up for lost without knowing why.

My aunt's stubborn refusal to speak of him plagued me into what Mother used to call a "murdering dump": a mood so black I could scarcely speak. I began another week thus, flinging myself about work like a pitchfork. At least it made me proof against attack. Any petty tyrant can tell when his victim feels no fear, and most will back away straight; I thwarted the approach of one would-be assassin over the planks with no more than a killing look. This put me in a slightly better humor. Later that day I was stacking kegs to make a delivery when a girl's voice sounded from over the quay: "Ho! You with the barrow!"

I turned to the same figure who had applauded me a few days before at my first triumph. She stood on firm planking today, the shawl sensibly wrapped around her head, since our loving English clouds had dropped a steady drizzle upon us all morning. I considered ignoring her again, then called without enthusiasm, "Ho, on the dock."

"Know you all the Psalms?"

"Over half." I was weak on 119 and 107 and other long ones, but the rest of them tripped off my tongue readily enough.

"And do you read?"

I stared at her; what meant this examination? "Passing well," I said, "and write, too. English and Latin—d'you need a clerk?"

"What be your name?"

This was too much; I dropped the last keg of wine on top of the handcart, stepped to one side, and turned to her briefly. "Richard, Earl of Quayside, so please you," I called, and made a sweeping bow with one leg turned out in the courtly manner. I performed it too well, however—dipped so low I knocked my forehead on one corner of the barrow.

She laughed—not a mean laugh but the delighted one of a child whose favorite uncle has performed a trick to amuse her. As I picked up the prongs of the handcart and trundled away, blushing furiously, she shouted, "Look for me tomorrow, Your Grace! We are destined to meet again!"

What the Knife Said

Early the next morning, Master Motheby, acting alone for once, set me to a clerking task. He thrust a ledger and a piece of slate into my hands and steered me to a corner of the dock. "Behold!" he said, waving toward a collection of barrels, all one size, piled haphazardly as though they had just been unloaded. "What do you see?"

"Barrels, sir."

"Nay. You see a foul insult to the noble English palate. Sack from Spain, boy, and abominable stuff. Is it any wonder we're at war with the Spanish, when they foist on us bilge like this? Figure these up at one pound six per head so our clerks can write a receipt. Then, figure the least space needed in a ship's hold to send them back. Can you do that?"

He gave me a measuring line and I set to work. It

was a task to occupy my mind, but infuriating thoughts of Anne Billings intruded still. Where she was concerned, I was "long to burn" indeed—anger dug into me like a spade, gouging an ever-deeper pit until the cry of "Ahoy, Richard of Quayside!" sounded from the bank.

It was, of course, the girl who had shown such a prying interest in me. After making her salute, she walked down the dock and stood expectantly at one corner of the Motheby and Southern warehouse. I judged there would be no harm in meeting her—to discover why she was plaguing me, if nothing else. She hiked herself upon a malt barrel and swung her legs from side to side, watching my approach with a lively interest I could feel even from a distance. I guessed she was a little older than me, by a year or so, plainly dressed in a kirtle and bodice, but neat and clean. Her pleasant face was round as a pudding, framed by wispy curls escaping from her cap—curls of that mousy shade seen most often in tree bark. But her eyes glinted in the sun, green as bottle glass and more alive than any I had ever seen. I fancied they could catch any object of her curiosity and pull it in, like a skiff to bank. "How does Your Grace?" she called.

I shrugged. "Passable. What is it you want?"

"I want to make your acquaintance. My name is Starling Shaw, but some call me Star. And yours?"

"You already know it. I am occupied, as you see, and can't spare much—"

"Well then, my lord Richard, I am wondering if another occupation might suit you better."

This captured my attention fully. "Almost anything would suit me better, but I've fallen into the habit of eating well."

"We can arrange to see you fed."

"Who are 'we,' then?"

She flicked me playfully with the edge of her shawl. My humor flared up, for I was not in a mood to be toyed with. "Look you, girl—"

"I am not at liberty to tell you about the position. Would you know more, you must come to St. Mary's Parish just after dark. It's on Aldermanbury Street, just north of the church."

I was tempted. The girl's dress and manner suggested she was employed by some wealthy merchant. The market basket by her side was filled with items of quality and she spoke fair—better than the common housemaid. This made me wonder if her master was a man of letters, or a Court official. Yes, I was tempted, but cautious. "What's the object? Why this mystery?"

"There's no mystery about me—us. But there seems to be one about you."

"About me? How so?"

She tilted her head with a sidelong smile, much like a flirt at a county fair. The suspicion returned that she was playing me, and I felt tempted to tip her off her perch. Then she said, "You are being watched. There are two idlers on yon pier, and their chief object seems to be you. Don't look, you pumpkin!"

"But—" I blinked at her, slowly taking in what she'd said, and uncertain how to credit it. "How do you know they're watching me?"

"When you left yesterday to make your deliveries, they followed you. And today they are here again. I'm wondering what their business is."

"I am wondering the same—about you."

Her shoulders raised, with a little laugh. "I come here four mornings a week to shop for my mistress. I noticed you first on the day you thwarted those attackers by your inspired use of the Psalms—"

"And what of that?"

"You must come to Aldermanbury Street to find out. But I daresay those two yonder have some other reason for their care."

She laughed again, and I began to see that she was staging a little play for my watchers—if such they were. I sidled around to the warehouse wall, leaned one shoulder against it with my arms folded, and forced a sickly smile to my face. Courting, or even the appearance of it, was not one of my accomplishments.

"Where are they?"

She ducked her head coyly. "On the next dock, playing quoits."

I glanced around, with seeming indifference. On one side of Motheby and Southern stood the warehouse of old Roger Coverdale, a dealer in salt fish. On the other side was an empty dock, where masterless men gathered to pass the time or wait for work. Two fellows in leather aprons and hoods were idly tossing an iron ring at a post. I could tell little about them in that brief a look; one of them flickered his eyes to me, but that meant nothing. "Are they there all day?"

"How am I to know that? I don't have all day to watch them watching you." So saying, she hopped off the barrel and wrapped her shawl around her, brushing me again with the corner. "About tonight, what I told you—it should be an easy matter to slip away unseen after dark. If by chance I do not meet you at the gate, ask for my master, Henry Condell." She strolled past me with a little twitch to her hips, then turned for a last word. "But I will tell you this, if you are in some trouble, and seek a place where you won't be seen, it wouldn't serve you to come. Think on it."

Truly, she had given me much to think about but not near enough to come to any conclusion. After turning in my figures to the satisfaction of both Motheby and Southern, I set off on a short delivery just west of the Bridge. Though I glanced behind me several times, no stalkers in leather aprons appeared in view. Starling must have imagined their interest in me, or else she amused herself by making up tales and passing them off as true. I hoped she was sincere about the offer of a position. In any case, I determined to go to Aldermanbury Street and the house of one Henry Condell, to satisfy my curiosity if nothing else.

St. Mary's Parish is a fine neighborhood, with tall stone or half-timbered houses behind high walls. Lanterns glowed over the gates, each illuminating a brass plate inscribed with the name of the householder. Peaceful and homelike sounds drifted over those walls: the strumming of a lute, the voices of a man and woman lifted in song, the shouts of children at play in the yard, drunk with the joy of running wild on a warm spring night. Tall treetops whispered in the breeze and the scent of apple blossoms and lilac drenched all with sweetness, even the scream of an outraged child. Susanna used to scream at me in the same way, and for a moment I heartily wished myself back in Alford quarreling with her—except that Mother was no longer there to step in and make peace. The heavy iron gates of Aldermanbury Street leaned upon my loneliness. I walked slowly to read the nameplates and my face may have shown the melancholy I felt, for a watchman stopped me to ask my business.

I straightened and donned the look of an honest youth. "I seek the house of Henry Condell, sir. He expects me."

This seemed to increase my worth in the watchman's eyes. "Master Condell? Three doors further, on this side. Mind you don't try him; he is a man of obligations."

I thanked him and hastened down the next three gates. A high shriek answered my knock, then a scurry of threaded footsteps like a dozen giant mice crossing paths in a hayfield. The gate swung wide and I looked into the pert upturned features of a boy about six or seven, rosy in the lamplight. "Who's it, then?"he demanded.

Starling Shaw appeared behind him, her round face flushed, tucking strands of unruly hair back into her cap. She looked almost pretty, her green eyes snapping. "Stand aside, Neddie. This is Lord—this is Richard."

"Has he come courting you?"

"Hold your noise! He's the new apprentice, if all goes well. Now go on about your game."

The boy went, but not before giving a vigorous tug to her apron. "Caught you." Then he whirled away, calling, "Olly, olly, all! I found Star!"

The girl retied the strings of her cap, head lowered. Had I not known her for a bold thing, I would have thought she was a little undone by the jibe about courting. "We were playing hide-and-seek," she explained. "Were you followed?"

"If so, it was by the phantoms of your own imagination."

"I'll have you know—well, never mind. Come and meet my master." She took my arm and started me toward the house.

"What mean you by 'new apprentice'?"

"That's what you will be if you take the position, won't you? Master Condell will reveal all."

She led me into a long room with a low ceiling held up by heavy timbers. Everyone in it clustered at one end—so many, they seemed to tilt the room in that direction: servants, hounds, a number of young ladies and gentlemen. A kitchen maid and a waiting man were clearing away the remains of the evening meal, throwing scraps to the dogs. Several of the young people were singing to the mingled tones of a recorder and lute, while two girls drew and gossiped in a corner, and the children, rushing in after their game, began to get underfoot. Near a huge fireplace (unlit on this mild evening) stood the master of the house, instructing an elderly servant while the mistress tied the second sleeve to his gray velvet doublet. I could have taken him for no one but the master, for all attention ran to him. His face was sharp with a high-bridged nose and strong chin—kingly, I would call it, though I had never seen a king. But his eyes, when he looked at me, were dark and soft. His wife, a handsome, willowy lady almost as tall as he, paused with her hand upon his shoulder as they turned their heads.

"Master Condell," Starling said, with a little bob, "'tis the youth I told you of, come to recite."

"Ah. You catch me in haste, young sir. I'm due for a vestry meeting, but I can give you a brief hearing. No!" he exclaimed as I took a step toward him. "Stay where you are. Rather back up, back up toward the wall yonder. Alice"—this to one of the young ladies—"fetch me my ruff, so please you, the second-best. Now, lad." He turned back to me. "Starling says you know the Psalms. Declaim to us Number 137: 'By the rivers of Babylon,' et cetera. Speak it lovingly at first, and no louder than I can hear."

By now I was wholly confounded, having been greeted, measured, backed against the wall, and ordered to recite from memory before speaking a word on my own. But the man had a commanding way about him. Accordingly, I opened my mouth and began in what seemed to me a "loving" manner: "By the rivers of Babylon, there we sat down, yea we wept when we remembered Zion. . . ."

"Good!" he spoke over me. "Now bitterly, bitterly! And louder!"

More puzzledly than bitterly, I continued. "We hung our harps upon the willows in the midst thereof. . . ."

He paced me through a range of feeling, from sorrow to amazement to hurt to anger, of which I managed the amazement best because it was nearest to what I felt. His mention of the vestry meeting made me think his church was in want of a reader, but to my knowledge that was not an apprentice's job. The room fell silent as I spoke, except for the dogs and little children, and having all eyes on me made my chest feel tight. The stares were thoughtful, not surprised, as if they all knew something I didn't. This made me rather irritated at Starling for being so infernally tight-lipped as to my purpose here, and when Master Condell called for rage at the conclusion of the Psalm, I could almost comply. Then I self-consciously folded my arms.

"He speaks well, Henry," remarked the mistress to her husband.

"Stands well, too. Your age, boy?"

"Fourteen, sir, so please you."

"Your voice has broken, yes?" I nodded, rather abashed. It was a disappointment to me that my voice had changed without becoming notably deeper, only fuller.

"Do you fence?"

"Ah—no, sir. I never learned to fence."

"Dance?"

I shook my head, as notions of church reading departed from it.

"Sing?"

"Passing well, sir."

"Sing for us—But no time for that now."

His wife tied on his ruff, with a glancing smile at me. "The voice is the vital thing. The rest can be learned. Though fourteen is late to start. Cole, Mary—kiss thy father good night." Two small

50

children leapt to his arms in turn, as one of the young ladies helped him on with his cloak, another handed him his hat, and the whole party swept over him in a wave of love and goodwill, as though he were setting out for an ocean voyage. He emerged from this fond farewell and approached me with hat in hand, brisk and cordial. "As for you, lad, you show promise and I shall tell my associates of you. If you wish to be an actor, I bid you come—"

My jaw dropped. "An *actor,* sir?"

He stopped abruptly as the room felt silent again; often I wish that my voice did not carry so well. "Why, yes," he said mildly. "An actor. What did you think you were being sounded for?"

I looked daggers at Starling, and said, "To speak true, sir, the position you were sounding me for . . . was not made clear to me."

"Hmmm." He glanced from Starling to me and back again. "Well then, I must leave it to be explained. Perhaps both of us were imposed upon, young sir. Please accept my apology."

With a most gracious nod, he left us. I made my own farewell to the lady of the house, my face flaming, and as I passed took Starling firmly by the hand and pulled her out the door. "Why didn't you tell me?" I hissed, once we were outside.

Her face, near as I could make it out in the twilight, had turned sulky. "Because I feared you wouldn't come. You Puritans paint the whole theater with one brush, and I wanted you to see Master Condell for the fine Christian gentleman he is, though an actor."

"What makes you think I'm a Puritan?"

"Who else would be spouting Psalms on a quay?"

She may have been half-right. My mother leaned toward the Puritan sect, far enough perhaps to fall into their camp. The rector who taught me Latin and figures was a Puritan, and always kind to me. I loved and respected them, but perhaps did not agree with them on everything. Taking my silence for hesitation, Star bent forward urgently.

"Look you," she said, "a chance like this won't come again. My master acts for the Lord Chamberlain's Men—there's no finer company in all of England. Every Christmas they are asked to perform before the Queen! Apprentices would almost cut their throats to get in, and at any other time you wouldn't stand a prayer. But the Company's lost three boys in two weeks and they have to fill those positions now. Tomorrow night there's a hearing at the Mermaid Tavern—"

"Why would I have a chance, with boys all over London cutting their throats?"

"They won't all be there, you berry-brain. This has happened so sudden, there's been no time to get the word abroad. Besides, you have the voice." Her manner turned solemn, as though The Voice were a gift bestowed by angels. "It's the one thing that cannot be taught, the one thing you must be born with."

Her words, or the way she made them sound, gave me pause. The temptation to regard myself as extraordinary had a strong pull. But an *actor*—even with the stately image of Henry Condell fresh in memory, I could not shake my notion of actors as capering clowns or red devils falling through trapdoors. And another thing:

everyone knew that any woman's part must be played by a boy, since women were not allowed on the stage. If I were to appear in a play, it would be pranked up in a gown and wig. No; impossible. "It's impossible," I told her.

"*Richard.*" She all but stamped her foot. "All right then, be a fool."

"No fear for that," I said, making my way to the gate. "You've seen to it this night."

"At least think on it. If you change your mind, come to the Mermaid Tavern tomorrow at seven o'clock. It's on Bread Street."

I turned at the gate, one hand on the latch, and sighed mightily. "Do me one good turn, Starling Shaw: leave off taking such a tender interest in my welfare." Then I opened the gate and stepped through it, fully believing I had exchanged my last word with her.

On the following day, I looked for those two silent overseers in every nook and shadow of the quay, but they were not to be found. No wonder—I had decided they were figments of one girl's overwrought fancy. The air breathed damp but warm that morning, my belly was full, and the other boys had begun to treat me with some respect, even friendliness. Master Southern had commented upon my knack with figures and hinted there might be an opening in the counting house. No need to assume that I would have to toss kegs forever, with the ability to rise beyond that. And God willing, I would rise; I was an Englishman.

Just after breakfast I glanced toward the street and felt a faint twinge in my guts: a lonely, furtive part of me missed Starling Shaw, a little. But London was full of meddling females, or any other kind of friend or companion I might wish to meet. I picked up the prongs of the barrow and gave it a shove to start my midmorning delivery to the taverns of Cheapside, in the neighborhood of the Royal Exchange.

The route was an easy one I had traveled three times already: most of the deliveries were to inns and taverns along Lombard and Fenchurch streets. After the Golden Bear came the Lord Loudon, then the Sail and Cleat, then the Unicorn. At each stop I unloaded a keg or two of Italian claret or Spanish sack and usually took an equal number of empty kegs to return to the warehouse. Each tavern had its own account with Motheby and Southern; payments, whether in coin or credit, went into a leather pouch tied to my belt. I was pleased that after so short a time the masters trusted me with their money.

The streets were full, as always, with so many people on so many errands they made me dizzy. In the village where I grew up, everyone's business was known even before he did anything: when the blacksmith crossed the street at ten o'clock he was making for his morning dram at the Red Lion, and when Mary Fable ran from one house to another she was looking for "that devil Stephen," her youngest. But in London, aims multiplied with the populace. Every carter, beggar, housewife, and lord spun his thread, weaving in a huge intricate pattern the life of the city. The liveliest threads were spun by apprentices. Most, like me, went about their work with more or less willing hands, minding their own business. But the shiftless ones were always roaming in packs and looking for trouble.

I was between the Unicorn and the Roaring Bull at noon that day when—amid the shouts of tradesmen, the tunes of vendors singing their wares, and the groan of iron-rimmed wheels on cobblestones—my ears picked up the sound of running steps. Many steps, coming up directly behind me.

Without thinking I swerved the barrow to one side. Three figures darted across the street to my right, making toward a small group of young men who had gathered to pass the time. One of them clipped a fellow in the knees, another snatched an apprentice's cap, the third butted shoulders with a lad hard enough to knock him to the ground. The street seemed to freeze for an instant, as though caught in a flash of lightning, then out of no particular throat came the bloodcurdling cry: *"Clubs!"*

The street erupted. Women grabbed their children and dashed for shelter. Carters whipped their horses to the sidelines, snatched their halters, and covered their eyes. At the same time young men and boys boiled out of the shops and side streets, eager to join the fight, no matter its cause.

I was not one of them. No one had to advise me to push my cargo aside and hold clear. But the barrow was scarcely turned when I felt a pair of arms grab me from behind. A hand clapped over my mouth and a hot taste of pewter flooded my tongue as a heavy ring jarred my teeth.

With a strength born of panic I twisted loose, but not free. The grip that held me, unyielding as iron, pushed me into the rough plaster wall. Then a blow to the ribs and an exploding pain that forced all the air from my lungs. The riot entered and took possession of me, a steady roar in which no detail stood out separate and alone. Except for the knife at my throat.

Thin and cold, the edge of the blade bit lightly into my neck. A dead-quiet voice without inflection spoke in my ear, seemed to bore directly into my brain: "If you want to stay well, you'll fly away straight." The knife then glided across my throat, and after it trailed a thread of sensation that was not yet pain. Fear, rather, as pure and cold as spring water. It emptied me, so that when I was released I slumped against the wall, with no more strength to stand.

The city watch had arrived: constables with clubs and flails, dragging the warriors apart. None bothered with me, a mere piece of turf flung aside in the conflict. From the wall I gulped air like a cod, calling home my scattered wits. I felt a warm wetness on my neck and reached up to touch it; my fingers came away bloody. The words were burnt into my mind: "If you want to stay well . . ." Who could wish me ill? What danger or threat was I to any soul alive? I remembered hands clutching my chest—too many hands for one person only. There must have been two. My watchers? I leaned forward, felt the pain in my ribs, and caught my breath sharply.

My wallet was gone. I searched my clothes and the ground all about, but knew it had been taken—that, and nothing else. The

56

coins and receipts were still in the leather pouch at my side, the barrow lacked not one keg of valuable wine. What they had wanted was the one possession I would have fought to the death for.

I felt my loss, cold as a gust of air through a bad tooth. They went right for it, as though knowing where it was, and what it contained. I blinked, taking in the scene before me: young men limping away or still prostrate on the rough paving stones; cracked heads, broken bones. Had it all come about because someone was after me?

At that, rational thought deserted me entire. I abandoned my barrow and ran like a rabbit, darting down the nearest by-lane, scattering a knot of children who were playing some game in the street. They shouted abuse at me, but I ran on until I came to an alley, then dove into it to catch my breath.

Though the stench almost gagged me, I waited there until I was satisfied no one had followed. Then I picked my way between the dark and fetid walls to the next lane, and stole down that one to the next, and on through the narrow crooked streets until I emerged on Cheapside, with St. Paul's directly ahead.

Booksellers dominate the south common of the cathedral; here in a forest of fluttering ballads and broadsides I took refuge. A right unsavory-looking character by then, sweaty and begrimed, with blood staining my shirt, I sought to fend off notice by burying my nose in a small book of poetry. The quarto was poorly printed and cheaply bound, and the poems in it may have deserved no better. Still, they served as a painful reminder of what I had lost.

On the day after my mother died, I had broken the lock on the small lead casket that held her dearest possessions. Susanna and I divided the contents: a ring, two silver spoons, a pendant passed down from our grandmother, the medallion rubbing, and a sonnet, which read in part

> *But soft within the layered petals keep they curled,*
> *These poor sighs of mine by the rose concealed*
> *While in thy sweet possession rise to fly unfurled;*
> *My secret wound enbalmed, my hidden hurts healed.*
>
> R.M., 1581

"It should be buried with her," Susanna had decided.

My reply came after a long pause. "I want to keep it."

"Whatever for?" Her voice rose, becoming shrill. "'Twas not written to you. Only our mother had a part in it, and that little enough."

"I want to keep it, though." I could not have found the words to say why, but these lines were of my father's heart, and in his hand, and seemed to give back a little of what he had taken away.

"Poetry," Susanna muttered bitterly. "A treasure indeed. You can guess how much comfort it brought her." But she put up no further argument, especially when I offered her the ring and pendant, and the spoons to keep for me. Only the papers had I taken, and thought them a fair trade. But now they were gone. And the rector's testimony, and those silly beads I had bought in my mother's memory, and the shilling given me by my first friend in London—all gone.

"Will you be buying that book, sirrah?" The bookseller, a portly dame who looked better suited to selling iron skillets, folded her arms and glared at me meaningfully.

For answer I replaced the quarto and turned away, speechless. Drawn toward the cathedral by a need for quiet prayer and reflection, I climbed the stone steps and passed through the arched doorway into the nave—where I paused for a moment, blinking in surprise. The interior of St. Paul's was almost as boisterous as the grounds. It appeared to be a kind of public meeting hall, where money changed hands over the very font, and hopeful tradesmen angled for work, and lovers whispered together in dark corners. London had confounded me once again; in a daze I made my way past all these doings and into the unoccupied south transept, where a row of short high-backed benches stood in a pool of light falling from the clerestory overhead. Here I knelt, with my elbows on a bench and my head in my hands, and tried to think.

By now my fright had ebbed away, and another sensation was stealing in to take its place. I recognized this new arrival—a quality that was my mother's bane, the one thing in me that drove her to violence. "Ah, thou'rt ever a stubborn lad!" she would cry. One time I refused to apologize to Susanna for an offense I did not see myself to blame for, and Mother took my head and slammed it against the heavy oak door of our cottage. "Stubborn, stubborn lad!" she cried, and then clutched one hand with the other as though to restrain them, while I bit my lip so hard it bled, forcing back tears. She had a temper but also true humility; it was she who begged my pardon later, not the other way round.

Alas though, she was right. When crossed, I am apt to dig in my heels and refuse to shift in any direction. I do not attack; I resist.

And now I was crossed, as never before. I struck my head on the back of the bench and cursed my aunt, the so-called Holy Nan, with more passion than I had thought was in me. Without doubt she was responsible for this—she, and those she had set on me. "Fly away straight," they said, but I hereby vowed not to oblige them. Those who had stolen my heart evidently expected me to run home with my tail between my legs. But I would not. I found myself knocking my head against the wood over and over, hard enough to hurt. Stubborn, stubborn lad. Almighty Lord, I prayed: let them not escape. Deliver me from unrighteous and evil men, and bring them unto thy most speedy judgment.

Surely that judgment would fall, and soon. In the meantime I meant to stay, for no better reason than my enemies wished me gone.

Returning to work at Motheby and Southern was out of the question. Somehow I must spirit back the pouch that held their bills and receipts and leave them to draw what conclusions they could. This was the very day we were to draw up the papers binding me to an apprenticeship, but fortunately that had not come to pass—I need not add bond-breaking to my list of woes. Most of my possessions, except what I carried on me, would have to be written off as lost. I dared not show my face on the docks; *they* would no doubt be watching, as they had before. Starling had been right about that. Perhaps she was right about other things as well.

What I needed was a place in London where I might be free from detection and still earn a living.

A place where I could fit immediately into a set or trade and go about in company—unnoticed, perhaps even disguised.

A place where no one watching for me would ever think to look.

o, lad," were Master Condell's first words to me. "You've had second thoughts about acting, have you?"

"In a way, sir. If you still want me, I am willing to bind to you."

"You are willing." His tone was dry. "That's all well, but I don't comprise the Lord Chamberlain's Men by myself. The rest of the Company must approve."

"Yes, sir."

"Then take a place at the board, and we'll hear you anon."

So I seated myself at one end of the table with six other boys, most younger than I, and all more presentable. My afternoon had been spent in outfitting myself by any means at hand to one who had no change of clothes, nor tiring place to change them, and scarcely two coins to rub together. I did manage to wash my shirt in a rain barrel behind the cathedral, and scrubbed most of the blood from it. With my next-to-last farthing I bought a strip of linen and tied it to cover the cut on my neck, hoping to create an impression of uprightness. In truth, I probably resembled an undersized street brawler, but no one at the table paid me much heed. The men at one end were deep in discussion about a trial, trade, and the city of Venice, carried on a tide of names all ending in "o." The boys were engrossed in study—each held a piece of paper and scanned the words on it intently, with a fluttering of lips that told me they were memorizing the words thereon. No sooner had I understood this than Master Condell passed a scrap of paper down to me: "Con these words as best you can. You'll soon be asked to speak them without reference to the paper."

This was all the instruction I received. I looked down at twenty-odd lines of verse, and panic struck, hard as a blow to the side. I had not seen an entire play in my life, and my only notion of acting was pieced together from my memories of inn-yard performers and our village rector's dramatic reading from Scripture. The scheme I had determined in the clear, pearly light of St. Paul's appeared as insubstantial as a dream in the smoke and noise of the Mermaid Tavern. The speech began thus:

> *The quality of mercy is not strained;*
> *It droppeth as the gentle rain from heaven*
> *Upon the place beneath. It is twice blest;*

It blesseth him that gives, and him that takes.
'Tis mightiest in the mightiest; it becomes
The thron'd monarch better than his crown . . .

And so on for another sixteen lines in praise of mercy, the glory of kings and gift of God. I reckoned that these were the words of a play; the speech appeared to take place in a court of law and was addressed in part to a nameless Jew. But who was speaking, and to what end, and upon what occasion, I knew not. To make matters worse, scarcely five minutes after I had begun my study, one of the boys at the table was called upon to recite for the Company. My turn could not be far away.

For the first two soundings my mind was cruelly divided between the hopeful young actors and these words I must somehow drive into memory like a peg. But by the third I had gathered from their example some notion how to stand and hold my head, along with a conviction that there would be no harm in seeing this thing through. My memory, when not distracted, soaks up words as the plowed fields take rain. Therefore I shut myself in by a huge effort of will and made a clean, straight furrow in my mind: "The attribute to awe and majesty, wherein doth sit the dread and fear of kings . . ."

Then I was called, and the next moment stood before the Lord Chamberlain's Men. Their stares were neither soft nor hard, only the intent study of workmen who wish to see their work well done. "Thy name, lad?" asked one.

"Richard, sir," I said firmly. It had occurred to me that spilling my

64

last name might not be wise if anyone was looking for me. My first name was safe enough—one could hardly throw a rock in London without hitting a Richard. To my relief, the questioner let it pass.

"Have you parent or guardian?"

"None, sir."

"Well then." I saw a pot of ink upon the board, a hand with a pen coming down to scrawl my name upon a sheet of curled paper. "You may begin."

I drew a long breath, and began. "The quality of mercy . . ."

A calm approach seemed best suited, so I did not stride or pace or leap forward as some of the other boys had done. My arms stayed bent and my palms rose slowly, pleading but not groveling for mercy to a poor orphan without hope or prospect. As I spoke I began to hear my mother reading from Scripture: "For thy mercy is everlasting . . . Thou dost not regard us as our sins deserve, nor punish us according to our iniquities . . ." And as I spoke, I know not how, my voice became hers, rounded to her pauses and inflections. No one ever read the Word with more depth of feeling. She might have been holding my hand, so smoothly did I walk through that speech. I thought, when all was done, that it had not gone so badly.

One or two heads nodded. All looked thoughtful, and after a brief spell of silence they launched into a comparison of the seven of us and our merits. I felt suddenly faint and heard little of it. So earnest was the discussion that no one noticed I had remained in place, until one of the actors glanced up and made a little start.

"I'll vow," he said, as frankly as if I were deaf, "see how he stares! If wishes could build kingdoms, this boy would be emperor of us all!"

His resounding voice sent a shiver down my spine. I blushed, and bowed, and returned to my seat, noticing how intently Master Condell was watching me. "True enough, Richard," he said (not to me). "A lean and hungry look, if ever I saw one."

"I like his manner," said the scribe of the company, who had spoken little thus far. His eyes were the kind that seem to pierce through the styles and habits one may assume, and into the soul of a man. "'Tis plain, but eloquent. He speaks from the heart."

"As thou dost, Will." Another player affectionately thumped the said Will on the back. "The boy shows promise. I vote for a trial. What say you, gentles?"

Through a haze I perceived that the Lord Chamberlain's Men voted to take me in on trial. Henry Condell alone appeared to hesitate, and no wonder: my abrupt change of heart about the theater must have aroused his suspicions. Yet after I was elected with two other boys—Richard Worthing and Adrian Ball—Master Condell was the one who offered to board me in his household. He may have wished to keep a curious eye upon me, but I cared not for the reason at that moment. My state was one of exhilaration and terror. God help me now, I thought, barely attending as these men settled my future among them.

"He'll be pretty enough once he scrubs up," said the man called Richard, with a jerk of his head toward me. "I'll give him that."

And this was a revelation. With my wide eyes, broad jaw, and short chin, I have always thought I possessed the face of a rabbit.

Starling almost squealed when Master Condell brought me into the great room of his house. He sent her to fetch another shirt and hose for me, and upon her return, she whispered, "I knew you would be back." I made no reply; she had been right too often already.

The master led me up two flights of stairs to a short hallway with a door on either side. Here he opened the right-hand door to reveal a youth about my age, sprawled on a low bed and covered with small boys. "Thomas! Ned! Cole!" scolded their father. "Get to bed. You know Robin has to study."

"I have my part, sir," the youth offered. "The boys were only plaguing me, like always." The children had jumped into their own bed and pulled the blanket over their heads and pretended to be fast asleep while Master Condell introduced me to Robin Bowle: "This is Richard, our new apprentice. Take him under your wing, pray."

"You're in for it," Robin told me cheerfully, after the master departed and I confessed I had never been on a stage before. The little boys, who clearly worshipped him, had crept out of bed again and now were fighting each other for his attention. "I'll toss thee out the window, see if I don't," he cried, dangling little Cole above the sill while the child screeched with delight. A banging from the room below broke upon their revels. "There," said Robin as he set the little boy on the floor, "'tis thy sister Lady Alice telling you to

67

muckle down. Peace now, or she'll be upon us all like a tiger." He bared his teeth and made his fingers into claws and chased the boys around their bed.

"But," I tried to resume our conversation, "I don't know—that is, I am not certain—"

"Aye. You seem right green to me—about the stage. You could probably teach me a thing or two about the street. How did you get that cut on your neck? By my guess you were taken in so quick because of our sharp need of 'prentices just now. One broke his leg in a fall from the gallery and another died of the pox on Saturday last. Poor James," he sighed. "He sang like an angel. God grant he's singing *with* the angels now. Then there's Ned Bly—sweet baby-faced Ned. Within a sixmonth he's grown the iron jaw and hammy arms of a blacksmith, and we had to let him go. We doubted our audience would take to him as Juliet, say. But fear not; the Company would never have voted for you, did you not show promise. They're no fools."

"No, but—"

"So I am to take you under my wing." Robin flapped one elbow and squawked like a chicken. "You may squeeze under with these brats. The Lord Chamberlain's Men produce almost as many children as they do plays."

"Why are they called that?"

"The Lord Chamberlain's Men? Because he is our patron. And our protector."

"Do you mean the chamberlain of the Royal Court?"

"Is there any other? His name is Henry Carey, Lord Hunsdon—a cousin of the Queen, and the best patron we could have. Without him the Lord Mayor would have us playing on the street, can you imagine? The finest company in London!" I tried to look shocked, as he continued. "Lord Hunsdon arranges our appearance at Whitehall, during Christmastide—"

"Whitehall?"

Robin flipped the howling Thomas over in a somersault. "To play before the Queen, country lad. I can see you've a deal to learn."

This was putting it gently. I undressed and got into bed as Robin went on in his high, rippling voice, piling information upon me with such generosity I felt my brain collapsing. The Company was composed of ten master players, plus hired actors and apprentices and stage help and extra players as needed. The names of the ten I promptly forgot, save of course for that of Henry Condell and Richard Burbage, who had commented on my face.

"Master Richard is the tall fellow with the rolling voice. And the big nose. No actor in London rivals him. His brother Cuthbert manages our receipts."

The Company determined the plays and the casting and divided the profits amongst themselves.

"The rest of us follow their direction and work our bums till there's hardly enough left of them to sit on."

As he spoke, Robin prowled the room with the thoughtless grace of a cat, stripping off his round hose and netherstocks, scrubbing his teeth with a frayed twig, delivering an affectionate kick to the Condell boys, finally settled in their low bed. He was handsome and solid as a seal; his auburn hair curled upon his shoulders and his long-lashed blue eyes laughed at everything they saw—including me, but without malice. One glance told me that girls went wild over him, though he told me he was only twelve. Just before getting into bed he knelt and rattled off a prayer.

"How long hast thou been in the Company, Robin?" I asked— very low in spirits, for if this boy was my measure I had too far to stretch.

"Since I was nine. Most don't engage so young with the Lord Chamberlain's Men, but my saintly widowed mother did marry again, and my most excellent stepfather desired me out from underfoot. You're fourteen, you say? That's late to begin."

"How would you advise me?"

"Why, like any apprentice, at any trade. Listen much, say little, do as you're told. Haven't you some notion of the stage?"

"I've never even seen a play, entire," I answered miserably.

He sat up and swore like a sailor. It unsettled me, this tendency of Londoners to swear by the body parts of God and Christ. "May the Almighty Grace defend you, then," said he, in a tone that clearly suggested the Almighty had a deal of work ahead.

Imagine a puppy seized by the scruff of the neck and flung into the foaming Thames at flood tide, and you will have a fair picture of my life for the next many weeks. Dick Worthing and Adrian Ball, both of whom came into the Company with some experience, seemed to adjust to the current and swim right away. But I barely kept my nose above water, and every day found a dozen opportunities to wish that I had sped directly to Newgate in that fateful hour after the riot, and kept on to Scotland.

My first view of the Theater, on a damp and overcast April morning: a round barnlike structure with three circular galleries surrounding a center court. The posts supporting these galleries were pranked up to resemble fine marble pillars and the wooden railings were painted to suggest the balustrades of an Italian villa, or something like. It was clearly meant to look grand, and perhaps did so at one time, but the stern gray light showed its obvious pretense. The stage was a rough board platform, about fifteen feet square. As we arrived, boys were spreading sawdust on the ground to soak up some of the rain that had fallen before dawn. Most of the Company were gathered at one corner of the stage, discussing business matters.

Master Condell turned to me before joining him. "Today you watch. Watch Robin and Kit, especially, and I'll not take amiss any opportunity you find to make yourself useful."

Robin eagerly introduced me to Christopher Glover, or "Kit," a thin youth with straight black hair, a milky complexion, and gray eyes shaded by soft black lashes. He raked his icy gaze over me and stalked away with the haughtiness of a prince. "Don't mind it," said Robin, "'Tis just his humor." He went on to explain that Kit was approaching sixteen, an age when most apprentices had either quit the stage or moved on to male roles. But young Master Glover remained unsurpassed in playing imperious queens and duchesses.

A sharp voice sounded from overhead: "Avast! Mind your ears!" Immediately after, the stage shook with a roar, followed by a sprinkle of cinders. In answer to my wide-eyed stare Robin told me it was only Harry Smithton, in the "hut" over our heads. I glanced up to a boxlike structure built high above the stage, with a trapdoor in its floor. Master Smithton, it seemed, liked to get off a preliminary shot or two before any play that involved a battle, to "warm the gun."

"The stage boys must be handy with buckets, in case he sets the thatch on fire," Robin added. "I'll be off. Watch the play, so you'll know what to do tomorrow."

I helped hang curtains around the stage, to hide the forest of trestles that held it about four feet off the ground. Black curtains signified that the play was a tragedy; the boy I was assisting informed me it was called *The Greek Warriors*. "What's it about?" I asked. "I dunno. Somewhat to do with the Trojan War." The rehearsal that shortly took place left me no wiser than he. Actors moved in and out through two doors at the back of the stage, spoke lines that were cut short, corrected each other, made grand exits, and entered again in what seemed to be another character. Toward the end of the rehearsal my attention was drawn more and more to Kit, who was playing the role of Helen. His voice fell into a melodious alto that could ring with command or sigh with affection. His face, now in transition from boy to man, was too angular to be considered beautiful, but somehow he created an impression of beauty. By merely putting out a hand, he made me see a sweeping skirt and train. Watching him, I felt hopeless: here was another standard I could not match. Even Dick and Adrian, the other new boys, were masters in comparison to me; they were to be used today as servants and messengers.

Noon came, and Starling soon after. I was surprised to see her, and to learn that she took fares for the gallery seats and sold fruit and gingerbread during performances. "How goes it?" she asked me, with ill-concealed delight.

I sighed. "It's bedlam. I'm lost."

"Be patient. In time it will all make sense. I'm in a pother to ask you, though—what drove you here from the docks?"

I was not comfortable with outright lying, so I merely shrugged. She jabbed me in the ribs, I poked her back, and a shrill-voiced woman called her to her station. Already, patrons were filing into the Theater, though the play wasn't to begin for another hour. "There's more to this tale," Starling whispered to me before scampering off. "And I *will* have it."

During the performance I stood on the floor with the "groundlings"—the apprentices, clerks, and maids who could only afford a penny to get in. Mindful that I was supposed to be in hiding, I pulled my cap low and added nothing to the noisy comments made by the audience. It was my first real play to watch and I wish I could remember it better, but too much lay on my mind. After the third act, Dick Worthing came to fetch me to the tiring rooms behind stage.

If the play was confusing, what went on behind it was in-comprehensible. I dared not offer to help, but stayed out of the way and wondered how anything could be made of the mad rushing about. Only toward the end did peace reign in the tiring room, and that because every available player was on the stage, battling before the gates of Troy. The cannon roared, the actors howled, the audience cheered, my head ached. Immediately after the play, the Company assembled on stage for a dance, and then the happy crowds poured out of the Theater to go their ways.

I had expected the players to take a rest then, but after chang-ing their clothes and making a quick survey of the day's receipts, they walked through some scenes of the next day's play, in which I was to perform as a servant and a soldier. Rehearsal, for me, meant being grabbed by the elbow and pulled into this place or that, like a piece of furniture. After about an hour (and me still as confounded as before) the day was finally over. By then it was six o'clock, almost twelve hours since we had arrived at the Theater. The Company scat-tered; Master Condell and his neighbor John Heminges walked home to St. Mary's Parish, a distance of one mile, followed by me and Robin and Kit (who boarded with Master Heminges). After supper that evening Robin showed me how to stage-fight with staves, then laid out the plot of the morrow's play and told me what my entrances were, then studied his part while I lay in bed in a blank stupor. So ended the first day of my blithesome life as an actor.

My expectation of theater life was that once or twice in a per-formance I would glide upon stage in a gown and make a speech loud enough to be heard in the third gallery. Two things I did not reckon on: first, that plays must be acted, not merely spoken, and second, that Londoners have an insatiable appetite for them. Citizens of the provinces may be well content with two or three performances in a year. But the London public has been fed so often it is like a beast, hurling itself at the theater doors demanding, "Plays! Give us more plays!" When I began my term of service with the Lord Chamberlain's Men, the city boasted four theaters open to the public, and each performed its own schedule: a different play almost every day, six days per week, for at least eight months of the year. Yesterday a comedy, today a romance, tomorrow a tragedy, and so the cycle continued, as relentless as the tide. I found time the first week to write to Susanna and tell her what I was doing (which I knew she would not approve); after that the stage swept me out to sea.

"Forward, march!" barked Master William Sly, who had served some time as a soldier and knew his drill. "Wheel right! Up with the pikes and engage!" He was built as solidly as an ale tankard, with thick wavy hair and a bull neck and a lower lip that bowed up combatively when something displeased him. "To the right I said, Richard, thou thick-pated shrimp—to the right!"

The play in which I first "acted" was about King Henry VI and the French wars. Wars make excellent dramatic material, so the first lesson for an actor is how to march on with a pike on one shoulder, then leap about the stage in a semblance of hand-to-hand combat. Since Robin was busy with his own part, I was paired with an actor hired for the day, a lanky, clownish street player who nonetheless knew his business. "Stick close to me, little brother," he told me with a wink. "I'll show you the ins and outs." This is exactly what he did, for we shared all our entrances as soldiers and serving men. To signal my speaking cues, he covertly kicked me, but as I had only two lines to say, my shins did not suffer overmuch. Both were in the same scene, where we entered fighting with bloody bandages wrapped around our heads. Master Condell, as King Henry, commanded us to cease, whereupon I cried, "Do what ye dare, we are as resolute!" Shouting such words with passion proved to be easier than I thought—the difficult part was making the fight seem natural. I had doubts about my performance until Dick Worthing accidentally brained me with his staff and knocked me near-senseless to the ground—that probably looked natural enough.

For two weeks I was used as a figure of action, and seldom spoke more than four lines together, usually as a messenger bearing news of some bloody event. My plan to disguise myself as a female may thus have been thwarted, but I could often wear a helmet or a hood, or smear my face with sheep's blood in a battle or street grime in a fight. I could don a beard or pull my cap low or simply melt into the crowd. "Stand forth, Richard!" the players shouted more than once, in rehearsal. "What are you doing in the theater if you don't wish to be seen, eh?"

The acting, in itself, made few demands on me during that first fortnight. When I was required to look something other than attentive, the sentiments were extreme ones—terror, rage, exaltation— all of which any child can, and often does, perform several times in the course of a day. So quickly did I master screaming upon the stage that I could almost begin to fancy myself a gifted actor except for what went on behind the stage.

The tiring rooms remained in a state of mayhem during a play, with actors throwing off costumes, searching frantically for misplaced properties, or scanning the plot to determine their next entrance. The cues for the actors on stage were often supplied by Cuthbert Burbage, who sat behind the door holding the playbook. But he could not divide his attention two ways, and thus the need for the "plot": a long scroll hanging from the centerpost, on which were written all the cues for every scene. Never was a piece of paper more ardently courted than during a performance. Every member of the Company possessed incredible gifts of memory, but no mortal could remember all the cues of a different play every day. Traffic around the plot was heavy and sometimes I could get nowhere near it. On one occasion I missed a cue entire, and found myself hurled a little late upon the boards by Master Cuthbert. There I blurted my alarm about the approaching barbarians with all the terror that the bloodthirsty warrior played by William Sly could have wished. Only at *that* point in the play he was expecting an announcement of the birth of his son. There followed a very brief pause, then Master Sly took two steps and fetched me a blow on the ear not entirely feigned, demanding, "Have done with thy madness, dolt! What ails thee? What news of my *wife*?"

"Keep your feet in line!" Robin had to remind me over and over. "You walk like a stork—turn your toes in! Heel-to-toe, remember? Round your steps, roll them—and keep those knees together when you sit! No maid sprawls like that."

Walking and talking like a female is a matter of observation and practice. Robin made an exacting teacher, drilling me in the garden if the day was not too far gone. Starling often joined us once her chores were done, and sometimes she was a help. More often she was a nuisance, collapsing with laughter on a bench or hopping up beside Robin to show where he was in error as to how ladies behaved. "That's all well," he said once, "but these are stage ladies."

I agreed, rubbing my neck wearily. "He's right. Everything has to be done broad upon the stage."

"Oh, listen to the veteran," Star scoffed. "I know that. But Rob should spend less time aping Kit and more looking around him."

"I do not ape—"

"You do. Mind how Kit walks, Richard, like he had an iron rod for a backbone. A real woman bends once in a while." So saying, she spread her arms like wings and bowed her back in a graceful curtsey, one toe pointed.

"Not in a corset, she doesn't." Robin imitated her curtsey with his back faultlessly straight, then spoiled the effect by making a vulgar noise. "You should lace yourself into one sometime; 'twould force all the wind out you."

"I don't pack near the wind you do!"

"True; what you pack is somewhat more solid. Ow!" he yelped, as she poked him in the ribs. "Pecking fowl! You be the instructor then, since you know so much." With that, he ran off to join a game of battledore which the Condell children were starting on the lawn. Star sat next to me on the bench.

"I have been thinking," she said. "Your coming here owes somewhat to those two men on the wharf. Did they chase you hither?"

I had to swallow before answering. "What men?"

"Just as I thought. Be comforted: I would know them again should they ever come to the Theater. I will be your sentry." With a reassuring smile, she dashed back toward the kitchen, leaving me not in the least comforted.

By the third week I had learned enough about walking and curtseying to be trotted out in a corset and gown, as a lady of the court. The part itself required little of me, merely to stand and look shocked or alarmed and make exclamations now and then. It was what I had imagined doing all along, but it proved, of course, to be nothing like I expected. In the midst of a harrowing scene, while a king accused his most trusted advisor of base treachery, I became aware of an itch deep within my laces and petticoats—in a place where no lady would ever scratch. The more one dwells upon such trifles, of course, the more intense and demanding they become.

My predicament was approaching a kind of agony which could not last much longer—when abruptly I thought of my sister Susanna's face, could she see me now. From uncontrollable itching I went to uncontrollable mirth. I happened to catch the eye of Dick Worthing, who was likewise decked out beside me. The two of us broke into sniggers that put a strain upon our corsets and drew stern looks from the actors nearby. One of them, Thomas Pope, put a stop to it by coming down with an armored foot upon my toes—pain can cut a fit of the giggles right short.

At least once every week the Company met at the Mermaid Tavern to set schedules, assign parts, or discuss any other business that came up. When parts for a new play were to be handed out, apprentices joined them, though they were expected to keep silent.

On the first Tuesday in May all gathered at the tavern to hear the plot and casting of the latest play by William Shakespeare—he who had "liked my manner" when I first read for the Company. Master Will, I was told, penned two or three new plays every season for the Lord Chamberlain's Men, though how he found time I could not say. As an actor and partner in the Company, he was as busy as any of them, and his reputation as a poet brought other work to his door. When we arrived at the tavern, in fact, he was engaged with two gentlemen who were trying to persuade him to write a funeral ode. The object of the ode was not yet dead, I gathered, but his death seemed likely, and the gentlemen were adamant that only one poet in London was up to the task.

"My humble thanks for the honor you give my poor pen," said the poet, "but I fear I have not time to do justice to Lord Hurleigh."

"'Tis not for ourselves we ask it, good sir. Lord Hurleigh admires your verses exceedingly. A request from such a kind and noble patron as he, so loyal a subject and kinsman to the Queen, is not to be despised."

"Alas," said Master Will, spreading his hands. "I am exalted by his regard, but the stage is my mistress. And demanding she is, too."

"If you would but consider—"

"I pray you, gentlemen." Richard Burbage rose from the table, with all his actor's presence about him. "You have received your answer, at least twice. Your business is done; we still have ours."

The two left, most reluctantly, and the Company seemed to think Shakespeare had done well to get rid of them. "Though it's a fair purse they were offering," he sighed.

"That's no matter," said Master Burbage. "Everybody knows Lord Hurleigh is a Catholic."

"A suspected Catholic, we must say."

"A suspected thief can hang as easily, and blot all he touches."

The conversation was only of passing interest to me, at the time. But before long my attention was riveted by a debate concerning whether I was ready for a real part—an actual, named character, not merely "first soldier" or "third lady." Masters Burbage, Pope, and Sly expressed some doubt—for the very good reason that I had made no impression on them. Masters Condell, Heminges, and Cowley spoke in my favor. They knew me best:

Henry Condell had taken time from his many duties to teach me elocution, while Richard Cowley served as dancing and fencing instructor to the boys. Their support was lukewarm, however—they saw me as barely competent, and no more. Master Will kept silent and merely nodded when the men came to agreement, then wrote my name beside the part of "Nerissa," and passed down the papers that contained my speeches and cues.

Robin, at my elbow, whispered, "Now thine arse is in the skillet." He grinned to reassure me, but I could almost smell my own flesh fry, and was not reassured. Events were moving too fast, and every day brought further indications that the stage required much more than I had anticipated. More, it seemed, than I was able to give it.

FLOUNDERING

✤

"*I* can make no sense of this tale," I complained to Robin. We were drilling each other on our lines for the new play. The hour was late; little Condell boys twitched in their sleep and a soft spring breeze sighed through the narrow window as the night watch called eleven o'clock from below.

"'Tis only a story," Robin yawned. "Why worry it to death?"

"Because I don't understand it. Here I am to play this serving maid—"

"Not a serving maid. Nerissa is a grand lady who waits upon an even grander lady."

"Aye, the lady Portia, who is so beautiful—and rich—that princes come from far and near to woo her. But why does she make them choose between three caskets? Why can they not strum lutes beneath her window at night?"

"You know that! It's all in the speech Nerissa makes at the beginning. Do you not remember your own part? Portia's father fixed it before he died: three little caskets, one gold, one silver—"

"And one lead. Yes, but—"

"Peace! I am explaining to you. Her picture is in one casket only and the suitor to choose the right one wins her hand. A man who picks gold will love her only for beauty. The man who picks silver desires only her wealth. But he who chooses lead . . . what was the writing on the lead casket?"

"'He who chooseth me must risk and hazard all he hath.' But anyone who chooses wrong must swear he will never again seek to marry. Who would take a risk like that?"

"Are you our master critic, now? It's just a story."

There was more that bothered me about the play, which they called *The Merchant of Venice.* The merchant, one Antonio, foolishly promises to lend money to his friend Bassanio so the latter can go wooing the lady Portia. But, as Antonio's money is all ventured in ships, he must borrow it in turn from a Jew named Shylock, who requires a pound of the merchant's flesh if Antonio cannot pay him on time. "What reasonable man would agree to those terms?" I demanded of Robin.

Of course, Antonio is unable to pay on time. Shylock, who hates Christians and is further angered when his daughter, Jessica, elopes with one, insists on claiming his pound of flesh. Bassanio, meanwhile, succeeds in winning Portia by choosing the lead cas-ket, but when he hears of Antonio's distress he rushes back to Venice to stand by his friend in court.

Shylock will not be swayed either by mercy or reason, and Antonio is about to go under the knife when a learned lawyer appears—who is really Portia in disguise, accompanied by Nerissa in clerk's robes. She also appeals to Shylock's mercy (in the same speech I recited at my hearing), but the Jew will have his bond, and the law is on his side. Cut away then, says Portia, but remember: the bond calls for flesh only. If Shylock spills one drop of Antonio's blood, then the law he appeals to will come crashing down on him. The Jew is thwarted, Antonio saved, Portia revealed, and almost everyone is married in the end—even my character, Nerissa, who has managed to fall in love with one of Bassanio's friends.

But what lover would fail to recognize his beloved in the weak disguise of an attorney's robes? What court would fail to rule that shedding blood is necessary to cutting flesh?

"What apprentice would quibble over a story?" Robin, tried beyond patience, heaved a pillow at me. "Go back to quayside, if you've no more touch for the theater than that."

Going back to quayside was impossible, of course, but what Robin said struck home: I seemed to lack "the touch." True, by now I had begun to decipher the mysteries of the plot sheet, and could get through most performances without some player hissing, "Now, Richard!" or "Not yet, Richard!" I had gained some notion of how to stand upon the stage and pitch my voice low or high and conduct a tolerable fight. But all were pieces, fragments of some greater whole that my mind failed to grasp. I was looking for a good reason to dress up in a gown and wig for the amusement of Londoners who might better be spending their time elsewhere. What value did they draw from the stage?

More to the point, what good was it to me? Almost a month had passed since I was attacked and robbed, and my simple intention to remain in London and spite my enemies had grown to a hope that I might somehow get my property back. But the theater claimed body and soul—I had scarcely time to think of a plan, much less act on one.

These thoughts ran faster through my head as the date approached for our first performance of *The Merchant*. The Company did not slight its schedule to prepare a new play; all our rehearsals were squeezed in before or after each day's offering. For three mornings I rehearsed with Kit, who played Portia, under the watchful eye of Master Condell. My master took some pains with my first speech: "On you rests the burden of letting the audience know why Portia's suitors have to go through this guessing game with the caskets. But keep your speech light and sharp—if you turn dull, you will lose their interest."

Kit was never dull. Portia's lines glittered like a needle as she described her failed suitors, skewering each one. As Portia he charmed; as Kit he made me feel like a fool. Our rehearsals went thus—

Me (as Nerissa): "What say you then by the French lord, Monsieur . . . um . . ."

Kit (as himself): "Le Bon, you blockhead. 'Tis an easy enough name to remember." (As Portia): "God made him, and therefore let him pass for a man."

Me (as Nerissa): "What think you of the Scottish lord—"

Kit (as himself): "What think I of nitwits? The *English* lord comes next!"

After three days my lines were firm, I had suppressed my fear of sharing a scene with Kit, and Master Condell claimed to be satisfied. But he had yet to tell me, and I knew not how to ask, what it was all about. Only once did I catch a glimmer of what acting could be.

It was during our one rehearsal of the entire play, with all actors present. The middles were dropped out of the long speeches and many of the shorter ones—I had scarcely begun my first and longest speech when Master Will called out, "Hold, enough! Jump to the end, so please you." Walking through the play helped me see that the story held together better than I supposed, but Shylock as portrayed by Master Burbage was the real surprise. He made a proper villain, rubbing his hands in glee at the prospect of cutting up Antonio's sweet Christian flesh. But in the middle of the play Burbage swept aside the villainous outline and revealed the beating heart of a man scorned all his life by the society that fed off him: "Hath not a Jew eyes? Hath not a Jew hands, organs, dimensions, senses, affections, passions? If you prick us, do we not bleed? If you tickle us, do we not laugh? If you poison us, do we not die? And if you wrong us, shall we not revenge?"

Watching from the back of the stage, I was spellbound—caught up, feeling *with* the greedy Shylock. Burbage had brought him to life. And that, I guessed, was the aim of the Lord Chamberlain's Men: to serve up rich helpings of life to their audiences, to introduce them to people they would never otherwise meet, to stretch their minds and hearts to fill a greater world.

But in realizing this aim, I doubted more than ever my ability to achieve it.

Now the dreaded day has arrived and all the actors are behind stage getting into their costumes. The second trumpet has just sounded, signaling half an hour until the performance begins. Kit and I are in the upstairs tiring room because we need more space than the others. We have each stripped down to breeches and hose, then pulled on a shift and one stiff petticoat. The dresser hurries to lace us into corsets, very tight at the waist but looser near the top, where he skips every other point. Stage apprentices generally do not stuff themselves in the bosom. Real ladies of the court, in fact, aspire to a shape much like our natural one, with a smooth front tapering down to a very long waist.

The garments are not designed for comfort or ease in dressing. They are the same clothes, minus a few petticoats, that any of the Queen's ladies might don of a morning, with hours to prepare and a bevy of servants to assist. The farthingale goes on over the corset—a sort of oval pillow that ties around the waist and flares out at the sides, lending a woman the shape of a Spanish galleon. A corset-cover next, then the gown—silk, satin, velvet, or quilted versions of the same—always heavy, with skirts that could conceal a troop of dwarfs and separate sleeves shaped like giant sausages. Most of these dresses are embroidered all over with seed pearls or silk thread—one sleeve would have fed us for months back in Alford.

After the gown is laced up the back and the snag-ends of gold thread are clawing at our necks, on goes the ruff—as subtle an instrument of torture as man has ever invented. It ties around the neck and locks your head in such a vise you can scarcely turn it—that, and scratchy too. The ruff stands out in stiff pleats, with a grandeur of width to match the rank of the wearer; some are so wide they make one's head look like a pea on a plate—a pox on them all! By now we are so trussed up that the dresser has to complete us, buckling our shoes and setting a jeweled wig, which reeks of many wearings and not enough washings, upon each head. Portia wears a tiara glittering with paste diamonds. And I am topped with a headdress of plumes.

All this takes place in near-perfect silence. Off the stage, Kit behaves as one who thinks very well of himself, but in the hours before a performance his manner is passing strange. He might never have trod the boards for all that a stranger could tell: so tightly wound that if I bumped him accidentally he might whirl back and slap me. I have seen him bite at his lips until they bled.

Most actors will jest with one another while waiting for the play to begin, or run quickly over a scene together, or clasp hands and wish themselves well, for a play like a ship sails smooth only when all hands are working in accord. But Kit steers his own ship, and the Lord Chamberlain's Men take care not to jog his sails; that is his humor, and everyone works around it. He has powdered his face white and lined his eyes with kohl; now he rubs a bit of rouge on his cheeks and lips, then hands the mirror to me—still without a word—so I may paint my own face.

Robin, agile as a monkey, clatters up a stairway so steep and narrow it is little more than a ladder. As Shylock's daughter, Jessica, he does not appear until the second act and is waiting until we quit the tiring room to dress himself. "Fair Venus, descend!" he cries to Kit. "The play begins anon, and the house is packed. We'll have silver in our pockets tonight. Then ho for the Southwark stews!" I was pretty sure the brothels and gambling houses across the river had never seen Robin's face, though he liked to speak as an old familiar. The bit about the silver might well be true, for the Company charges double for seeing a new play and apprentices receive a bonus from the profits.

Robin scurries back downstairs as the third trumpet sounds. The peculiar, breathing hush of the theater falls upon our audience, suddenly weighty in their silence. Kit glides to the stairway, turns, and looks at me directly for the first time. "Your feathers are tilted," he says before descending backward, sinking like a bright sun behind the floor's planked horizon.

Before this, all I had done with my short lines and brief actions was help push a story forward, like one of the stage boys moving trees or pillars. Now my task was to enter the story, give flesh and life to a play, and I still had no idea how. For the first time, I understood why acting is a profession, not a trade. Delivering extreme emotion is easy; carrying on everyday conversation is hard. Scarcely three sentences into Nerissa's first speech, I became aware of whispers and flutters in the audience. My part, which I had rehearsed so many times it might have been carved on my brain, crumbled like chalk.

In the course of their conversation, Nerissa names the suitors and listens to Portia's witty judgments on each, but I soon became so rattled that the names came out in a very haphazard order—one I mentioned twice, and two others were left out altogether. Kit took over the naming, carrying on a dialogue with himself while I nodded when it seemed appropriate, and tried to smile, and prayed for a quick end to my misery.

Once off the stage, he called me a gaudy string of names hardly befitting a lady, and it might have come to blows had not Master Heminges taken him aside for a lecture on self-control. Most thankfully, I had no speeches for the next many scenes and only short ones thereafter, of which I missed about half. I did make some impression on the audience: when Portia reveals her plan to pose as the doctor of laws with her clerk, Nerissa says, "What, shall we turn to men?" "Aye, lad," cried some wit from the audience, "and that is the trick, for thou art a mouse so far!"

Kit refused to speak to me thereafter. Nor did anyone else except Master Will, who as Nerissa's suitor had sent me looks closer to pity than love. But not even he addressed the issue directly. "Here, Richard," said he as I descended the stairway in lawyer's robes for the court scene. "Let us be true to life. A law clerk always wears his tassel on the left side to show he does not yet aspire to the profession." So saying, he moved the tassel on my cap, and in my distraught condition I remembered leaving it on the right side for a reason, but could not think what it was. This simple act of kindness helped, for Master Will coaxed me into showing a bit of spirit in the last scene. Then I turned to exit and tripped over my petticoat, falling on my face.

The audience enjoyed this, as much as they had enjoyed the entire play. The business with the three caskets delighted them and while Bassanio pondered his choice, they did not hesitate to help him decide. "Choose lead! Choose lead!" they called, and laughed when Bassanio pointed guardedly to the said casket and winked at them. They loved to hiss Master Burbage as Shylock, with a red beard and a leering grin, and cheered loudly when he was dealt his defeat in court. But his speech about revenge silenced them. I noticed its effect even while sunk in gloom behind the stage, waiting for my next entrance under Kit's scorching disdain. ". . . and when we are wronged, do we not revenge?"

The Merchant was deemed successful enough to play for two more days running, and in those performances I managed to not butcher my part—although I did no special kindness by it either. Nerissa could scarcely speak three lines together before the whispering and nut-cracking began. Try as I might, I could not enter the play; I felt almost as if the play had locked me out. After church on Sunday I took to the garden, dumpish and tight-lipped, to study my prospects: namely, whether to leave the Company now or wait until they dismissed me at the end of the season.

A letter from Susanna had arrived the day before, full of reproach, as I expected. Though we were twins, she was born older than me, and considered herself wiser: "It doth maze me that you who claimed to know our mother's heart best could shame her by making a fool of yourself upon the ungodly stage. . . ." More followed in this vein, before she assured me that I could always return home if I changed my mind. But Alford was no longer home. It had nothing for me besides living off my sister or hiring out for farm work. What to do?

In the two months since my mother's passing, life had spun me around so many times I had lost all sense of direction. I recalled the opening scene of *The Merchant,* where Antonio described his state of melancholy in words that suited me well: "Such a want-wit sadness makes of me that I have much ado to know myself."

"I'll tell you this," came a voice behind me. "If you keep moping, you'll never get anywhere. I'll wash my hands of you."

I considered not answering, then sighed. "Is that my Lady Consolation? How sweetly falls her voice. Truly, 'tis the voice of an angel—from hell."

Starling swept in like a gale from the north bringing cold comfort, and perched upon the back of the stone bench. She had kept mostly clear of me while I was learning my new profession (or drowning in it, more like). But her prying nature could not be put down forever. "A wise youth would wait until he knows his angel better before deciding where she's from."

"How can you wash your hands of anything that was never on them?"

She snorted. "Were it not for me, you wouldn't be here."

"For that, I know not whether to thank you, or push you off that bench."

"Oh, peace!" she burst out, suddenly angry, unless she had been all along. "I didn't drag you by the heels into this company. You were chased here, as we both know."

"It's no concern of yours how I came here."

"That may be, but there's a thing I've been turning over in my mind. Something odd about one of those men."

"What was it?"

"Probably no concern of yours." She hopped off the bench and took two steps before I grabbed her by the apron-bow.

"What's your price?" I asked.

"Only your story."

Very well then, thought I; I'll take this bait and tell her all. If a choice of allies were offered me, I might have passed over Starling, as she was tart and inquisitive and talked when I had rather she wouldn't. But the friend market was not a large one at the time, and I had to admit she was clever. So I started from the beginning and told her of my arrival in London and the man who directed me to the quay and the infuriating interview with my aunt. I finished with the street riot and the threat upon my life, which drove me to the theater. She listened avidly, her eyes widening. "Faith, it's better even than I thought!" she exclaimed, when I had done.

"What is?"

"Your tale. Like something out of Robin Hood."

I laughed, though grimly. "Robin Hood never soaked his breeches, I warrant, while the sheriff's men held a knife to his throat."

"Did you do that?"

"Very near. Now you must tell—"

"This law clerk, who sent you to the wine merchants—what of him?"

"Him? He was kind to me. He gave me a shilling."

"Did he? Why?"

"He liked me, or pitied me. Of course, the shilling was stolen, too. But I have kept my end of the bargain; now you must keep yours."

"Well. I told you that I would recognize those men again, but to speak truth, I would know only one. You came to us on a Wednesday. The day after, I was on the docks as always, at the fish market, and noticed a man leaning against the wall of Coverdale's warehouse. Old Roger Coverdale himself laid into him. I've seen this before; he hates idlers. He's such a little rooster." Here Starling darted her head forward and back, so like the gentleman in question I had to laugh, a little. "The stranger left, with Master Coverdale railing at him all the way down the wharf. I noticed his bearing. He was dressed like a common laborer but walked like a man of quality. Somehow you could see that he despised Master Coverdale."

"And you think he was one of the two who followed me?"

"I am sure of it. Before, he wore that leather hood that shaded most of his face. But he could not disguise his walk, or attitude. He was there to make certain you were well and truly gone."

"Perhaps. But this is speculation."

"Then let us go back to what we know." With a start, I saw that she had taken over my case. "We know that your aunt was not telling you all."

"She was not telling me anything. 'Tis certain that image of the medallion meant something to her but I can't go back and ask her."

"True, but she's never met me."

"What's your meaning, pray?"

Squirming with suppressed excitement, Starling proposed that she pay a visit to the lady and see what might be seen. My objection to this was swift and firm—but unfounded, as she quickly proved to me by a series of logical arguments that would have done credit to Aristotle. I most truly did not want her taking a hand in my affairs, but the longer she talked, the more sense she made, and I could not deny a desire to know more about Anne Billings.

Starling proposed to present herself as a poor wronged maid who had left her infant child on a church step and now, conscience-stricken, was searching all the foundling hospitals for a dear little boy, six months of age, with thick black hair and a green ribbon tied around his right wrist. She tried this out on me, with such tears and pleadings I had to wonder if she harbored a thwarted ambition for the stage. But I saw how it might put my aunt off-guard, and Star's sharp eyes might discover something. Neither of us had a clear idea of what there was to be discovered, but action seemed better than speculation.

I insisted upon going with her as far as the hospital, to see that she did what she pledged and no more. We wrangled over this for some time, her objections being, first, that I could trust her, and second, that I might be recognized. Then she hit upon a solution: I could go in disguise as—what else?—a young lady, in clothes borrowed from the mistresses Condell. That almost killed the expedition. She said it would be good practice for me, but I knew enough about the theater to recognize that stage deportment is nothing like real life, and it is only in plays by Will Shakespeare and the like that one sex is easily taken for the other. But somehow within an hour I was in the garden shed, corseting myself in one of Alice Condell's day dresses. Since we had no wig, I brushed my hair back under a French hood, which was a little out of fashion even though older ladies still wore them.

By then I most heartily regretted letting Star into my confidence, and could not fathom how she had talked me into this. But there comes a point in any dubious venture when turning back makes less sense than going forward, so I straightened my back, lowered my eyes, and went forward, in the short, rolling step Robin had taught me.

Of our journey to east Southwark, my long wait outside the foundling hospital, and an unpleasant encounter with two Italian sailors who mistook my character, there is little to tell. When Starling finally emerged, after at least half an hour, her face looked thoughtful.

"Well?" I demanded, almost wild with the effects of an anxious wait.

"Not here. Let us walk a ways." We walked all the way to Southwark Street and turned north for the Bridge before she spoke a word.

"She's a close-mouthed woman. All I could get out of her was that she's operated the hospital for twenty-one years."

"Could you have asked too many questions, and made her suspicious?"

"All my questions were reasonable. I don't think she suspected me, or my story; it's just her way with all. And I can guess why."

"Why?" I asked, so exasperated I forgot to soften my voice, and two passing gentlemen gave me a very startled look.

"She's a Catholic. Perhaps even a nun."

"You know this?"

"Almost certain. Those beads around her neck—rosary beads. 'Twas hard to tell in such dim light, but I know they are."

I considered this in silence. It could explain much: why my aunt had never married, why she was called "Holy Nan," why she and my mother disliked each other so. Her faith meant nothing to me, so long as she practiced it in secret. But suppose my father turned out to be a Catholic, too? That would be a bitter dose to swallow, and I began to wish we had never come. "There's something else," Starling went on. "She is supposed to be running a home for foundlings, yet there are no children about."

"Yes, I wondered about that. But can you be sure?"

"Think of the Condell house. Is it ever wholly quiet, except in the dead of night? And around the room I saw no little stools or books or toys or birch rods. I searched every corner of it while sobbing my eyes out." Directly we came to Cheapside and turned west before she spoke again. "One thing more, Richard."

I kept silent, knowing she would come to it.

"'Twas all I could do to keep her as long as I did. I kept asking and begging to see the infants in her care—which she never denied—and going into long teary spells, until finally I tried her patience past its limit. She stood up with her shoulders back and took a deep breath and ordered me from the house. But in that breath I saw it. 'Twas just under her bodice, and her chest rising pushed it out to make a shape upon the gown. I saw it only an instant, but I am sure it was the outline of a medal just over the breastbone."

I commenced nibbling on my thumbnail until she told me it wasn't ladylike. "What size?" I asked.

"About an inch and a half across, just as you told me."

"It could have been any sort of medal. Catholics hang all kinds of charms and talismans around themselves."

"That's true," she said, smooth as cream, and I could tell she did not believe for a moment that it was "any sort" of medal.

We progressed up Cheapside with little conversation, pondering these things until after another couple of turns we had reached St. Mary's Parish. There I intended to slip down the alley behind Aldermanbury Street and come upon the Condell house by the back gate, then hide myself in the garden shed before anyone spotted me in my outrageous garb.

But we had reckoned without Mistress Condell's custom of taking Sunday-afternoon walks. Halfway down Cattle Street we raised our eyes to behold her, flanked by Alice and Mary and chatting with a neighbor beside one of the hawthorn trees that lined the avenue. I froze in terror at the very moment Mistress Condell glanced my way. The girls were still engaged in their conversation. I might have so forgot myself as to pick up my skirts and make an ungraceful dash in the opposite direction, but Starling seized my elbow.

"Get behind the trees," she hissed, "and on down the alley. I'll distract them."

I took a last look at Mistress Condell before following these instructions and knew that one lady, at least, was not about to be distracted.

A FOOTHOLD

✢

After supper and prayers, Mistress Condell called to me: "Richard, do stay awhile below stairs. I need your help with winding some yarn." This caused everyone in hearing to turn and stare, and at my side Robin murmured, "Set apart for yarn duty, then? What have you done?" I was soon to learn that when a member of the household required a dressing-down, the Lady Elizabeth was apt to sit him in a corner of the great room, drape his hands with a hank of wool taken off the spinning wheel, and dispense the lecture while winding yarn from the skein onto a bobbin. Thus tied to the mistress, the victim has no choice but to listen.

"I will not ask you to explain what you were about this afternoon, Richard," she began when we were settled in our corner. "I spoke to Starling, and she told me it was a personal matter which only you could divulge." She paused then, while four lengths of yarn wrapped round the bobbin. I might have divulged my whole life story, had I been able, but my throat was so tight I could scarcely have given her the time of day. After a long moment she continued. "But I feel called upon to warn you of a certain danger. 'Tis a temptation peculiar to actors, and as subtle as any devil might devise." I gazed intently at the bobbin while feeling her eyes on me. "You strike me as a gently reared lad, and you know the Scripture, yes?"

I cleared my throat. "I do, lady."

"Then you know how your soul and body were knit together in the secret place by God Himself, and all your being is owed to Him?"

"Of course, lady."

"You say 'Of course,' as if the thought hardly needed minding, but ofttimes the greatest thoughts are soonest overlooked." Two more lengths of yarn went onto the bobbin. "Acting is a gift, and has its uses. It can lift a plowman's eyes from the ground and give him a vision of the greater world. It can offer food for thought to a dull brain. At his best, an actor can stir the flagging spirit with noble words, or model courage for the fainthearted, or teach a lesson in virtue. Even at his least, he can beguile an hour or two from the laborer's weary life and make him laugh. This is worthy. But—"

The bobbin halted abruptly, and my gaze jumped to her face, looking grave at the moment, with delicate smile lines chiseled about the firm mouth. "Here is where you must be careful, and learn this now while you are young. Acting has its place, but that place is in the theater. A player who is good at what he does may be tempted to take the characters he portrays upon the stage out into his own life, that life that God has given him to live as himself. And soon, his friends lose sight of who he is. What is worse, the player may lose himself. Do you follow what I say?"

"Yes, lady," said I, thinking her words would have had more salt if I were any good at acting.

"This is what you must guard against. When you take off your costume, you must take off the character you played, and put on yourself. Acting is a worthy profession, but a dangerous one for this reason: the better you are at it, the more perilous it may be to your soul."

I made bold to speak my mind. "Pardon, mistress, but there seems little to fear for my soul on that account." Her hands, which had resumed their bobbin-winding, paused as though considering my words and what they meant. Then they moved on, swift and sure as fate.

"Perhaps not. I have seen you on the stage, Richard, and I will allow that the profession does not take easily to you. Or you to it. But I would not yet give it up. There is something in you—my husband sees it, and one or two of the others. If you leave the stage, may it be for the best. But if you stay . . ." The skein I was holding felt suddenly lighter, and I noticed with a start that she had wound almost all of it. "If you stay, you may find that you are one of the truly gifted, and my warning holds double for you. See that you heed it.

"And when you go about in the city, you must go as yourself, and not as what you most surely are not. If I catch you in my daughter's clothes again, we will have to find you another lodging. Do you understand?" I nodded miserably. "Now, rest your arms a moment while I ready another hank of yarn to put upon them."

I feared a two-skein lecture, but she turned the talk to more trifling matters: where I grew up, and how I got my schooling, and how my sister got along. Mistress Condell possessed a stately bearing that caused even the high-born to bow upon meeting her, yet she glowed with an underlying warmth—not merry but deep, and as soothing as the scent of orange and cloves that wafted from the pomander ball at her waist. Little by little it loosened the knot in my guts and allowed me to speak almost freely. That knot had been some weeks in the making, so steady a companion I scarce knew myself without it. But by the end of the third skein, her calm had spread to me, with a feeling I suddenly recognized as happiness. Another thought struck then: I did not want to leave this house. Here was the order and peace I had been craving, ever since circumstance uprooted me from Alford. With all my heart, I wished to stay. But one great difficulty stood in the way of that. I would have to secure my place with the Company.

May was drawing to an end and the season had scarcely more than a fortnight to run. Warm weather brought the plague time, when

London theaters closed for fear of contagion and actors left the city to tour the countryside. Robin was to accompany the Lord Chamberlain's Men on tour for the first time, and every night he bent my ear with the glories of life on the road. Having myself spent some time on the road during my journey to London, I could have told him about the glories of sleeping under hayracks and begging bread, but Robin was better at talking than listening. Further, I had the sense that most of his relish owed to disappointment: he had been awaiting his mother's call to spend the summer with her, but the invitation never came. So I held my peace and let him talk.

Kit harbored no such longing for his own parents, who were grocers on Cheapside; he would join the Company for his third tour. Dick would pass his summer with cousins in Surrey. And Adrian Ball had left the Lord Chamberlain's Men to join the boys' company of St. Paul's Chapel. Master Condell said nothing about my situation, either because he was too occupied or because he knew not what to say. Or more likely both. In the meantime I was back in harness as a soldier, a messenger, a nobleman's daughter who speaks seven lines and is brutally murdered off the stage. All this I managed without disgracing myself, and the month of May was lumbering peacefully to a close, when Kit ate a piece of boiled goat on Thursday night and was violently ill by Friday morning.

The first word I had of it was Alice Condell charging into our attic room well before dawn. "Up, Richard! We're in a coil today— Kit is puking up his guts and Father says you must take his part!"

I sat up halfway, squinting at the sheaf of papers she waved before my face. "'Tis Lady Constance, in *King John*. Master Heminges has made cuts in it, but you must get your lines in the second act before breakfast. Father will quiz you on it. You may con the rest at the Theater. Up, I say!"

She leaned over Robin and gave my shoulder a hard push, which, as I was resting half-awake on my elbows, overbalanced me and sent me crashing to the floor. This uncovered Robin, who sat up in his skewed shirt, blinking. "What's this about? Out, you froward female!"

"Mind what I say, Richard," warned Alice, just before disappearing swift as a wind.

"What was it she said, Richard, that warrants stealing my sleep?" When I told him, Robin groaned and threw himself back against the pillow. "Constance is a demon's part. You'll be hard-pressed to have the second act before we reach the Theater. What are you gaping at me for? Strike a flint and light the candle!"

King John is a historical play, another of Will Shakespeare's works. It concerns the John who was brother to Richard Lionheart and who took over the kingdom after that great crusader met his premature end. But, as often happens in history no less than drama, the king must contend with a rival. Though Richard died childless, he does have a nephew, Arthur, who is next in line for the throne. But John has ruled England since his brother Richard joined the Crusades, and does not intend to surrender his crown, especially since Arthur is but a child.

Arthur's mother, Constance, enlists the aid of King Philip of France and the Duke of Austria to secure the throne for her son. War breaks out between the forces of John and Philip, then a truce, then more war. Arthur is captured and John plots to have him murdered, but instead the boy is killed in a fall while trying to escape. His mother Constance dies of grief (off the stage, fortunately), and eventually John himself is poisoned by a fanatical monk.

Master Heminges had pared down the lines so that they were not too much to learn in a morning, but all of them were to be strongly delivered. It was a "demon's part" indeed—Constance is a she-lion, completely devoted to the advancement of her son and ready to tear apart anyone who stands in her way. She snipes at Queen Eleanor, her mother-in-law, taunts her allies when their zeal appears to falter, whips up flagging spirits with bloody rhetoric. When Arthur is captured and taken from her, she spins into a grief so profound her allies think she has gone mad. "I am *not* mad," she rails at them. "I would to heaven I were, for then 'tis likely I should forget myself!"

Reading over the part, I felt my heart sink. Dick Worthing had been trotted out as a madwoman the week before without much success, and I guessed why. Rage and grief may be easy to play, but I had noticed, in comparing Dick to Kit, that one can go too far with it and fall into parody. Audiences have been known to laugh at an over-tragical interpretation of the lover betrayed or warrior expiring. That is what I feared would happen to me when Constance appeared with her hair all unbound, spouting lines like "Death!

Death, O amiable lovely Death! Thou odiferous stench! Sound rottenness!" To say such words as though they came from the heart, rather than from a poet's overheated pen—that was the task before me, after first getting the lines in my head.

And all to be done in a matter of hours. Robin, who was cast as John's daughter, helped where he could; a year before he had taken Arthur's part and still remembered some of the cues. As he fed them to me, I stumbled over my speeches in Act II, all the while getting dressed and combing down my unruly hair and washing out my brackish mouth with rosewater, continually tripping over little boys who couldn't stay out of the way.

Then Robin and I hurried down to the great room, where our master met us in company with John Heminges and William Sly. Master Sly had sped from Southwark as soon as the news of Kit's misfortune reached him. He was to play the Duke of Austria, a pompous bag of wind who parades about in a lionskin and offers Constance endless occasion to jeer at him. Masters Condell and Heminges were Kings Philip and John respectively. Together we made up enough of Act II to lurch through it, and did so while hastening toward the Theater in the milky light of an overcast morning, tossing lines back and forth. I staggered to keep up both literally and figuratively, clutching the sheaf of papers in a sweaty hand.

While the Company rehearsed Act I on the stage, I practiced my lines for Act III in the tiring room, with Master Sly offering uncertain instruction: "Put a hand to your head. Nah, nah, take it off—

you look like a sailor! Now Salisbury says"—he consulted the prompt book—"'Pardon me, madam, I may not go without you to the kings.' That is your cue; continue."

"'Thou mayest,'" I read. "'Thou shalt. I will not go with thee. For my grief's so great that no support but the huge, firm earth—'"

"Hold awhile. Make a note here. At this point you are to sit upon the stage."

". . . Do what, sir?"

"Mind what she says about no support but the earth. She sits on the ground and bids the kings come to her, fractious female that she is. Do you, sit down. Do it! Then the kings enter, arm in arm after making their alliance. . . ." So we continued, and after several more lines I was standing again, trying to respond fittingly to William Sly's cues. But I was distracted, remembering a recent scene in my own life that seemed to have some bearing on this play. I wished to give it more thought but could not, with Master Sly barking cues at me. At the end of our time together he seemed less than confident. "That's all I can do for you," he said. "I have my own business and you must get this part in your brain. The task is yours, Richard; you must sink or swim, as God grants."

After walking through Acts II and III with the Company, I was released to study while the others practiced the remaining scenes. History plays brim over with more characters than any company can supply, and actors often doubled on the smaller parts. The Lord Chamberlain's Men also hired unattached players to fill out a large cast, and a number of these were milling about today, adding to the confusion as I sought refuge deep in the bowels of the tiring room.

The rooms behind stage are like a rabbit's warren: dark, complex, and busy, smelling of starch, powder, paint, and too many anxious bodies crowded together. Racks of costumes and properties form little coves in the clutter, to which is added all the furniture necessary to a particular play. I worked my way to the back wall, where light from a narrow window fell upon King John's throne—a masterpiece of gilt and velvet, with richly upholstered arms and a high pointed back. In Act V the dying king is carried in this chair by the stage boys, and fortunately it is made lighter than it looks or the boys would be serving notice.

I chose the throne for my study, though even in this out-of-the-way place actors came and went. Richard Burbage plunked a severed head on a shelf nearby with the words, "A bit of company, eh, lad?" It was a plaster replica of William Sly's head, who, as the Duke of Austria, would lose it in battle. It stared fixedly at me until I turned it aside. The ceiling over my head rumbled at a blast from the Company cannon, which Harry Smithton had touched off from the hut.

A memory was needling me, and it would have to be dealt with before I could concentrate on getting my lines.

On the day our mother was buried, Susanna had cleaned out the cottage, hauled all our pots and dishes to the stream to scrub them, aired the mattress and washed the linens, and worked herself to little more than a frayed twig. She could hardly stand during the short burial service. It struck me as irrational and dis-respectful, and I took her to task for it. This led to the biggest row we had ever had, with me claiming she was bent upon scrubbing all memories of our mother out of that place—which I would admit now was not fair. For her part, Susanna wept and wished herself dead. Then she dropped cross-legged on the plank floor of our house. "How dare you reproach me? How dare you? She was my mother, too, though she may have loved you better."

I tried being conciliatory. "I should not have reproached you. Now get up."

"I won't! You come to me, if your knees will bend."

"Stop playing the madwoman," I said, exasperated. "You can't stay on the floor forever. We still have to live."

"That's easy for you to say. Oh, it is easy for you." She pounded the splintered boards with her fists, working herself to new heights. "Everything is easy for you!"

We made peace later that night, but it remained a painful scene I did not like to recall. Yet the part of Constance had forced it to my attention. I looked down at her lines: "My grief's so great that no support but the huge firm earth can hold it up. Here is my throne; let kings come to it!" The words blurred before my eyes. Susanna, I thought. So this is what you were feeling. . . .

"Art dreaming, lad?" a mild voice interrupted my thoughts as Master Will's head appeared above a row of feathered hats on a costume rack. The tiring room had begun to fill with actors seek-ing cloaks, helmets, and armor that would transform them into warring princes for an afternoon. The sun's rays fell steeply through the window and I knew that Harry Smithton had run up the white silk flag to signify a performance at two o'clock.

"Not dreaming, sir," I replied. "Pondering."

"A worthy occupation," said he. "God gave you wit, but it remains your charge to use it."

Another head popped up in the thicket of feathers, a pleasant face very similar to the first but without the retreating hairline. This was Edmund Shakespeare, brother to the playmaker, who had joined the Company that spring at the age of eighteen. As the son of the French king, Edmund was acting his largest role to date. His face glowed with anticipation and—well might I recognize it—a touch of terror. "Come, Will," he cried with a gaiety somewhat forced, "I would parry a word with thee over a rapier's point."

Master Will nodded at me before going off to practice a bit of swordplay with his brother, and I had the sense he had meant to say more. He listened far more than he talked; there was always a listening look about him, as if the whole world had his ear. Suddenly, I understood what he was listening for: it was life. And he heard it, too. This was how Richard Burbage could breathe a soul into such a character as Shylock the Jew; Master Will had given him life.

I turned back to my part with an eagerness I had never felt about anything touching the stage. Reading over the lines again, I saw more and more of Susanna in them. She was, and is, a most capable person: a quick study and a tireless worker, with ambitions to rise higher than her station. Yet when our mother took sick, Susanna found herself at a loss. It so happened that I was a better nurse: gentler, more patient, capable of sitting an entire afternoon at the bedside while my sister could manage no more than half an hour. The trial of our mother's illness and death had fed her long-standing resentment of me—I saw it now. Susanna could spend all day being better than me at a score of things, even my own job of managing the horses. And yet she could be defeated an hour before bedtime because, at the end of the day, I was the one who could make our mother laugh. "Everything is easy for you!" she had cried. The words seemed absolute nonsense to me then; I understood them now. Constance was like that, collapsing in despair because all her hard work and strong will had counted for naught.

So I could do it. I could speak her impossible lines from the heart, because I had found my way there.

I felt a sharp sting on the ear, where Robin had scored me with a paper pellet. "Up, bedslug! The dresser is taken sick today and we must lace each other. Stop thy sulking—this performance stands to pass like all the rest."

The ensuing flutter of preparation left no more time for study, but as we helped each other dress we ran through my lines one more time, and found them fast. "All well, then?" Robin asked, taking a closer look at me.

"Very well," I replied.

"We'll try to whisper any cues you misplace, won't we, Dick?" Dick, who had started down the steps to be ready for his entrance as Queen Eleanor, nodded amiably—though he knew no more cues than I. My heart warmed to both of them, as though we were comrades-in-arms before the battle. Robin clapped me briefly on the arm. "God be with you, Richard."

And indeed, I can give to no man or woman the credit that belongs to God for seeing me through that performance. What I did was not perfection, for I lost some lines and repeated at least one, and twice the Company had to smooth over a cue I had missed. But for the first time I caught the current of a play. My mistakes were snags that hindered for only a moment. The other players recognized the change almost at once and began playing to me rather than away. It was a subtle difference, hard to explain, but it meant that they felt free to call attention to Constance, instead of distracting the audience (by countless actor's tricks) from a weak performance.

On my last entrance, when I appeared with hair unbound, mourning for the captured Arthur, I heard a ripple through the audience, a gasp of alarm. Like a strong wine, it went straight to my head. "Lo, now!" I wailed. "Now see the issue of your peace!" A woman in a nearby gallery cried out in sympathy.

"Patience, good lady." Master Condell, as King Philip, extended his hands. "Comfort, gentle Constance."

"No!" I cried. "I defy all counsel, all redress, but death!" The utter stillness of audience made my voice ring with authority. They were on my side. It was like nothing I had ever known—a power, a sense that I could sway hearts and draw tears. "Oh death! Amiable, lovely death . . ." I took Constance to the brink of madness but not beyond it; some cool hand of restraint kept me from overplaying.

King Philip spoke soothingly: "Come, bind up your hairs."

"Yes, that I will. I envy their liberty, and will again commit them to their bonds, because my poor child is a prisoner." When the lady began to put up her unruly locks, it became obvious to all that she knew not the first thing about hairdressing. I covered the awkwardness by pacing, like a princess striving to remember herself even as her hands forgot the simplest task. My steps took me far left, where the second gallery swings so close to the stage that patrons therein are all but sitting on it. ". . . and so he'll die; and rising so again, when I shall meet him in the court of heaven I shall not know him . . ."

An experienced actor can risk looking directly at the audience, and even addressing them in asides. I did not dare, but nevertheless, while sweeping near-sightless eyes over the gallery, my gaze caught and stuck on one face: a face neither old nor young, with round eyes and a wide mouth, shadowed by the square brim of a scholar's cap.

". . . Never, never, will I behold my pretty Arthur more—Oh!"

Martin Feather's law clerk and I recognized each other at the same time, and his body jerked, as though pulled by a string.

As for me, I forgot the rest of that speech.

I paced back to the center of the stage wringing my hands and crying out "Oh! Oh!" while one of the men reproached me: "You hold too heinous a respect of grief."

"He talks to me that never had a son," I snapped—remembering that line at the last moment. I turned back to the gallery, in time to see the clerk stepping over the feet of patrons as he worked his way out of the row. The tassel of his cap swung from side to side—his right side, though I recalled Master Will telling me that clerks always wore theirs on the left.

King Philip: "You are as fond of grief as of your child."

Constance: "Grief . . . grief fills the room of my absent child! It . . . it lies in his bed, walks up and down with me. Up and down . . . up and down . . ." Here memory failed me as I walked up and down, and my eyes strayed to that spot in the second gallery, now empty. It was no use, and my exit almost due anyway: with one more "Up and down," I gave it up and left the stage.

King Philip then stated a fear that Constance might do harm to herself, and followed directly. "By heaven, Richard," said Master Condell, once we were clear off, "that was *well done*. Thou hast caught it, lad; I know not how, but well done."

Such fulsome praise was uncommon for him and at any other time it would have pleased me no end. But the law clerk, if such he was, had set the afternoon at a tilt. I pulled off my wig, which was suddenly too hot to bear. "Thank you, sir. But if I could be excused—I've just thought of a thing that wants doing, and if you could grant me the afternoon, I'd be grateful."

He hesitated, being famously stingy with the time he allowed off. But I had never made such a request before, and he presently decided I had earned it. So I set about divesting myself, dumping my fine garments with a haste that did them no honor, ignoring Robin's jibes about calls of nature. He thought I had done well also, and told me so by an especially hard punch on the shoulder. I spared no time in trading compliments with him, but slipped out the back door of the Theater so quickly I was still buttoning my doublet on my way down the Shoreditch Road.

My destination was Middle Temple and the chambers of Martin Feather, attorney.

STRANGE ECHOES

❖

I knew the way from my wine-delivering days.
Though I had made the Châlons run with Ralph
Downing only once, it was as simple as following
Cheapside through the city and out Ludgate, then
taking Fleet Street to Middle Temple. What I hoped
to discover there was less clear to me—not the clerk
himself, but perhaps something about him. All I knew
was that seeing him again had spurred me to action.
In the half hour it took to reach my destination and
locate Master Feather's chambers, I hatched what
seemed a reasonable line of presentation for myself.

I climbed a set of creaky stairs and pushed
open an arched door. A clerk and a young scrivener
at his copy desk paused in the midst of a dictation
to stare at me.

"Is Master Feather within?" I asked, in my best London accent.

"He's gone to the country," the clerk informed me shortly. His narrow face wore a sour expression, or perhaps that was its natural cast. "Who wants him?"

I ignored the question, so rudely put. "The other clerk, then— do you know where he might be found?"

"You are raving, boy. And too much in haste. Your doublet is buttoned wrong, know you that?"

I glanced down at the slovenly gap where I had missed a button and winced. No help for it now, though. "But the other—"

"There is no other clerk here. I am Master Feather's sole assistant for the last sixmonth. Why should you think there was any other?"

Something in his tone—a sudden sharpness, an attention too pointed—warned me to take care. "I may have been mistaken. I understood him to say he was a clerk."

"Who, sirrah?"

I took a chance and described the man I sought, and directly saw the gamble rewarded. For as I spoke, the scrivener's eyes lit with the eager glow of young climbers everywhere who see a chance to show off their knowledge. "It sounds like John Beecham, Master Merry."

I saw one side of the clerk's face twitch. "The same thought crossed my mind, Samuel," he remarked dryly. "Though my tongue be not so limber as yours." He folded his arms, then absently ran his index finger along his lower lip as he regarded me with a prosecutor's stare. "You saw him, you say? In this room?"

"No, sir. Outside Master Feather's lodgings in Cheapside."

"Oh?" There was that sharp tone again. "What was he about?"

"Sir?" I was confused now; the man seemed as eager for information as I myself.

"What business? What was he doing?"

"Well . . . he was leaving."

"What is it *you* want with him?"

I had an answer ready for this. "If you please, sir, he lent me a shilling once, and I want to pay him back."

The clerk blinked at this, then let out a harsh laugh. "You owe money to *him*? You must be the only one in London—with everyone else it's the other way round. When was it you saw him, pray?"

The air had become too thick for me; I began backing toward the door. "I disremember, sir—"

"Come. The month, at least. Surely you recall the month."

I paused and screwed up my face like a half-wit in an effort to surrender as little as possible without lying outright. "April, I believe—or was it March?"

"How many weeks past? *Think,* boy."

I goggled my eyes at him, as though thinking were beyond my skill. "Truth, sir, I do not mark the days so well—"

"Leave off, you caviling calf-brain!" Patience and pretense flew away together as Master Merry advanced toward me with murder in his look. This was all the push I needed; I was halfway down the stairs before he reached the landing and had soon outrun even his voice as it bellowed, "Stop!"

"It was ill thought," Starling said firmly. She had latched on to me when I came in early and dragged me to the garden to hear all. "You should not have let them see your face."

"What was the harm?"

"Someone could have followed you back here and discovered who you are."

"I thought of that," I informed her loftily. "At Ludgate I stopped to watch a juggler and carefully looked all around. There was no figure in robes behind me. Or the scrivener, Samuel. He was such a pretty little fop I would know him anywhere."

"It's easy enough to throw *off* the lawyer's robes and look like a common man."

That, I saw belatedly, was all too true. "Well . . . at least I learned two things sure. The man I saw at the Theater is not Martin Feather's clerk, and his name is John Beecham."

"So he lied to you. And it seems they have an interest in him as great as yours."

"It does. This fellow Master Merry—what a name for one so grim!—he was right startled to hear where I met the man—"

"—as if Beecham were in a place he had no business being. Did you mark anything about him that day? Think."

I cast back to my meeting with John Beecham, and the longer I thought, the more curious it appeared. There was that rustling behind the door, which ceased when I knocked, and those papers spilled, and the iron grip of his hand on my wrist—

"The paper you picked up," Starling interrupted. "Did you see anything on it?"

"A name. It seemed a proclamation of some sort. Not a letter. 'By order of,' 'By the will of'—something like that."

"And the name?"

"I disremember. Something with a ford. Shallowford, Streamford, or the like."

"It meant much to him that it not be seen. Do you suppose he stole the papers from Master Feather?"

I was thinking the same, and my clerk was taking on a darker color. I liked it not, but what other conclusion? His violent start upon recognizing me at the Theater, and the fact that he saw fit to disappear immediately after, only added to my suspicions. Starling went on, "You say he's the one who sent you to the wine merchants in the name of—who was it?"

"Peter Kenton."

"I wonder if we should try to uncover this Peter Kenton."

"How? I can't go down to the docks and ask for him."

"True." Her mouth was stopped but not her brain; I could almost see it working behind those clear green eyes.

"Starling, have a care. If you take this up on your own, you could bring me harm."

"Would I bring you harm?" Her tone was all light and innocence—a very angel she sounded. "By the way, you were excellent today as Lady Constance. I knew there was an actor in you. What brought him out?"

I lacked the words to explain, and doubted whether I could bring him out again, but fortunately our conference was interrupted by Alice Condell coming across the lawn.

Lady Alice was not one to be denied. At a mere sixteen, she was one of the most daunting people I knew—tall and handsome like her mother, with much the same air of command but lacking the subtlety. Like a troop of cavalry she bore toward us now with her un-mincing walk, ribbons streaming like banners from her cap and a folded paper in her hand. "Here, Richard," she called while still yards distant, "My mother bids you carry this message to Father. He's at the Mermaid. You must be quick about it—'tis a church matter."

I took the message with a bow. "Never mind," Starling said when Alice was out of earshot. "I will think of something."

I already knew the sort of thing that happened when Starling proposed to think, but there was no time to argue over it. I took the back gate out of the garden, then followed the alley all the way to Bread Street, arriving at the Mermaid just as dusk had curled around the city and tavern keepers were setting out their lamps.

Yellow light gilded the smoke of a dozen pipes inside the tavern. Spanish tobacco from the West Indies had become all the rage in recent years, biting hard into the Lord Chamberlain's Men. At least half the Company were puffing on clay pipes lit with coals off the grate, and the sight was still wonderful to me—like so many genial, smoldering dragons gathered about the hearth of their dragon kitchen. In this blue-gold haze I spied Master Condell seated at one end of the board, gazing toward Will Shakespeare. That gentleman occupied a space at the middle of the table surrounded by listeners, a stack of papers before him. With broad actor's vowels and eloquent pauses, he was reading all the parts in his latest play. This was the custom for a playmaker, to declaim his work before the company he hoped would perform it. If the work failed to please, they would silence the author and send him packing, with his hero's love unfulfilled, the lady's virtue unavenged, or the knife still planted in some hapless victim's chest.

But Master Will was never silenced; his readings held all listeners spellbound to the end. He was at that moment conveying to his audience the sorrow of a man compelled to carry out a hateful act. I did not grasp all the particulars, but it seemed that the character he was reading had taken an infant child to a distant land, where he must leave it exposed on a rocky beach to die: "Blossom, speed thee well! There lie, and there thy character—which may, if fortune please, still rest thine. . . ." His listeners were silent in the brief pause that followed this speech, except for a sniff or two.

"Then," said our reader in his everyday voice, "there follows a clap of thunder and Antigonus makes ready to fly back to his ship. But a bear appears and chases him off the stage, and we soon understand—"

A sputtering from across the table interrupted him. "A bear? Come, Will, a *bear*?" This came from a stocky, square-faced man with dark hair and deep-set eyes, who stared at the playmaker with a look that managed to be belligerent and affectionate at the same time.

"Yes, a bear." Master Will showed no offense at the badgering tone. "Antigonus must die, you see. The bear is as good a means as any to finish him off."

"But you allow us no preparation for the beast. There are no bears in the plot, no warnings from a madwoman or wise fool or any of the usual devices. And I daresay the animal never reappears after dispatching Antigonus? I thought not. At least give us a verse on the subject from the Oracle, otherwise shalt be an unbearable play."

"I'll think on it, Ben. But what hurt to have the beast appear as a stroke of divine judgment?"

"Oh, by your leave, no hurt at all to the louse-bait audiences you play to. May as well let Jove himself descend on a lightning bolt, and 'twould please them equally. They are not even like to know you've put a seacoast on the land of Bohemia."

Richard Cowley, seated next to Master Will, wrinkled his brow. "But isn't there a seacoast on Bohemia?"

The square-faced man swore and slammed a heavy fist on the board. "Why did our Drake sail around the globe, if Englishmen hold no more knowledge of geography than that? Bohemia is land-locked entire, Master Cowley! At least, Will, call the land by some other title than Bohemia. A coast by any other name would smell as sweet, eh? Sweeter, in my nose, for being true."

"I will think on it, Ben," Master Will repeated, with the ghost of a smile.

I noticed Kit, perched raven-like on a stool drawn up behind John Heminges. Looking a little peaked from his encounter with the putrid goat, he sipped ale sparingly from a wooden mug as he followed the conversation. On his face was something that, small and tight though it was, I could not recall seeing there before—a smile. It encouraged me to step over to him and murmur, "Who is yon professor, with the soul of a poet?"

Kit may have gained a particle of respect for me after I carried his role that day—enough to answer, though he did not trouble to look. "You speak wiser than you know. He is a poet, though not as great as he thinks. 'Tis Ben Jonson."

I gave the man another look; so this was Ben Jonson. All the talk in the Company that week was of his recent release from Marshalsea Prison, where he had spent a time for writing a play that annoyed certain officials of the Court.

Kit said, "If you came here to angle for my part tomorrow, I assure you I am recovered quite." I felt a sting in his last words, and wondered if it was only my imagination.

Shakespeare had resumed his narrative, a comic scene involving a shepherd and his lame-witted son. I worked my way through the crowd (for the reading had attracted almost every patron in the tavern) and over their laughter delivered my message to Master Condell.

"Stay a little, Richard." He scanned the paper, refolded it, and stuck it in the pocket of his sleeve before returning to me. "You write a clerkly hand, d'you not?"

"I have been told so, sir."

"Hold, then. We may have work for you."

I would have held till Doomsday on the promise of work, but it was less than an hour for the play to run its reading, especially since Master Will would begin a long speech, then break off and skip to the last two lines. Since I had missed the first half, the story made little sense, but given the run of a Shakespeare plot, this may have been true even if I had heard it from the beginning. Even so, it was pleasant to sit among the players, gathered close in the warm night while crickets tuned up in their corners and smiles came and went like fireflies. Strange, how a trifling story can lure the mind away from its worries.

The Lord Chamberlain's Men clapped and cheered when the reading was done, and decided by unanimous vote to perform the play during the autumn season. With that in view, it wanted copying. "For which I propose," said Master Condell, "that young Richard here will serve. He writes a fair hand, and stands in need of work."

The Company approved with no debate and went on to discuss where and how deep to make the cuts in the play. With a start, I realized that the riddle of my situation was answered: I now had a place. By his proposal Master Condell implied that the Company could use me in future and thought it worthwhile to keep me on through the summer. I felt a bit dizzy at first, then relief filled me, warm as mulled wine. The smoky, stuffy room glowed with a new light, and every face looked more dear. Even Kit's, as difficult and distant as it was, took on a softer cast as he listened intently to the talk around him. I lingered until my master stood to meet his

127

appointment with the vestry, indicating to me with a nod that I must now go home. I went with a will, almost floating.

"Copy work?" Robin exclaimed, in our room. "That pleases you? Copy work is the gate to hell, in my view."

"I am good at it." Nothing could shake my mood.

"I am good, too, at any number of sins." He unlaced his breeches and slipped them off in one swift motion that rid him of shoes and hose as well. Then he flopped on our mattress in his shirt, bent his elbows, and stretched until they popped.

"None of which you will indulge tonight, I take it." The approach of summer worked like strong ale on Robin, who had lately embarked on a new enterprise. At least once per week, during the changing of the watch an hour before midnight, he would slip through our narrow window, cut light-footed over the tiled roof, and climb down a stone trellis by the kitchen garden. Then he would join Kit at a designated spot and roam the streets for three or four hours, jesting with tavern maids and sailors on the docks, hovering on the outskirts of a dice game or bear fight. I was told of these excursions in detail, but never invited to join them—a snub, probably from Kit, that troubled me more than I cared to own.

"Do I look like a fool?" snorted Robin, in answer to my remark. "We depart on tour two days hence, and I must restore myself. The wenches and the bears must wait"—here he yawned greatly—"until I return."

"No doubt there will be general mourning until then."

"Puritan!"

The Company set off on their tour the third week in June, with little fanfare. Master Condell kissed his wife and children, instructed the servants, appointed his son Harry as co-ruler of the household, and bade me make myself useful until the play was delivered. "And no carousing in the streets at night," he warned. "Take your needful recreation, but if you reflect poorly on this house you will not be in it, come fall." I nodded solemnly, thinking that nothing could lure me into the streets after dark if it meant risking my job.

Every play which seeks a performance must first be read by the Master of Revels to insure that there is nothing inflammatory or indecent in it—nothing to incite its hearers to lewdness or riot. Since my copy work could not commence until the play came back from the Revels office, I set about making myself useful. Mistress Condell decided I would make an excellent summer Latin tutor for Thomas and Ned—who, until now, had seen me as fit for nothing but jumping on. They did not take readily to instruction. While struggling to make them sit still and listen, I was distracted by Starling, who kept very busy and regarded me with a smug expression that she refused to explain, or even admit to. I welcomed the arrival of the manuscript ten days after the Company's departure: here at last is something I can manage, I thought, little dreaming how that play would come to manage me.

Certain authors made bitter complaint of the butchery performed on their works by the Revels office, but not the gentle Shakespeare. His play came back with modest, almost apologetic cuts that did little harm to it that I could see. I was to make one master copy for the prompter and a complete set of lines for each character, with cues—a week's task for a professional scribe. But I intended to write slowly and do my best work, even if it took a month. The play was called *The Winter's Tale,* a romance that begins in sorrow and ends in joy.

Two kings, Leontes of Sicilia and Polixenes of Bohemia, grew up as bosom friends, though adult responsibilities have kept them apart. As the play opens, Leontes is playing host to his friend in a long-delayed reunion. But then, for no apparent reason, Leontes becomes convinced that his queen, Hermione, has fallen madly in love with their guest and that the two are conducting an adulterous affair under his very roof. Directly, he accuses them outright, and the entire court of Sicilia is appalled—not at the beautiful Hermione, whose character and conduct have ever been above reproach, but at the irrational jealousy of Leontes. Polixenes, fearing for his life, escapes by ship to his own kingdom, leaving Hermione to be locked away while awaiting trial for treason. Mamillius, her young son, falls desperately ill of shock and sorrow.

While in prison Hermione is delivered of a girl child, which her husband believes to be a bastard. He orders a nobleman, Antigonus, to take the baby to a distant shore and abandon her to the judgment of the gods. Antigonus departs with great regret, and soon after Hermione stands trial. No evidence can be brought against her; even the Oracle of Delphi is consulted and testifies to her innocence. But Leontes will not be swayed from his mad course until word arrives that his son Mamillius has died of grief. Hermione swoons and is soon after reported dead. This double stroke of divine judgment brings Leontes to his senses, but by then it is too late.

Meanwhile, Antigonus has landed with the infant child on a seacoast, which happens to belong to Polixenes' kingdom of Bohemia (much as Ben Jonson would vigorously deny it). He leaves the baby on the shore, but before he can reach his ship he is dispatched by a bear. However, the baby is rescued by a simple shepherd and his oafish son, who guess that she must be of high birth by the baptismal cloth wrapped around her.

Sixteen years pass. The baby has grown into a lovely maid of noble bearing called Perdita, "the Lost One." She has captured the heart of Prince Florizel, son of Polixenes, who visits her humble home disguised as a shepherd. During a sheep-shearing festival, he proposes marriage to her—not a wise choice of time and place as it happens, for Polixenes is present, in disguise, spying on his son. The king flies into a rage and forbids the lovers to meet ever again, but they decide to flee together to Sicilia. There follows some comic business with an amiable thief known as Autolycus, by whose schemes Perdita and Florizel, the shepherd and his son, Polixenes and Autolycus himself all board various ships for Leontes' kingdom, Sicilia.

"So then," I explained to Starling, "it all remains to be tied up. Leontes has been living like a monk all these years, though his counselors are urging him to marry again. But Paulina reminds him—"

"Wait. Who is Paulina, again?"

"A lady of the court, the late queen's closest friend. She reminds Leontes what the Oracle said, that he will die without an heir if 'that which was lost be not found.'"

"I remember now." Starling was shelling peas, and I was resting my cramped fingers from copy work. We sat near the garden under a spreading oak whose leaves barely moved in a listless summer breeze. "It would serve him right to die without heir, the jealous tyrant."

"Perhaps, but the fates have decided that he's suffered enough, for soon Perdita and Florizel arrive, followed directly by the shepherd, who just happens to bring Perdita's baptismal cloth. And from that it ravels out—"

"'Ravels out.' Oh, such wit!" She was in a snippish mood, which I ignored.

"—and Polixenes, when he arrives, forgives everyone in sight and all are friends again. The only blot on all this rejoicing is the memory of Hermione and poor little Mamillius, long dead. But Paulina has a surprise in store . . ." I paused, to bait her a little.

". . . Yes?" Starling asked, when she could bear it no longer.

"She claims to own a statue of the late queen, which is so lifelike it could deceive Hermione's own kin into thinking she lives. So of course all must go to Paulina's house to see it, and it seems she spoke true. The statue shows Hermione as she would appear in the present—still beautiful, but older, even to the lines on her face. Both Leontes and Perdita long to touch it, but Paulina forbids them. Instead, she commands the form to step down. The statue moves, then speaks, and behold! It is the real Hermione, who only pretended to be dead all these years and has hidden herself in Paulina's house until her husband is well and truly sorry. So all's well that ends well."

"Oh," Starling sighed. "I love the way it ends."

"Well, I think it's too bad nobody produces a statue of Mamillius, full grown. The boy stays dead."

She made a little sniff and went back to shelling peas. "It is a beautiful story. Why do you mock it?"

She had misjudged me. If I mocked, it was only because the play had touched a deep place in me that disliked being stirred. In this tale I heard echoes of my own life. I knew firsthand how Mamillius had suffered, with his mother falsely accused and his father become strange and distant. I knew how a faithful wife could be rejected and spend long years waiting for her husband's repentance. When I pictured Hermione waiting through those years, I saw Rebekah Malory, sitting by the window in a plain gown with neglected mending in her lap and a hurt, fretful look in her eyes—only my mother's wait was never rewarded.

But it was the character of Leontes who haunted me. He was the villain of the story, yet there was nobility in him, a greatness, both in his sins and his repentance. He had done terrible things, but forgiveness restored him. One night I dreamed that Leontes was my father, carrying me around on broad, kingly shoulders and laughing a rich, rolling laugh. He set me down and went away. I was searching for him in the tiring rooms behind the stage, in coves and closets that ever multiplied, while over my head the third trumpet sounded. Only it was the Oracle that spoke in its windy tones, warning that something terrible would befall us "if that which was lost be not found. . . . "

It was the kind of dream that makes you wake feeling wrung out like a rag.

Not that I wished to explain any of this to Starling. "Master Will's plays always have something awry," I said. "It's as if he were twisting life to fit the story he wants to tell. First, there's Leontes setting out to destroy his family, for no reason—"

"There is always a reason," she said sagely. "It may not be so soon apparent, is all."

"—And the way people just die, of grief or whatnot, when it suits the plot. I watched my mother die—it's not that easy. And then," I hurried on, "there's that bear. He shows up with no rhyme or reason and kills a man and disappears, and we never see him more. What purpose does he serve?"

"Whatsoever God pleases. Sometimes we are granted to know, or know who to ask. If my own father were alive, I would ask him."

"Was he so wise as you?" Now I was the one being snippish, but her knowing manner had begun to wear on me.

"Not in most ways," she said, gravely. "But he *was* a bear."

This was so unexpected I could think of no clever reply. "Oh?"

"Indeed. A most burly, furry, and fearsome bear. To be sure, he started out as a man, else he could never have got me. But he was wedded to the forest and we never saw him, my sisters and I, except when he showed himself with a haunch of venison over his shoulder or a brace of rabbits in his fist. Big, hairy hands he had, and his laugh was like a roar.

"Then one day he went into the forest and we never saw him more. Or not as a man. For you see, he passed so much time amongst the caves and the trees and the leaf-mold that his hair grew out into fur to keep him warm, and his fingernails hardened into claws to protect him. His round, whiskery face doubled up in a muzzle so he could smell out his food. He curled up in a cave one snowy winter's eve to sleep and when he woke, the sky was weeping warm tears and the trees had put out a fuzz of green. When he came forth from the cave, he found himself walking on his hands, and when a squirrel chattered at him from a branch overhead he brought it down with one swipe of his paw. Then he ripped it open and scooped out the flesh and cracked the bones between his huge yellow teeth."

Starling was a renowned storyteller among the Condell children, but this was the first she had worked her wiles on me. I let my breath out in a shallow stream. "How do you know this?"

"I saw him," she said calmly. "Two years ago last Whitsuntide. He had been caught, you see, and was on his way to the bear pit. They had him chained to a post in Smithfield, where they matched him against two champion dogs and he broke them easily. Then he looked over the clearing and found me. His eyes were ever small, even as a man, and shiny as onyx stones. Those were his eyes staring at me, and they told me all."

With a jolt I remembered the eyes of Benjamin in the Smithfield market, and how I, too, once fancied that a bear had talked to me. "Did you ever see him after?"

"Nay. But heard of him. He ruled the Bear Garden for almost a year, until his wounds finally made him weak. There was a dog named Savage who got him square in the neck, where they could not staunch the blood. 'Twas a sad day at the Bear Garden, for many a wagered shilling was made off Black Jack. That was what they called him—as chance would have it, Jack was my father's name. He made a sad end but died fighting. Truth to tell, I don't think he minded being a bear, though he'd as lief be one in the freedom of the forest."

She had finished with the peas; her fingers sifted idly through the limp green pods, their papery skins so thin I could see the tiny veins in them. Suddenly, she gathered a handful of these slivers and threw them at me. "'Tis all true, I swear it," she laughed, springing to her feet and shaking pods off her skirt. She trotted off toward the kitchen, her gait so smooth that not a single pea jumped out of the pan.

As for me, I felt as though I'd had a hat pulled over my eyes and my nose tweaked.

"Jack Shaw?" young Henry Condell repeated, in answer to my question. "I remember him well. He was gamekeeper for my aunt and uncle Fredericks, in Barkshire." Harry drew hard on his pipe to make it catch, then blew out smoke with the satisfied air of a youth who's mastered a manly art at the age of eighteen. He was in a mellow humor, having worked out a tangle in the household accounts with a bit of help from me. "Jack was a big, hairy fellow. Great for telling tales—the children loved him. He lived to hunt. That was his downfall. A hardened poacher, poor man; no one could break him of it. The wardens caught him on the neighbor's land gutting a deer—red of hand, as the saying goes—and in the scuffle Jack was killed. A sad tale."

"Was it an accident?"

"Oh, no doubt." Harry put one foot on the accounting table and puffed contentedly—two things he would never have done had his mother been anywhere about. "I know Starling has . . . enriched the story. One thing sure, the deed made three girls orphan. All named after birds—Starling, Skylark, and . . . I forget the other. Raven? Nuthatch?"

"Titmouse," I suggested.

"Hah! That wouldn't bear shortening, would it? Starling is the eldest, and my mother and father took her in out of kindness. She used to be a flighty wench, but she has settled down to earn her bread in the last year or so. She's told you the bear story, then? As I thought. Had you believing it, didn't she?"

❧

✢

few days after bewitching me with her "Black Jack" story, Starling burst into the master's study, so agitated she could scarcely draw breath. "Richard! You must come at once. He was just here, at the gate. If you hurry, you might catch him!"

I was industriously copying, and she had made me skip; I glared at the ugly blot left on the paper and demanded, "What—"

She stamped her foot. "Don't argue. He's getting away."

"Who?"

"Peter Kenton!"

That was all I needed to move me—why had she not said so in the first place? The next instant we were out of the house and pelting down the street in the direction she had seen the man go. "What did he want?" I asked, on the lope.

"Not now. Hurry!"

We ran to the corner, where a row of trees compromised the view. Starling pointed east. "I watched him down the street, and he turned that way." But except for a carter, a dustman, a sprinkling of housemaids, and a distant, black-robed scholar, the street was empty.

Star wrung her hands while her mouth went sideways. "Ah, what a simpleton I am! I should have followed him straight and not gone to fetch you. My faith, what a foolish—"

"Never mind that!" Neither of us believed she was simple, and I cared not to waste time. "What did he want?"

"The most wondrous thing—he had a message for Richard Malory!"

I stared, wondering what this might mean. By now my name was no secret in the household, for Susanna had sent me two letters under it, but it was seldom used. The only others who knew it would be Motheby and Southern (if they happened to remember) and my aunt in Southwark. "I offered to fetch you, but he forbade me. 'Just tell him this,' said he. 'On no account is he to go to Martin Feather's chambers or lodging. His friend Beecham will not be there and Feather is a dangerous man to know.'"

It was too much to take in at once. "Describe him."

She did: a man of middling height with a golden beard and a proud manner. He wore a fine cape of dark orange velvet and a

139

square-crowned hat with a partridge feather sweeping off one side. The brim shaded his eyes so she could not make out their color. "And he didn't linger. As soon as the message was out, he turned on his heel."

I glanced at the opposite corner, where Betty the kitchen maid, a market basket on her arm, was passing the time with a young man. Little Ned Condell, who had accompanied her to market, tugged impatiently at her apron. I thought of asking Betty if she had noticed where the stranger turned next, but her attention was obviously taken. I must follow blind, and sort the matter on the way. I struck east then, walking very fast, with Starling at my elbow. "Suppose it was not Peter Kenton at all," I mused. "We've never seen him."

"I think it was, most like. This man answers to the description they gave at—" Starling broke off, and I whirled around to meet her face, now wide open with alarm at what she had given away.

"You went down to the warehouse, didn't you?"

"I did. And asked for him."

"Why should they mind the demands of a housemaid?"

"Because the housemaid stuffed a cushion under her gown and let her condition be known."

I blew out an explosive sigh. "When was this?"

"Two weeks ago, just after the Company left on tour."

"What were the words you used to describe my visit to Master Feather's chambers?" I demanded. "Did you not say it was 'ill thought' to show my face there?"

"We said nothing about showing *my* face. And you seemed not to mind when I played the same ruse on your aunt."

"We agreed on that. Whereas this you've undertaken on your own with no leave from me—"

"You are not my master."

"But this is *my affair*. What have you to do with it, when all's done?"

Her fingers had pleated up the edges of her apron like a ruff; she stared down at them. "I am your friend."

This was obvious enough, but seemed to leave us both at a loss for words. Then she looked up briskly. "I must get back, or they will miss me. Here is what happened: I spoke to Southern, the stout one. I asked for a description of Peter Kenton first. When he gave it, I wrung my hands and cried, 'Oh! 'Tis he!' and asked when they hoped to see him next. It seems he usually comes around the beginning of each month to discuss business and add up accounts, but sometimes he skips a month. Master Southern said he would pass along my message, and wanted my name and house, but I refused to give it. He was amused—easy for a man to laugh! But this is the fifth of July, so Master Kenton must have made his usual stop at the warehouse and heard of me. The question is, How did he know where to find us?"

I shrugged—more of a shiver, though the day was warm. "It's probably hopeless now, but I'll try to catch him. We'll shake it out later."

So we parted, she returning to the house and I continuing on to Cheapside, watching all the while for a strolling gentleman in a velvet cape. Of course he was nowhere to be seen, but it helped me to walk, pacing out what had happened and what it might mean.

That Masters Kenton and Beecham shared each other's confidence was not strange; the so-called clerk had allowed from the first that they knew each other, when he sent me to the quay in Kenton's name. The true mystery, as Star said, was how the latter had known where to find me. One of us may have been followed—either I, from Middle Temple, or Starling from the docks. Or John Beecham could have asked about my whereabouts after discovering me among the Lord Chamberlain's Men. And what of the warning, which I had now from each of them—avoid Martin Feather? The advice (at least, as I myself had it from Beecham) sounded sincere and well-meant, but the man had lied to me at least once. Suppose they were in league with my aunt, and Master Feather was my true friend?

Such questions only tangled up my thoughts. I envied King Leontes of *The Winter's Tale*, who could at least inquire of the Oracle, even if he chose not to listen to it.

The streets were less crowded than usual, for during July those who can afford it remove themselves from the steaming city and head to the country. But as always, music spilled from tavern doors and street corners. That was the divided character of London—to sound like heaven and stink like hell. Trade was slow, leaving the laboring public with time on their hands and none but low amusements to occupy them: bear baits and cock fights, roving fire eaters, sword swallowers, clowns in motley.

One of these independent performers had set up at the forks of Cheapside. He was a man of multiple gifts: first he juggled flaming torches with consummate skill, then yelped in mock pain as he flipped them between his legs, then doused them one by one in a mouth so wide it could have swallowed a cabbage whole. Something about his clever face and pale hair seemed familiar; I watched to the end of the performance, when he got a smattering of laughter and a few farthings tossed into a straw hat. When the coins had ceased, he picked up the hat and swept it toward the onlookers in a bow that took his head a whisker's width from the street. On his way upright, his bright blue eyes snagged me. "Hey! Little brother!"

As I stared, he beckoned me near. "Fear not. We're comrades, you and I. Dost recall?"

Then it hit me. "Wait—my first play, at the Theater. We made our entrances together—"

"Aye. I went by way of breakin' you in, and it was good work I did. When we played together in *King John,* you should've thanked me."

"I don't remember you in that one."

"I was, though. Marchin' and shoutin' with the armies, and spoke one line as the Prophet Peter. But well I remember you. 'O death! Thou odiferous, rottenous death, pluck the eyeballs from this barren skull and come smack me with a big slobbery kiss!'" This was a mangling of Constance's "mad" scene, delivered with such reckless abandon he might have been arrested as a public hazard had he gone on with it. After one startled moment I found myself laughing, and it felt as though the laughter had built up for weeks and burst like a thundercloud. He dropped his tragical manner and joined me, throwing back his head to show all his remaining teeth. He put me in mind of Autolycus, the amiable scoundrel in *Winter's Tale* (a character I had thought to be exaggerated). "But truth, little brother," he went on, judge-sober now, "'twas a fine performance. Made me as proud as your own dad." He shook out a loud red handkerchief and blew his nose. "Need a bit of work?"

The man changed tack so often it was like being jerked upon a catherine wheel. "How's that?"

"Got a job for the morrow. Lord Hurleigh's funeral at Westminster. There's a call out for mourners."

"Oh." Lord Hurleigh, I recalled, was the nobleman who wished Master Will to write an ode for him. I had heard of such "calls" for players to walk behind a funeral hearse with mournful garb and expressions to match. It reeked of hypocrisy—the very sort of thing Mistress Condell had warned me against. "I think not. . . ."

"Mayest think again. They're paying double, I hear, plus the funeral feast. Mourners are scarce in summer and the gentleman hasn't many to weep for him of their own accord."

"Why is that?" We were strolling away from the Exchange now, while he took a penknife from his motley garb and idly dug under his fingernails.

"Oh, a widower, with no remaining heir. Under a papist cloud to boot. A Catholic, they say. Poor Philip Shackleford! All his gold won't buy him a proper funeral. But he's the Queen's kinsman and can't be stuck in the ground without some ceremony."

"Will she attend?"

"Nah, she's on progress."

Of course, I knew that. The Queen and her court were "progressing" through the northern provinces, a system by which they descended upon some hapless nobleman's estate and stayed for a fortnight or more, draining his larder and stretching his devices to come up with entertainment. "So," said my companion, "if you change your mind, come to the north common of St. Paul's an hour before noon and ask for me—Zachary of the quick hand."

He touched the knife to his forehead in salute, turned, and disappeared down the nearest side street. Something in his look, a meaningful flicker of his eyes, made me glance down at my side. The small canvas pouch that tied to my belt was now decorated with a neat slice, about two inches long, and felt lighter by threepence.

Autolycus was a cutpurse, too. I would never again consider one of Master Will's characters to be overdrawn.

In low spirits I turned toward home. Threepence was all I had left from a bonus paid by the Company at season's end. Most had gone to Susanna, but I was keeping this much for myself alone. The money that came to me did not stick; it was the same with John Beecham's shilling, mysteriously given and just as mysteriously lost. Perhaps I should attend the funeral after all, if only to

145

get my threepence back from Zachary the light-fingered. It might be a worthy act of charity besides, if the deceased had so few to mourn him. Poor Philip . . . what had the clown called him? Something with a ford. . . .

I stopped dead at the corner of Coleman and Cattle streets, seeing as clear as day a paper picked up from the road muck, and scrawled on its lower edge a line reading, By order of Philip—

"Shackleford!"

Starling's eyes went wide when I told her. "You must go to the funeral. There's no argument."

"But now the stakes are higher. Master Feather's clerk, and probably Feather himself, and Beecham and Kenton—they all know me. Should I show my face in this setting?"

"If you enlist in the first rank of mourners, they'll give you a robe and a hood. Pull it far enough over your face and no one will look twice at you. But you must go."

I had to agree.

That night the household was livelier than usual, for Mistress Condell and most of the children were packing for a visit to her sister in Surrey. By the time Thomas, Ned, and Cole were tucked in their bed it was nigh unto midnight, and they had no energy left to wrestle me. But they always demanded a story. Though not so free as Starling at making them up, I told tales from the Bible with enough spirit to hold them still. That night they heard of Elisha and the bears, a timely warning about the just reward of exasperating little boys. It settled them, except for Ned, who popped upright in bed and remarked, "I saw a man turn into a bear today."

"Did you, then?" I knew well the operation of his brain; oft he lulled us all to sleep on some wild notion that promised great things and ended nowhere.

"Aye. 'Twas just past noon, when we got back from the market. He came toward us and turned at the corner. A fine gentleman in a gold cape and a hat with a long feather."

"How's that?" I rounded on him. "A long feather—with a curl in the end, like a partridge?"

"Aye!" Ned bounced in excitement. "You saw him, too?"

"Not I. But Star did. Ned, think: you say he turned at the corner. Did you see him make a turn after that?"

"But list what I tell you." I was spoiling his tale. "I saw him turn at the corner and disappear behind that row of trees. The leaves—the leaves drew a curtain about him. And then—"

"*What?*" I could have choked the story out of him in my impatience.

"When he came out from behind the trees, he was a bear!" Thomas, who had become skeptical at the ripe age of eight, groaned loudly, but little Cole squealed in delight. "A round, furry, black bear," Ned continued in a growl, catching Cole about the neck.

"Don't strangle your brother," I chided, my mind elsewhere. The hawthorn trees that he mentioned were planted along a wall. The branches spread low and were full and leafy—they could hide someone walking behind them, at least in part. "Where did he go after you saw him come out from behind the trees?"

"How would I know? I didn't follow him—I had to watch Betty."

Betty always went to market in company with one of the boys, who were supposed to discourage her courting. A worthless strategy, in my view. I sighed and shook my head.

"But would you hear more about the bear?" That was the best part, to Ned. I let him chatter on about it until the boys fell asleep, leaving me no wiser.

Mistress Condell and the children departed for Surrey in the mid-morning, leaving me ample time to make myself respectable and get to St. Paul's by noon. The groundskeeper of St. Paul's common directed me to a shed behind the cathedral, a stable of sorts, where a ragged troop of "mourners" were getting themselves outfitted. Two members of the Queen's Yeomen, in their black-and-yellow tunics, were leaning against the wall—perhaps to make sure that the distinguished company did not steal anything as they tried on robes and hats, washed at the stone trough, trimmed each other's hair. One was getting a tooth pulled by a barber wielding a pair of pinchers. The air of cheerful mayhem reminded me of the tiring rooms at the Theater. Zachary was easy to spot, even with his pale hair covered by a black judge's cap—an uneasy match to his red-and-pink motley. "Little brother!" he sang out as I approached. "I knew our paths would cross again. Was it fate?"

"No; threepence," I said, unsmiling. "And I want it back."

"With good will." He opened the pouch at his side, then paused. "If you stay to follow the corpse." I nodded and he handed over the coin. "I was only keeping it as surety, and sure you've come. And turned out like a gentleman, too—we'll put thee in the second rank. I've a fine black hat that would look fetching—"

"No. I must be in the first rank."

His face fell, as resoundingly as the walls of Jericho. "But lad! Thou wouldst be an ornament to the procession. And second-rankers get more in pay." I surveyed the other mourners and guessed why. Most of them looked as though they'd been scraped from the city's underside—beggars, brawlers, and cutpurses who could be made respectable only by covering them head to foot. One seemed a notch above, if only by his bearing. He sat on a stone bench beside the cathedral, with the hood of his mourning robe pulled over his face—so unearthly still he seemed the very image of death. A cold presence, on this sweltering day.

I turned back to Zachary. "It's first rank, or I'm off."

He sighed gustily, then shrugged. "So be it. Am I correct in taking thee for a scribe? Take this slate and set down these names. First rank: Sly Jack, Old Blind Peter, Mark the One-Handed, Ned Cut-Nose, Flat-Faced Francis. And thyself, if it must be." I paused, then wrote "Tom Brown" for myself. "Second rank," Zachary continued: "John Pinch, John Wood, Black John, French John, Simon the Jew . . ."

Once the names were listed, he took the slate from me and

counted them, to ensure he would not be slighted on his commission. Next I was outfitted, but the robe they gave me was so long I looked like a child dressing up. Zachary tied a pair of pattens to my feet, which elevated me a couple of inches but made me feel as though I was walking on stilts. While this was going on, two gentlemen arrived on horseback, followed by two ladies in covered chairs. The gentlemen dismounted and crossed the common: one an elderly fellow dressed in gray velvet, of noble bearing and amiable countenance. In one hand he carried a paper, rolled up like a scroll. A younger man followed, bearing a parcel tied with ribbon. He bore some resemblance to the elder man in face, but not in attitude—by the pinched look about his nose and mouth he might have been wading a sewer.

"Look sharp!" Zachary hissed to his comrades. "'Tis our chief mourner, the Lord Chamberlain himself with his noble progeny!"

I watched with renewed interest as the gentlemen approached, for I had never seen our patron. Henry Carey, Lord Hunsdon, proved to be a pleasant-looking man with an easy manner that did not stand on ceremony. He nodded to Zachary, who had made one of his earth-kissing bows, and turned to consult with the Yeomen. Then he spoke to all of us, raising his hand with the paper.

"I have here an ode, written in honor of the deceased. If there be anyone here who can read it, it will be worth a shilling to him. Is there such?"

A long moment of silence; it seemed I was the only mourner who could read, unless the robed figure on the bench was able but unwilling. At my side, Zachary became fidgety. He gave me a jab or two with his thumb, shifted from one foot to the other, finally whispered, "Come, we'll split the money." Then he burst out, "My lord! Here's a youth can read passing well. An actor, my lord. In fact, a member of—"

I lifted my left foot and brought it down, patten and all, on his right. Zachary took it like a stoic, though his eyes bulged out a little and his smile turned grimacy. "—A member of a proud and honorable profession." He made another low bow, quick of thought as well as hand.

Lord Hunsdon looked at me, but I saw no recognition in his eyes. To my knowledge he had attended no Company performances since I joined, so my identity remained safe. "Is this true, lad?"

"True enough, my lord."

He extended the paper to me. "Will you, then?"

His manner was so gracious I could not refuse. So I took the ode, vowing that whatever happened they could not make me read it with my head uncovered.

The hearse arrived directly, pulled by two black horses and bearing an open coffin. In the confusion of sorting ourselves, I stepped up on a ladies' mounting block in order to see into the coffin. His lordship Philip Shackleford had shrunken a bit in the heat but appeared respectable otherwise; no rosary beads or other telltale symbols about him. The procession formed: first the drummers and halberd-carriers, then Sly Jack, who dolefully rang the mourning bell. Lord Hunsdon, resplendent in his gold-trimmed mourner's robe, occupied the place of honor before the hearse. He was flanked by the two ladies while his son, looking supremely bored, held up his train. Then came the hearse, followed by Zachary's crew. Last of all the silent figure on the bench stood, picked up a pottery urn, and brought up the rear. As the procession filed out of the church-yard and headed for Ludgate, he solemnly dipped ashes from his urn and spread them upon the road.

"Who's that fellow?" I asked Zachary. "Never saw him," was the reply. "For all we know, it's just a robe with no body inside, eh?" I was glad he bore me no ill will for his sore toes, but this was a right chilling thought to lay upon me.

Our destination was Westminster Abbey—a journey of a mile and a half under the remorseless sun, and by the time we arrived our countenances were sorrowful indeed. As we progressed down Fleet Street and the Strand, Londoners stopped and uncovered, and a few knelt in prayer. Some appeared to be truly grieved, others smug that it wasn't their funeral; a few seemed outright hostile. After turning at the Abbey gate, the procession finally entered the cool stone walls. There were more people inside than I expected, though from the looks on their faces it was curiosity brought them in, not sorrow.

I got through my ode reasonably well, but later could not remember a word in it, or guess whether Master Will could have written a better one. I pitched my voice as low as it would go and ignored the repeated motions from Lord Hunsdon at one end of the coffin and Zachary at the other, indicating I should uncover my head. When I finished and stepped down, the latter made an apologetic bow to my lord as though to say, Forgive the boy; he has a ready tongue but a dull wit.

The Archbishop of York read the service; the choir sang their responses; the congregation knelt, and stood, and knelt again; we first-rank mourners beat our breasts on cue. Lord Hunsdon gave a short eulogy, which made his peer out to be a model subject and most worthy gentleman; then he paused and the urn-bearing specter approached the coffin and sprinkled ashes on the corpse's chest.

"Ashes to ashes," intoned the Archbishop. "Dust to dust. To earth we consign thy bones, to heaven commend thy soul." The younger Lord Hunsdon came forward with his wrapped parcel, suppressing a yawn. His father untied the ribbon and rolled out the grave cloth in full view of all. I took one look and uttered an involuntary cry, which I covered with a cough. And once the coughing started, I found I could not stop.

The device on the cloth was a hand holding a cup with Latin words arched over it.

When I felt in control enough to look up again, the grim figure of the ash carrier was the first thing I saw. It seemed that his eyes were fixed upon me. If, indeed, he had any eyes in the smoky depths of the black hood.

❖

Starling worried my account of the funeral almost
to death, but could make no more sense of it than I. If
the cup-and-hand device was connected with Philip
Shackleford's house, what interest did my aunt have in
it? Or my father, who had carried that very image on his
own person? "It's not a symbol of the house," she
decided, "not like a coat of arms. Perhaps it's more the
symbol of a society or faction. Perhaps a secret society,
like the Knights Templar."

"Secret societies don't fly their flags," I pointed
out. "Yet they rolled out that grave cloth as bold as the
Queen's arms. If it's a Catholic symbol, could it mean
that the Lord Chamberlain has papist leanings?"

"No," she said, quite firmly. "Lord Hunsdon has
been the Queen's own man from the very beginning,

and true as gold. If he was flaunting that cloth, it would be for some good reason." But neither of us could fathom what that reason might be.

In mid-July came a report that the Queen had fallen ill in Northumberland. The news varied widely: she was recovering; she lay at death's door; she leapt from her sickbed and danced a reel; she was taken by seizures. Within days, some were saying that she had been poisoned—by a Catholic. I recalled how King John, in the play, had met his end likewise. As I was beginning to learn how art could echo life, the rumors gave me a terrible foreboding. True, Catholics had not threatened the Crown for eight years, or not since their last plot was cut off along with the Queen of Scots' head. But Elizabeth was old—destined to go the way of all flesh in God's good time, and had yet to name an heir. Surely the papists would not let her do so without an attempt to maneuver one of their own into the line of succession, and perhaps even hasten the Queen's end if she took too long to die.

This is what the servants were discussing late one afternoon, in the coolness of the great room. With the mistress and children gone and Master Harry usually out, they had the run of the house and liked to gather during the hottest hour of the day for a cup of ale or cider. Almost the entire household was present—Nell the cook, Tobias the butler, Jacob the gardener, Starling, and me—when Betty rushed in with flushed cheeks, waving her hands excitedly.

"Disporting with the neighbors' footman again!" Nell chided.

"But wait until you hear what he told me!" Betty fluttered. "Such news!" Of course, that got our attention, and she went on to impart what she had learned from her swain: at noon that very day, an apprentice was pushing a loaded wine cart through Ludgate when the little keg on top worked its way to the edge of the pyramid, overbalanced, and fell to the street. There it bounced on the rough cobbles, struck a curbstone, and broke apart. Amid jeers and laughter from the bystanders, a young music master happened to notice a flash of paper between the two oak disks that had formed one head of the keg. He picked it up.

The exact message of that paper was never made known, but within an hour all of London buzzed with the news of a conspiracy. The excitable music master had been heard to shout something about foreign agents and treason, and soon the crowd was a mob. The city marshal, ever vigilant during the plague season, arrived quickly to put down the disturbance. But word was out, and rumors can never be put down. "These devils are called the Knights of the Crossbow, or some such," Betty concluded.

"What sort of name is that?" asked Jacob. "Belongs back in the Crusades, sounds like."

Nell clucked her tongue. "Such foolishness."

"No, it's their device. The keg was marked with a little crossbow burnt into its head."

Old Tobias began one of his lengthy explanations of the obvious. "The French, now—"

"Wait!" I interrupted. "A crossbow, did you say?"

"Aye, upon my honor and virtue," replied Betty, with a little simper. She flirted with everything in breeches, even me. But my mind was wholly taken with the image of a crossbow about two inches square, stamped upon every keg of wine from the Châlons vineyard in the southeast of France. Very choice, very select, and imported only by Motheby and Southern. I pushed away from the table. Starling followed me from the great room, through the buttery, and out to the stone walk.

"What is it?" she asked.

I stood for a moment beside the herb garden, deep in thought. "What—" she repeated, but I held up a hand. The heavy, golden afternoon hung so still and sullen I could almost feel tempers kindling, fevers breeding throughout the city. A clang of bells sounded in the distance: not remarkable in itself, for bells were often tolling the hours or the news, or a birth or a death somewhere in London. The more I listened, the louder they grew, clamoring from the direction of the river. "I am going down to the quay," I said then. "Will you?"

For answer, she took off her apron and hung it upon the drying bush nearby. I fetched my cap and we set off swiftly down Cattle Street. As we went, I explained what the crossbow meant. "Not many would recognize it. 'Tis only sold at the Lion and Lamb, near Middle Temple."

"What sort of people go there?"

"Professional men, mostly. Solicitors." I paused briefly in mid-stride. "Lawyers."

"Ah. And you have been warned away from lawyers—lately by a man who imports wine from France. . . ."

"But what was on that paper? It may amount to nothing."

"Aye, but you know it does not."

I did know it, and that was precisely why we were on the street headed toward the wharf. The bells grew louder at our approach, and as their noise increased, so did my suspicion that I understood their meaning. Turning the corner at Cross Keys Inn, we could see a bloom of gray smoke pouring out upon the sky over the river, sparked near the roofline by busy points of flame. I knew without being told that what fueled this fire was the warehouse of Motheby and Southern.

"Come on!" I shouted, and Starling nimbly tucked up her skirts and ran beside me. Our haste attracted no undue attention, for everyone was running in the same direction.

Fires are common in the city, especially in the dry days of summer, but this one burned with a ferocious heat, throwing flames twenty feet into the sky. When we reached the scene, the confusion had just begun to sort itself, and sooty, shouting men had formed in two lines to draw up water in buckets from the river. The warehouse was beyond saving; all they could hope to accomplish was to keep the fire within bounds. They had already tied ropes around the counting house hard by; as we watched, the entire building was pulled down with a roar and men swarmed over the timbers, desperately dragging them out of the fire's path and beating out the flames. A molten breeze streamed past my face as the blaze leapt higher; the heat so intense it threatened to suck the air out of our lungs. Old Roger Coverdale, dealer in salt fish, was organizing a third brigade to save his nearby warehouse. But I saw no trace of Motheby or Southern, and only after intense searching did I spot Ralph Downing's moon face in the water line. I pushed through the crowd, leaving Star to follow as she might, and broke into line beside him just in time to take the empty bucket passing toward the river. "How goes it, Ralph?"

He squinted at me, holding up progress for a precious second. Then his soot-smudged face lit with recognition. "Richard! 'Tis you, then?" ("Keep it going!" roared a voice down the line.)

"The same. How did the fire start?"

"No one knows. Day of wonders, this." He took the full bucket on his right and passed it to me. "Agents from the court arrived before the tide and arrested my masters."

"Arrested! Both of them?" He nodded decisively. I felt the excitement about him; he relished his part in this affair, small as it was. "For what cause?"

"Can't tell you that. But mark me"—he paused to take an empty bucket from my hand—"mark me, it has somewhat to do with the upset this noon."

"What upset?"

"That keg spilled by Jemmy Burchett on Fleet Street. Had a message from the French king, promising to send an army to overthrow our Queen!"

"Impossible!"

"They've taken my masters to the Tower over it."

"And Jemmy Burchett—what of him?"

"Taken him, too, though he knows about as much as a cod. Lucky for me I wasn't with him. They sent only one load today. And that steward, at the Lion and Lamb—remember? I hear they had him on the rack within an hour."

I felt my stomach turn over. I did recall the steward, and how sharply he denied knowing any man by the name of Martin Feather. If he was on the rack, he would not be denying anything for long. Starling popped up beside me and spoke in my ear. "You must come. I've something to show you."

It was not difficult to find someone to take my place in the line, for a scene of public drama never wants for actors. I made a quick farewell to Ralph and caught his grin through the smoke. "See you at the Theater, Richard!"

I made but a weak smile in return and dashed after Starling, who was giving the flames a wide berth. In the confusion I felt her take hold of my hand as we climbed up from the river a short distance and turned at the head of a long pier. Here we joined the audience, who surveyed the frantic scene with an ill-concealed relish. Their talk was instructive: "Passing strange, eh? A wine keg breaking at noon and a wine warehouse aflame within hours?" "Aye, and they say it blazed up so fast, there was no time to get out the alarm." "No happenstance, this—"

"Look carefully to the right," Starling told me. "But don't stare. Those bales of wool, stacked along the wall—see them?"

"I see them."

"Now look to the topmost bale—that man on top? D'you recognize him? Don't catch his eye, whatever you do."

I found the indicated figure easily; he had cadged himself the best place on the waterfront to survey the action. Alone of that crowd, he seemed perfectly calm, though he studied the flames intently, rubbing a finger along his lower lip. This gave me an opportunity to study him, amid the gusts of smoke, and something in that beaky profile did seem familiar. "I cannot think where—"

"He's one of the men who were tracking you. Do you remember, I saw Roger Coverdale chase a fellow away from this wharf the day after you came to us? It's the same man."

I looked more closely. Starling was as sharp-eyed as anyone I knew, yet I could not place the man here; surely it was from some other quarter that I knew him, if at all. The high-bridged nose, the arch of eyebrow aroused in me a sense of discomfort. Such a face did not belong among riverside idlers—it was too refined, if not downright imperious, the sort of face to make you shuffle your feet and wonder if there was a smudge on your nose.

"Mark how calm he sits," Starling murmured. "Like God in heaven, surveying his handiwork. I would wager anything he set this fire."

There was a ring on his left hand, of some dull metal. As the hot wind fanned my face, I suddenly recalled the heavy taste of pewter in my mouth, a dead-quiet voice in my ear: "If you want to stay well, you'll fly away straight." Then I knew him—the clerk in

161

Martin Feather's chambers, who went by the name of Merry. I felt my head reel in the heat, as though turning a slow somersault.

"Let's be off," I said. "Back to the street. I know him."

Just inside a Thames Street tavern, now almost empty of patrons, I sat with my head in my hands while Starling tried to sort our findings. "So—he works for Martin Feather. Your aunt must be in some sort of league with the attorney, or at least in communication with him . . . unless she sends all her intelligence to this Merry fellow only. But John Beecham figures in it, too; surely it's more than coincidence that the very place he sent you to find work is now going up in flames, because . . . because . . ."

I rubbed my temples, which had begun to throb. "Because it's at the center of a huge devilish conspiracy that's about to crash down on my head."

"Well, that's more than we know—"

"Are they all against me?" I asked, in a muffled voice.

"Perhaps not." Star sounded overly brisk. "Your aunt, and this Merry, and Masters Beecham and Kenton all seem to be in communication, but they may not be in league. The link that binds them is Master Feather: one is his present clerk, another his former clerk; your aunt . . . how would she know the attorney, do you think?"

"Stop it!" I clutched my head. "It's enough for one night." By now all these names had the worn and grubby feel of disjointed parts that had been picked up and rearranged too many times in our attempts to fit them together. And one more factor had occurred to me: that my father also associated with Martin Feather

162

at one time. This was another line of speculation but I was too spent to follow it. A hot, slow twilight had fallen, thick with smoke, and the tavern was filling with men and boys who had done their part to put out the fire. The talk around us was of Catholics and plots, all in terms not fit to write. A threatening mood pressed down under the rafters. I glanced at Starling, who stared reproachfully back at me, hurt by my sharp tone. "Come along," I said, gruff but I hope not unkind. "This is getting to be no place for us."

She stood readily enough, and we threaded a path through the crowd, toward Gracechurch Street. Getting away from the smoke and catching a fresh breeze off the river helped my head. When we were halfway to Cheapside, Star spoke again, probably because the pressure of her thoughts would not allow her to keep silent. "You say the authorities have laid their hands on that steward at the Lion and Lamb. If they rack him, he'll spill all he knows, including names. So they may soon be looking for some of these people, like Martin Feather and Peter Kenton. . . ."

"They'll have a task finding him," I said. "He conjures himself at will."

"Meaning?"

I told her Ned's fancy of gentlemen changing themselves to bears. It was meant for a distraction, but to my surprise she latched on it. "Ned's eyes are sharp, in that flighty head. He must have seen something."

"Did he? You mean, something like you saw in the Smithfield market, chained to a post, that you thought was your kin?"

Her patience finally broke. "What has come over you? You're as sour as Master Merry. Do you wish to set a fire, too?"

We were now at the corner of Lothbury Street, and suddenly, the thought of going home seemed unbearable. My head was clearer now, and I clearly saw a chance that should not be missed. Master Merry had followed me, at least once; why should I not follow him? "You go along," I told Starling. "I must return to the quay."

"I'll go with you."

"That you won't. I can manage better on my own for this."

She flared up, I stood fast, and in the short but violent quarrel that followed I remember wondering why she seemed so passionate about staying with me. Eventually, she saw reason, for when tracking a prey there is no advantage in numbers. "But I won't sleep a wink until your return," she snapped, "so it had better be soon." I watched her partway down the street, then turned and raced back toward the river, where a pall of smoke now lay, sullen as a garden slug.

But of course, Merry was gone. I cursed my slow wits while scanning the scene for him, but it was no use. The fire was nearly out, only smoldering embers remained; it would be an imprudent criminal who lingers overlong at the scene of a crime. Thus thwarted, and the pain in my head stamping back with a vengeance, I rounded the corner of a tavern and ran headlong into a party of torch bearers coming up from the quay. My shoulder struck the chest of the foremost figure, a lad a little older and much bigger than me.

"Well!" said he, his voice raspy with smoke. "'Tis none other than the Psalm singer, bless his pissy name!"

It was one of the boys who beat me up during my quayside days—who had never bothered to learn my name, as a matter of fact. I reeled back at a flat-handed push from him, into the chest of another lad who had circled behind to wall me in. The sting of resin smoke from a torch burned my eyes and soured my tongue. "You've done well for yourself, Psalm singer," their leader continued, grabbing me by the undone buttonholes of my doublet. "Pranked up like a very schoolboy."

My voice was threatening to dry up, though I managed to choke out a protest: "L-let me by." He topped me by a hand's breadth.

"Let you by? Will you blast us all with scripture if I don't?"

"Let him go, Jack," complained one of his followers. "He's small fry. It's bigger game we're after." The company, none of them older than sixteen, cheered lustily at this, chanting warlike cries of blood and slaughter and vengeance on Catholic traitors. Like drumbeats, their shouts pounded in my head and matched the beat of my heart, and I saw a way to redeem my thwarted aims. From very far away I heard myself saying clearly, "Is it Catholic blood you're after?"

The shouting abated; Jack's grip loosened, allowing me to settle back on my heels. "Aye," he said, sounding puzzled. "Know you any?"

"I do. And I know where she abides."

He drew me close, up to his very mouth as though to take a bite out of me, and I received his rank breath in my nostrils. "Then take us there."

"Not as your prisoner. Loose your grip."

He grunted and did so, allowing me a moment to straighten my clothes and consider what I had done. In my present state of mind, it seemed only just: The woman had created a riot to steal from me and frighten me away. Why should I not bring a riot to her? If you prick me, shall I not bleed? If you wrong me, shall I not *revenge*? Jack struck my shoulder with his palm. "No more primping, you girl! Lead on!"

And I did.

Up from the wharf, down Thames Street, over the Bridge; past houses silent as stones, doors locked, windows shuttered. The air around us huddled close with a furtive whisper, disturbed now and then by a shout or a shiver of breaking glass. The boys fell mostly silent, their short, muttered queries goading me like knife points. I walked faster, my breath coming in sharp pants. With every turn I led them deeper into Southwark, into a maze of dark houses shut up against the storm. My heart beat louder with every step, pounding out a rhythm that nearly spoke: slow to flame, long to burn. Long to burn . . .

I found I was almost running, and they were running with me, until at last we reached the stone monastery wall. I put a hand to the gate and pushed, my heart thudding so hard it threatened to jump out of my chest. All was dark; in the hot silence a goat bleated from the corner of the garden. We ran up the flagstone walk and crashed against the house. I pounded the door until my fist ached, but already guessed the truth.

No sound from within answered my knock—Anne Billings had escaped. Fury blazed up in me as I gripped the iron door handle and howled, a raw screech echoed by all the fiends at my back. Jack picked up a loose flagstone and hurled it through the center pane in the front window. It was the work of a moment to hoist me through and get the door open.

I had some idea of searching the house. There were signs that the evacuation was recent: a plate of crusts and a half-drunk cup of wine on the table, an unmade bed in the servant's room. But the more I looked, the more it appeared they had made a clean break, she of the raisin eyes and her curd-faced maid Lydia. Meanwhile Jack found a picture of the Virgin and a breviary, which to his mind more than justified the destruction that followed.

It is difficult to wreck a stone house, but they tried: ripping down the shutters, smashing all the window glass, piling everything that would burn in the center of the downstairs hall. By then I had turned over my aunt's spartan-like bedroom and her study and found nothing of value to me. The upstairs was empty save for a straw pallet on the floor of one room—some pious beggar's refuge, no doubt—which I kicked apart in rage. By then reason and I had parted company and I joined in the wanton destruction. With all my heart, God knows; all my heart.

Downstairs they had set a torch to the pile of household goods.

I threw an armful of straw upon it, then dodged the live goat that two of the boys heaved through the open window. After a wild chase, we caught the terrified creature and dragged it to Jack, who cut its bleating throat with his dagger. He meant to roast it over the bonfire, but had hardly begun butchering when one of his lads burst through the door in a panic. "Run! It's the watch!"

"Every man for himself!" bellowed Jack. He bolted past, headed for the back rooms. All the boys followed, including me, but I lost ground when I slipped on something—candle tallow or goat's blood—and fell, striking my head on the doorpost. Sheer terror forced me to my feet again, though my head was spinning, and by some instinct I groped my way through the kitchen and emerged into the yard to see the last boy scrambling over the stone wall. I leapt after him, using a thick vine as a rope, and rolled over the top just as the torches of the watchmen poured through the open front gate.

❖

*A*fter that night, Anne Billings' house was the last place I would have wished to visit. But on the following day, near twilight, I was picking through the ruins with Star. She knew nothing about my part in the destruction; all I told her was that I had run into former quayside enemies who dealt me a hard time I didn't wish to talk about. The bruises and scratches I took during my frantic exit made the story plausible. By now she knew when to press me and when not; the state I was in upon arriving home that night (as hollowed and harrowed as a burnt-out house) was not a time to press me. But on her Saturday visit to the market she had heard about vandals sacking a former foundling hospital and brought this news to me in great excitement. She proposed we make a search. I could think of no good reason to refuse.

Even in July the house retained its chill, the stone walls clammy and silent, with no bleat of grazing goats to soften them. The bonfire had eaten a great oblong hole in the upstairs floor before the watch could organize a fire brigade. Seeing it in daylight made me feel sick. My sleep had been riddled with dreams of being marched into Newgate prison while the felons jeered at me.

"Are you well?" Starling asked, sharply. She thought we were searching for information and knew not what to make of my listless manner.

I nudged the corner of a charred mattress poking from the pile. A picture of the Virgin slid out from under it. The tin frame was bent, and I suddenly remembered seizing the picture with both hands and dashing it against my knee. "I'm well enough," I said, in a voice that seemed to lie flat on the stone floor.

We searched the downstairs, finding nothing, of course, then climbed to the second level and peered into rooms that still had a floor. "Someone has already set up housekeeping here," Starling remarked, standing in the doorway of a tiny room off the upstairs hall. The floor was scoured of mud and filth; the straw bed I had kicked apart was painstakingly put back together and covered over with rough canvas. There was no furniture, only a few pitiful possessions: candle ends, kindling wood, a length of rope. "I wonder if Mistress Billings was taking in beggars instead of orphans."

"It appears so."

"This beggar seems as cleanly as a Dutch wife. Look how he's sanded the floor." It was true; whoever made a home here had taken pains to carry sand upstairs and scour the floor and sweep it out. To think of him patiently bearing his loads and putting right the damage wrought by vandals like me turned my face hot with shame. Mother used to say that what a man shows in his anger is what he truly is. I was looking at myself, amidst these burnt timbers and wrecked goods, and hardly liked the sight. I turned and led the way back downstairs.

"What conclusion?" Starling asked in a small voice as we passed the remains of the bonfire.

I paused, took a deep breath, pointed at the Virgin's picture with my toe. "It appears Anne Billings was a Catholic," I said tightly, adding, "all the same, I hope she got away safe." And so I did hope, for the sake of my own conscience.

We had closed the front door and started down the flagstone walk when a movement at the gate halted us. A man in rags stood there, his legs bound in rough sacking, his head covered by a patched hood pulled forward so we could see none of his face beyond a scabby chin. He held a bag in one hand, and in the other a clapper made of two wooden slats—the kind that lepers use to warn of their approach. After standing motionless for a moment, he slowly raised the clapper and struck the air with it, informing us with an air of weary resignation that we must not come near.

Seeing this, I came near to breaking down. "Quick!" I whispered to Starling. "Have you any money—a twopence, or penny, anything? I'll pay you back." But she had none, and all I carried were two pennies. As I fumbled in my pouch for them, the beggar caught my intent and opened his bag. As we edged around him, I tossed the coins in the bag's open mouth. It was conscience money; the man seemed a living reproach to me. His gratitude, shown by tugging at the front of his hood, only made me feel worse.

Starling said little on the way back, having caught my somber mood. As we approached the Bridge, we noticed a constable tacking a broadside to the wall that shielded the riverside privies. No literate Londoner can resist a new broadside; as soon as the man moved on, Starling went over for a look, and I heard her gasp.

I came closer and read this:

BY ORDER OF HER MAJESTY

Any Person or Persons possessed of any knowledge soever of one

Peter Kenton, Esquire

or

John Beauchamp or Beecham, Attorney

should bring said Knowledge to the officer of the Guard at Tower Hill. All useful intelligence will be rewarded.

Long Live Elizabeth

In her service, John Clement

My mind was dry, barren. Before Starling could make any comment, I turned and made for the Bridge. She followed, by now so confounded I could feel it in her. We were all the way across the

Bridge before I could trust myself to speak. "I know what you're thinking. We should go to John Clement, whoever he is, and tell him what we know. But Beecham and Kenton know far more about me than I do of them. Besides . . ." I blinked fiercely, struggling for control. "I've had my fill of it. If I never hear those names again, I'll die content. Master Clement can manage without us, and all will pass. So let's leave it. Will you?"

"I will," she said, so faintly I could barely hear. For the rest of the way home neither of us said a word.

Rumors of the Queen's illness were proved totally false when an official proclamation arrived from her, assuring the good people of London that she was in excellent health and requesting that they stop their riots on her behalf.

Though I dragged out my copy work, it came to an end eventually, and by August there was nothing to do except help Jacob with the gardening. Besides church on Sundays I kept to the house, begging off on the few occasions when Master Harry asked me to run an errand. Starling and I managed to converse without bringing up painful subjects, but often found we had little to talk about. She did learn, on one of her shopping trips to the quay, that Motheby and Southern had been released from the Tower with no charges made against them. Their business was ruined, but at least their heads were where heads should be: on their shoulders and not decorating the Bridge.

A letter from Susanna informed me that she was well and her

master was pleased and Walter Hawthorne was far too attentive, even though she kept him at arm's length. It gave me an opportunity to lecture her for a change, advising her to allow him no liberties. Not for the first time, I wondered if my rightful place was in Alford, watching out for her, even though she always claimed she could watch out for herself. The narrow, stinking streets of London, dense and damp as a plum cake in the summer heat, stirred a longing in me for Lincolnshire's open fields and fresh-cut hay. The geese would soon be gathering on Squire Hawthorne's pond, and I recalled with a pang how my mother could sit for hours watching them.

But in mid-August Mistress Condell brought the children back from the country, and three days later the Company returned from their tour, sun-burnt and played-out. Master Condell's family hurled themselves upon him when he came through the front gate. After him trailed a hired man pushing a barrow loaded with presents: bolts of wool for the ladies, wooden toys for the children, local cheeses and brews from outlying provinces which loudly proclaimed their product to be the best in England. For me he brought a well-made copy of Foxe's *Book of Martyrs,* a happy find at a county fair. "I saw it and thought of you." I thanked him sincerely, moved that he should have remembered me in his travels—though I wondered what there was about Protestant martyrs that brought me to mind.

All Robin had for me was strong opinions. "Foxe didn't know what torture was. If Bloody Mary wanted to persecute Protestants, she should have sent them on a tour." He went on to describe the many shortcomings of wayside inns and county fair crowds, the roads choked with dust, the plague of gnats around every marsh, the miles of landscape in which one saw nothing but sheep and shepherds, and it was anyone's guess who was stupider. He sighed with envy when I told him of the anti-Catholic riots and the warehouse fire, and could not understand my loathing toward the same. "After performing on the heels of a dozen cattle shows, you would appreciate London better."

"Did you go through Lincolnshire?" I asked.

Robin swore and turned facedown on our bed, spreading his arms to catch the warm air from the open window. "Don't ask! One fly-specked town looks like all the rest. Just let me sleep, and tomorrow I shall wake in better humor."

No one told me I could stay for another season. Nor did I ask; I simply stayed.

The Lord Chamberlain's Men allowed themselves only a few days of rest before a meeting at the Mermaid Tavern that stretched to the small hours. They lined out a rough plan for the season: a "goodly blend" of comedy, tragedy, and history, beginning with *Romeo and Juliet,* a popular tale of thwarted young lovers. Robin did his second turn as Juliet, dying elaborately in full view of the audience, who loved him for it; Kit played Juliet's mother with some of the same controlled despair that I had seen in Constance; Dick drew the small part of Lady Montague; and Will Sly, with a cowl covering his beard, took on Juliet's nurse with a zest that made the audience forget his mustache. I played various serving men and added steel to the many stage fights, though I was rusty on my fencing after a summer's disuse.

Only one week into the season, I was already too harried by the demands of my profession to think of anything else. To my surprise, I took to it like a beached fish returned to water. Twice that first week the Company handed me a speaking part to learn the night before, walk through in the morning, and perform that afternoon. Every day I marched with the armies and shouted with the crowds, jostling properties and costumes behind stage and scanning the plot in a frenzy to find my next entrance. By Friday, when I was ransacking the property room to find the last helmet, an odd thought struck me: I felt as though I had been at this all my life. The tiring master bounded back to shout, "Never mind, then! The Duke's men are marching. Here, put a bandage about your noggin and get on!" I sighed and wrapped the linen around my head as quick and neat as any actor forced to improvise.

At the Mermaid Tavern that Saturday I delivered my copies of *The Winter's Tale,* then lingered with the other boys to follow the casting. As with all new plays, the parts were assigned three weeks ahead of the performance. Some of these sorted out predictably: Richard Burbage would play Leontes, the jealous king, with Henry Condell as Polixenes, his suspect friend; Richard Cowley would take the shepherd's role, with Will Kempe, the clown of the Company, as the swindler Autolycus. Will

Shakespeare was Antigonus, the faithful courtier compelled to expose the infant Perdita; his brother Edmund would play the ardent young swain Florizel.

This last was an obvious disappointment to Kit, who coveted the role for himself. He had turned sixteen over the summer and seemed to think more male parts should be coming his way, but in this play his regal bearing and presence were needed for Hermione, the wronged queen.

That left Paulina, Hermione's friend and Leontes' conscience, and Perdita, the castaway daughter. The young-maiden parts were usually assigned to Robin, who made the most of them with his wavy auburn locks and long lashes and lilting voice. Imagine our surprise then, when Master Will rejected this obvious bit of casting. "I've another thought," said he, "in which our Harry concurs." I saw Master Condell incline his head and felt a quiver in my spine.

"I think Richard should take Perdita's role," said Master Will.

Startled glances went to and fro. Robin looked ready to pop with indignation, but the next assignment pleased him. He was given Paulina, a mature woman of character and a stretch for him. Paulina's was the largest of the female parts and offered several opportunities for displaying fine disdain and righteous outrage. So Rob was in a buoyant mood as we made our way home that night. My own mood was difficult to describe.

On the one hand I was greatly flattered by the Company's trust in me. But there was a touch of uneasiness, too. I felt a deep sympathy with Perdita, "the lost one": raised in the country among rustics, separated from her mother by death, from her father by his own mad impulse. Some part of me knew that I could play this part well, or better than well. But I was almost afraid to play it. The line between stage and life was so fragile here that I felt a risk of losing myself somehow. The more I thought on it, the more did genial Master Will acquire the menacing shadow of a demon or sorcerer, for he had written the play and cast me in the part. How did he know so much?

"Fear not," Robin said, climbing the steep steps to our attic room ahead of me. "'Tis a deal of speech you have to learn, but I'll help you. All will be well."

His confident tone was meant to reassure, but of course he had not spoken to my fears at all.

The Winter's Tale was to be performed the first week in October, and I was not overburdened with speaking parts until then. We staged *The Merchant* again and I was amazed at how quickly Nerissa's lines came back. I employed some voice tricks learned from Master Condell and managed to hold the attention of the audience during the first scene. Then I brought about a minor set-to with Kit by moving in front of him during one of his speeches. It was not intentional; I suddenly remembered I must be somewhere else on the stage, and without thinking took the shortest route to get there. No veteran would have done it, but Kit refused to take inexperience into account. As we shed our corsets and farthingales in the upper room, he lit into me with the vigor of a sparhawk, ending with, "And don't upstage me again, you whey-faced turd." Robin told him he was crying murder after spilt milk, which made him hotter. We descended the stairs in a tiff, only to find the Company likewise. The object of their disgust was the Admiral's Men, a rival set of players.

"Lest any doubt their intention, here it is, writ large." Edmund Shakespeare, who had taken no part in the performance that day, jabbed at the paper his brother was thoughtfully reading.

"What is it, Will?" Richard Cowley asked.

"Oh," said he, with a wry little twist to his mouth, "'tis the most excellent and lamentable romance of *Fawnia and Dorastus,* to be performed two days hence at the Rose. They claim it is a new play, though I remember seeing its like some years ago."

"But that is the point," cried his brother, jabbing the playbill again with enough force to poke a hole through it. "'Tis said to be a new writing of it. But word is they've lifted it, all or part, from *The Winter's Tale.*"

"Ah," growled Richard Burbage from the back of the stage. "That's just their meat."

"Their sauce, more like." Master Will glanced up with a smile. "How could they steal from my play before it's even performed? And it must be admitted, I stole the story from Robert Greene."

"Stories cannot be stolen," protested Master Heminges. "And Robert Greene is long dead, God rest his soul. But if they've taken your words, we must call them to account."

"No one has seen the words yet," said Master Condell, "save the Revels office. And Richard here, who copied it."

They all looked at me, and the matter under discussion became abruptly and terribly personal. By now I understood what was at issue. The work of a playmaker is in no way protected. Once accepted and copied, it becomes the property of the acting company, which keeps the book under lock and key. But anyone might lift a few apt lines from one play and graft them into another; I had observed bookish young men in our audience furtively scribbling verses that took their fancy. Though not against the law, it was considered bad courtesy, and the more respected companies honored an unspoken agreement among themselves not to perform each other's works without prior notice. Still, any author might be tempted to steal from one of London's most popular playmakers; this was why the Lord Chamberlain's Men regarded me with more than ordinary interest.

"Didst show thy work to anyone, Richard?" Master Condell asked.

"None, sir." My voice broke; I steadied it. "It was locked up in the scribe's desk while I was not working on it."

"Take comfort, boy," John Heminges said. "No one accuses you. Suppose one of us goes to see this *Fawnia and Dorastus* and uncovers the truth below the hearsay?"

The Company agreed to this sensible proposal, then pondered whom to send. "The obvious choice," remarked Master Will, "is Richard. He knows the play."

Before I quite realized what had happened, my duties for two days hence were assigned to Gregory, the new apprentice. Robin wished to go with me and spoke so roundly for himself that our master allowed him, as he was marked for only a trifling part on the day in question. No sooner had she heard of our design than Starling insisted she must accompany us, and found a girl to substitute for her at the Theater. The more the merrier, apparently.

Our master gave us each two pence to admit us to the Rose. Robin, still flush with silver he had earned on tour, insisted that we be rowed across the Thames in fine style, laying out another two pence for the purpose. The September day gleamed like gold, beguiling me to lay aside my worries, and Starling reveled in the glory of being squired to the theater by two such gallants as we. She had put aside her cap and twined flowers in her wayward hair as though it were May Day, and smiled prettily at Robin as he handed her into the boat. I was the drab in this party, recognizing too late that if I wished to go unnoticed it was unwise to travel with either of them in a festival mood.

Robin, who could talk a snake out of its skin, persuaded our waterman to take a seat on the stern and let us boys do the rowing. Halfway across, when the fellow was gazing placidly behind him and no doubt thinking he had got the better of these young pillow-heads, Rob seized the moment and, with jab of his oar, tipped him into the Thames. Even before the splash had fully sounded with me, Robin suggested that we bend to our oars with a right good will, putting yards between us and the roaring waterman. Already an empty wherry was spinning to his aid. Its grinning pilot tipped a nod to us, and Starling squealed with laughter, stamping her feet on the floor of the boat. Never was I more glad to reach another shore than when we ran the boat up the landing stairs and tied it securely. "Now for the Rose," Robin said with a glance over his shoulder. "And let us blend artfully with the crowd."

We passed the Bear Garden—which is misnamed to my mind, being as stinking, noisy, and ungarden-like a place as any in London. Rob knew it better than he should and entertained us with a bloody tale of the last match between Old Tim and Ball of Fire, until even Starling begged him to stop. By then we had reached our goal.

The Rose is newer than our Theater, and looks it: a many-sided building similar in design but sparkling with fresh paint and a permanent stage. The boards of the Rose were smooth-planed and well-fitting, with none of the humps that the Lord Chamberlain's Men had to guard against tripping over. Each door and shutter bore a handsome florid rose carved into the wood, and the floor was covered in dry rushes that breathed a light golden dust under the scuffing feet of the groundlings. Many of these—apprentices, laborers, and serving maids—were avid theatergoers who had doubtless seen Robin on the boards any number of times, but appeared not to recognize him. This was probably because he blended so well with them, as loud and unruly as any. Starling suffered a pinch or two, for females were fair game out of the galleries; she made me put my arm around her shoulders to pose as her protection. She enjoyed this more than I thought seemly, but there were only twenty minutes to wile away thus until the trumpet sounded its third call and a Prologue stepped out to set before the audience the gist of the play.

How odd to think that, although I had now performed in more than forty plays, this was only the second I had seen in London. My ability to judge it as a spectator was compromised, for by now I knew too well the workings of a play, and could not enter easily into the spirit of it. Just as well, for my purpose was not to be swept away but to compare this work to *The Winter's Tale*. The names were all changed—Fawnia for Perdita, Dorastus for Florizel, Podosto for Leontes, and so on—and though similar in its unfolding, the story ended very differently: the ruined queen died indeed and the king, overcome by his many sins (not least of which is falling in love with his own daughter) kills himself. The words seemed inferior to Shakespeare's overall, in ways I could not have explained, and I caught no outright borrowings.

Edward Alleyn, one of London's great players, carried the role of King Podosto with such authority that when he trod the boards, the audience fell into his hands. Some scenes without him dragged out too long. The groundlings fidgeted and made rude remarks, and Robin found fault with all the boy players. To the queen: "Look to your hands, mistress! Meat hooks, more like!" Of the shepherd's wife: "A tub of guts in a dress, and a voice like courting cats." In my ear: "Kit could best them all together, with a meal sack over his head."

In the middle of the fourth act, while Dorastus paid court to his love (and took too long about it) the groundlings grew restless again. "Behold the beauteous Fawnia," Robin said to me, "simpering like a milkmaid—"

"Quiet!" I hissed, suddenly most attentive. For my ears had picked up, amongst the rustles and whispers, lines that rang out clear and silver as bell-tones:

> But soft within the layered petals keep they curled,
> These poor sighs of mine by the rose concealed
> While in thy sweet possession rise to fly unfurled
> My secret wound enbalmed, my hidden hurts healed . . .

"What ails thee?" Starling whispered, noticing my violent start.

I shook my head, unable to speak. Those words were set in my brain, chiseled as deep as our Lord's Prayer. My father wrote them to his love. They were on a piece of parchment folded up in a leather wallet, which was stolen from me. My father wrote them. "My secret wound enbalmed, my hidden hurts healed . . ." My father.

"And mark how Dorastus takes her hand," groaned Robin. "He eyes her like she was a side of beef in the market."

The rest of the play was dead to me, though I had to notice when Edward Alleyn stabbed himself in the final scene and expired in a fine crimson gush. The Admiral's Men have developed gory deaths to perfection with their artful use of sheep's bladders and blood. The audience, completely won over, roared their approval when the players assembled on stage for the concluding dance.

"I must know the playmaker," I said, once the dance was over and the audience thronged toward the open doors.

"Why bother with that?" Robin scoffed. "This piece of barnyard turf is so slight the public will forget it in two weeks. The Company has naught to fear."

"That matters not. I must know the playmaker."

"What's this?" Robin's dark, finely shaped eyebrows rose. "Did you hear something? Did he rob us?"

"No, it's not that," I said, backing away.

"Let it be, Rob," Starling put in, with a searching look at me.

"I'll let it be, but I'm not disposed to linger here among these— dabblers."

"Go on then," I said. "Start your way home and I'll take the Bridge if I miss your boat. Go on. I mean it." I left them staring after me as I vaulted onto the stage and aimed directly for the tiring rooms behind it, ignoring the outraged cries of a stage boy who was kneeling on the boards, scrubbing up sheep's blood.

One can ask nearly anything if it is done with an air of authority, and I went some ways toward my goal before the Admiral's Men caught on to me. To my repeated questioning, one player after another shook his head and declared upon his soul he could not remember the name of the author, even though the work was heralded as a new play. Some thought it was a wit from Oxford, others an unknown hopeful. One swore the playmaker was dead until reminded that he was thinking of Robert Greene. In time I came face to face with Edward Alleyn himself, who had stripped off his kingly robes and sheep's bladder and now was lacing a splendid velvet doublet while a dresser combed out his perfumed hair. "The author?" He wrinkled his handsome brow. "'Twas Owen Mercer—was it not, John?" This he addressed to another actor passing nearby, who thought about it for a moment.

"True, Ned—though he wrote the old version. Ben Jonson brushed it up for us last summer, dost recall? Wait, boy." The actor took a closer look at me. "I've seen you about, haven't I? On the stage? Soft! I have it—"

"Thank you, sirs." I bowed quickly out of their presence. "I am in your debt. Pardon, sirs . . . ." I turned then and made a hasty exit, followed by a laugh and an exclamation in Alleyn's rich, rolling voice: "Oho! A *spy*!"

My brain was in a whirl with this new name to ponder, but all the same, while passing through the door I felt a tug on my memory. I stopped and turned, and studied the rose carved into the upper hatch, wondering why it seemed familiar. Roses are seen everywhere about London, notably in the insignia of the Queen. But what set this rose apart was its stem, a curl in the shape of the letter "C," bearing three thorns. I knew I had seen it before, under quite different circumstances; then it came to me.

A curious bystander would have been much amazed at what he

saw next, for I stood in the entrance to the Rose Theater and solemnly banged my head against the door. The last time I had seen this design, it was stamped upon a leather portfolio clutched in the arm of a supposed law clerk, a man now known to me as John Beecham.

IF THAT WHICH WAS LOST . . .

✤

I took longer than expected getting home, first missing Robin's boat and then stopping at the White Horse Tavern on Cheapside, a gathering place for poets and balladeers. Here I looked for Ben Jonson. I did not find him, but after a few questions I learned where he was staying, and that was some compensation for the trouble I was in when I got home. Masters Condell, Heminges, and Shakespeare all pounced upon me, much annoyed after their long wait for my version of *Fawnia and Dorastus*. I had intended to ask them if they knew anything of a playmaker named Mercer, but in their current temper this seemed presumptuous. After my report, and a brief discussion, the men determined that the play offered by their rivals was not enough like

Shakespeare's to disrupt their schedule. Then the visitors departed and Master Condell laid a part on me to learn for the morrow. As I was also to double as a soldier, he insisted on putting Robin and me through the entire manual of arms in the garden, and by the time we finished it was dark.

I considered slipping out after curfew to continue the search, but decided to be a model apprentice instead: learn my part, obey my betters, and humbly ask for an hour off in the morning. Master Condell regarded me with suspicion when I claimed to have urgent business in the city, but in the end he let me go, "For one hour only. Mind you're back by eleven, or you'll be fined—or worse." I set off down Shoreditch Road as swift as winged-heeled Mercury.

Lucky for me, Jonson's current lodging was not far from Aldgate, on the northeast end of London, but still it was a long distance to take at a run. I arrived in a sweat, panting, "Where's Master Jonson's room?" The housemaid mutely pointed up the stairs, thinking perhaps that I bore an urgent message for him. When I pounded up the stairs and hammered on the first door, the landlady arrived and demanded loudly what this was about. Despite the shouting, my ears picked up the sound of a man's voice behind the door. Hoping it was an invitation to come in, I lifted the latch and stepped inside a shuttered room, dark and close as a den.

"This," came a voice from the bed, "had best be a matter of life or death."

I took a deep breath and let it out slowly. "N-not death, but something meaningful to my life, sir."

"Is it? What's o'clock?"

"About a quarter beyond ten, sir."

I'll not repeat his next remarks, but once they were out, his temper improved a little. "Open the shutters, boy, and let me see who you are."

I found the shutters by the slats of light glaring through them, swung them open, and turned back to the figure sprawled fully clothed upon the bed, now leaning upon his elbows and blinking fiercely at me. Ben Jonson had a boisterous reputation, but it appeared that literary pursuits had kept him up late the night before. The table by the window was covered with papers that drifted like snow around the inkpot. Blackened little commas—shavings from his quill pen—were sprinkled about randomly, as if in the heat of inspiration he dared not pause to throw them away.

"I give it up," he said then, in a voice as gritty as sand. "The face eludes me. State your name and business."

"My name is Richard, sir, and I apprentice with the Lord Chamberlain's Men. You've seen me—that is, I've seen you—well, what I was wondering . . . in your time in London have you ever known—or known of—a playmaker named Mercer?"

As I stammered to a pause, he lowered himself until his thick bricklayer's arms were stretched flat upon the mattress and his deep-set eyes fixed upon the timbered ceiling. "Apollo, god of wisdom, lend me patience," he said. "Half the poets in London could tell you of that scape-grace. Why drag *me* out of a sound sleep?"

My heart made a leap at this, but whether from joy or dread I knew not. "If you p-please, sir, I . . . trust your wit and memory. And because . . . you're right about there being no seacoast in Bohemia. I looked it up in Master Condell's atlas."

He stared at me, then tossed back his head and let out a great bellow of a laugh, as frightening in its way as a wild animal let from a cage. "Well flattered! I'll strike a bargain with you then, young sir. Fetch me a pint of ale from the Bull, two doors south, and I'll tell you what I know."

This put a strain upon my allotted time, but it could not be helped—I rushed down the stairs, ducked into the Bull Tavern, and completed my mission before Ben Jonson had fairly got out of bed. Then, after combing his hair and beard and taking a deep draught of the ale and allowing it to settle—during which time I nearly burst with anxiety—he told me what he knew.

Owen Mercer had appeared in London during the summer of the Armada, as near as my informant could recall, though it may have been a little later. He hailed from some northern province: no one knew precisely where, as the man was not consistent about his origins. He had set out to make himself the darling of the London stage, grinding out three or four plays per season, many of which were performed—"But ne'er seen thereafter," Ben Jonson said, with a snort. Jonson himself arrived in London much later, but his path often crossed Mercer's at the taverns where poets and playmakers were apt to gather.

By then Mercer's star was in decline, and he had stirred up much bad feeling against himself. A clever fellow, he was known for gaining one's confidence and looting one's mind. *Fawnia and Dorastus,* for example: scarcely had the ink dried upon Robert Greene's book than Mercer had tailored it into a play, never even bothering to change the characters' names. He also earned ill fame as a gambler and racked up debts he could not possibly repay. When Jonson saw him last, it was in a low dive surrounded by worthless companions, claiming that his latest work had attracted the attention of no less a personage than Lord Hurleigh (my ears perked up even more at the mention of this name). Mercer expected the gentleman to shower him with money, whereupon all the unfortunate misunderstandings of the past would be blotted out. In the meantime, perhaps Master Jonson could lend him a few shillings. "Hah," said Master Jonson, his scorn returning with the memory. "Money may not remain overlong in my purse, but I don't throw it down wells."

The tale ended sadly. Mercer had made enough enemies in the city to come to a violent end any number of times, but finally crossed swords—literally—with a London gentleman in a private quarrel. It was put about that they were rivals in love, but Jonson suspected that the matter was money. The two met at Finsbury Fields early one morning, but only one walked away. Owen Mercer, gravely wounded, was carried to his poor lodgings and buried the next day in a pauper's grave. All this happened . . . here Ben Jonson took another gulp of ale and rubbed his forehead trying to remember. 'Twas sometime touching Robert Greene's untimely end, he thought. Not during the plague summer of 1592, for the theaters were closed all that year, and Mercer's death caused a stir because his latest play had been performed that season. It was about a titled young rogue who dabbled in the theater, lost huge sums of money, and eventually received his just deserts in a duel over a woman. *The Fortunes of a Fool* was the title my informant remembered, a work remarkable solely for the way it seemed to foretell the author's fate. That was probably some time in 1593, then. A few of Mercer's better plays were still performed, "although they must needs be oiled, to get the screech out of them. *Fawnia and Dorastus* is a crime against poetry, but I did what I could with it, and only because the Admiral's Men dangled a purse before my eyes."

"Please, sir," I asked, after a long pause. "Could you tell me what he looked like?"

"At this distance? 'Twas over four years ago, lad, and I hardly knew him."

"But . . . anything at all."

The man shrugged his heavy shoulders. "A gingery beard. Not a large man, nor a handsome one, for all that the ladies seemed to like him. Good teeth, a fetching smile. Now you must break with me, lad—you hang upon my words as though they were drops of wine. What is your interest in this ne'er-do-well?"

"I . . . cannot say, sir." This was strictly true. A line from *The Winter's Tale* came to me: "I cannot speak, nor think, nor dare to know that which I know."

For I did know. I knew the four lines of verse were written by a young schoolmaster in Lincolnshire, years before Owen Mercer appeared in London.

"By my guess," prodded Master Jonson, not ungently, "he was something akin to you?" I said nothing. "Not to fear, lad; thy secret goes no further than these four walls."

"I am beholden to you, Master Jonson." The stuffy room seemed to swallow up words. It took effort to speak again. "One thing more. Do you remember who killed him?"

"Easily. The man still lives under that cloud. An attorney, you see. What lawyer would get himself in such a broil? Name of Martin Feather."

The remainder of that day slips my memory. I went about, as Robin put it, with my head in a bucket. The few words I spoke upon stage echoed back at me and I missed one cue. Midway through the performance, Will Sly gave me a sharp jab in the ribs with his thumb. All actors have their bad days, but are expected to leave their woes behind the stage and carry nothing on but the part assigned them. I still had much to learn about acting. My tongue, which had felt thick and clumsy all day, locked up entire after the performance and soon even Starling gave up her attempts to get anything out of me.

This was grief, or close kin to it. I had felt much like this on my journey to London, numbed by my mother's death. Strangers on the road had tried to talk to me and I could not answer. So it was with me now, only what had died was not a man but a hope. In a sense, my father had died to me long ago, but I had sought to resurrect something good from the bones: some noble purpose, some redeeming grace that might make it easier to forgive him, as Leontes is forgiven. Ben Jonson's tale planted a dagger in that fond wish. And yet . . .

The lines of a poem kept running through my head: "My secret wounds enbalmed, my hidden hurts healed." That was my father also. The self-seeking, dissolute rogue Ben Jonson remembered could not have thought those thoughts or penned those lines or won my mother's honest heart. It was that man who would not let me rest until I had found him. The facts of his death might be known, but the truth still lay hidden. And so my search was not yet over. There was no help for it; I must have another try at Martin Feather.

Later that week the north wind blew in a cold autumn rain and the white silk flag did not rise over the Theater. After leaving the Condell house on a made-up errand, I spent a long afternoon at Middle Temple, huddled under the thatched eaves of a sausage vendor's stall opposite Martin Feather's chambers. The vendor was glad of my company; his trade was slow and we had time to strike up a little friendship as greasy steam from his brazier oiled my flesh and bones until I could have slipped through a keyhole. He showed no curiosity as to why a boy of my appearance was not in school or occupied in some trade. Like many people, he filled his own world, noticed little outside it, and enjoyed talking of what he knew.

"Master Feather? A goodly gentleman. Courteous to all,

though he's not the sort you can ask about the wife and children. Come to think, I believe he hasn't any. I'll point him out if he appears, but likely he won't. We've not seen him much since the riots."

"The July riots?" I asked. "Was there trouble here, too?"

"Trouble! They took that steward at the Lion and Lamb because he was receiving secret messages from France. Papist plot, mind you. I hear they racked all his bones out of joint but all he could say was who he got the messages from and who he passed them on to. Next we know, here come the Yeomen of the Guard all but rolling up the street in search of this Kenton fellow and Master Beecham."

"You know them?"

"Used to know John Beecham—we all did. A right amiable man, though he's used up all his credit here. Owes me a sixpence yet."

I bought a sausage from him and paid promptly to remain on his good side. "What was his position?"

The vendor scratched his stubbly chin and screwed up his eyes. "Truth, I never knew for sure. He was much in company with Master Feather at one time. A partner or some such."

"How long ago was that?"

"Oh, two or three years. It's been some time since he's showed himself."

"No wonder," I said, "if he's a sneaking plotter."

"Aye. I'd never have thought it of him, though. A fair shell can hide a black heart, eh?"

I nodded sagely and wondered where to go next. "Was Master Feather suspect, too, do you think?"

"By the Lord's sweet mercy, you'd think we was all suspect the way the Guard nabbed everybody in sight. Even questioned me. They did spend a deal of time in Master Feather's chambers, though there was no one to question but the clerk."

I cleared my throat. "Master Merry, you mean?"

"Aye." The vendor's lip curled. "Matthew Merry. Know him?"

"I met him once. He seems somewhat other than merry."

This primed the pump, so to speak, and for some time I heard many examples of the clerk's insufferable attitude toward all the vendors of Middle Temple. While listening with half a mind, I watched a stocky, red-faced man in brown wool carrying a ceremonial pike—an official of some sort—huffily ascend the stair. No more than five minutes later he huffily descended.

"Is Master Feather in some sort of trouble?" I asked, when the recital of his clerk's obnoxious behavior came to a pause.

"Just money, such as besets every gentleman from time to time. That fellow, with the face like a radish—he's a collector."

Small wonder the attorney had money trouble, as I had seen nothing like a client approach the stairway all afternoon. This opened an avenue for my last question, which I made to sound indifferent: "I hear that money was the issue when he killed a man, some years back."

"Old news, that. Some poet, I recall—but soft!" I looked in the direction of his gaze and immediately shrank back against the wall. The odious Matthew Merry had emerged and was now descending the stairway. I felt a dreadful chill, a reminder of that moment when I recognized his high-boned face, eerily lit by the quayside fire, and I knew him for the one who had held a knife to my throat. Hiking up my cloak, I leaned out far enough to see him pause at the corner of the building and glance in both directions before proceeding toward Ludgate.

"Aye," said my companion, too loud. "Off he goes, to worry widows and kick dogs." Shortly thereafter a customer approached, and I made a fateful decision. It had been at the back of my mind, and Merry's departure made it seem a God-given opportunity. While the vendor was occupied, I pulled my cap lower, wrapped my cloak higher, and crossed the street. I mounted the steps two at a time, fearing my nerve would fail if I gave it pause, pushed open the door to the outer chamber, and demanded, "I must speak with Martin Feather!" Then my nerve faltered indeed.

I had expected to deal with the cherub-faced Samuel, who could be tricked into betraying information. But it was not Samuel who occupied the scrivener's desk.

I had never seen him before: a gangly youth with carrot-red hair. Startled by my sudden appearance, he swept a handful of Paris wafers into his copy desk. "The master's gone to the country for the week," he mumbled, wiping his mouth. His shiny chin glared with pimples.

The cloak slipped away from my face as I repeated stupidly, "The country?"

"It's a place outlying from the city. With trees and ponds"—he paused to swallow—"and pigs. Do you have a case, or do you like standing about with your mouth open?"

How these chambers managed to contain two such upstarts as this fellow and Matthew Merry was beyond me. Like the Lady Constance, I felt continually out-maneuvered. I borrowed a saucy lip from her and a sentiment from *The Winter's Tale*. "Aye, a case. Something lost, that must be found."

"Shall I tell him that?" He was watching me, his hazel eyes very keen, and I guessed that for all the wafer crumbs about his desk and on his chin, this was no fool. He was older than the general run of scrivener—upwards of eighteen perhaps, while the displaced Samuel was close to my own age.

"Tell him that," I said boldly. "And tell him I mean to keep looking." I backed away on these words.

"And who are you?" he asked, rising from his desk.

But I was already out the door. Pulling an edge of my cloak over my head, I stalked down Fleet Street, dodging the puddles and despairing that I would ever meet Martin Feather. I had begun to doubt that such a man existed. He was like a phantom, who haunted every pathway but disappeared when I whirled around for a plain look at him.

At that thought, I stopped dead just outside Ludgate and turned completely around.

The youth was clever and almost too quick for me. He stepped behind a brewer's booth so smoothly I could have missed that flash of carrot-red sticking out from a cap. A little more thought may have caused me to doubt my own eyes, but instinct took over: I ran through the gate, cut across the south common of St. Paul's, and doubled back down Watling Street. After weaving through enough lanes and alleys to confuse even me, I headed back to Cheapside and took the lane behind Aldermanbury Street. By then I was winded, but satisfied that I had shaken off the scrivener.

In between regular performances, the Lord Chamberlain's Men knocked together *The Winter's Tale,* which was to be the first new play of the season. Its story presented a few difficulties to the tiring master, who had to outfit twelve "men of hair"—that is, shepherds who perform a satyr's dance in Act IV dressed in animal skins. To make it worse, the costumer had also to devise a passable bear. Rather than run one up from scratch, it was thought that the Company might fall heir to a real bearskin, which, tanned and dressed, would suit out a player. Perhaps Master Will's imagination misled him when he was inspired to write such a beast into the play: bears are no longer easy to come by in England. Most of the pit champions are imported from Germany, and all seemed to be enjoying wonderful longevity that season. The tiring master was nearly at his wit's end when Brutus, a favorite at the Bear Garden, met his end at a most fortunate moment for us. John Heminges, grumbling all the while over the expense, bid for the hide and won it.

"Now the question is, who shall wear it?" asked Master Condell. The hide had been delivered, dressed out according to instruction, only two days before the performance. It was constructed with a long opening in the belly through which an actor could step into the creature's hind legs, slide his arms into the forelegs, and set the head upon his own. The costumer had padded it out to resemble a well-made beast, but once on, it could suffocate a well-made man. It was not only hot but ripe, as the tanners had not time to do their job properly. One by one, players began to explain why they could not double as the bear, but the excuses ran thin; none of them *wanted* to play the bear, and none of them would have to. The job would fall to an apprentice—me, I feared, except that as Perdita I would be called upon stage shortly after Antigonus, the bear's bait, was chased off it. Gregory and Dick, playing shepherd maids in the same act, had the same excuse. That left Robin, who was too short, and Kit, who as Hermione would feign death in plenty of time to outfit himself. Kit it would be, then. I saw him smoldering over the Company's decision, and it did me good to see him put in his place by the men who indulged him overmuch, but I caught him glaring at me as if his misfortune were my fault.

On the first Wednesday in October, a white flag went up from the Theater at noon. "Now God guide the issue," said good John Heminges, as he always did when a new play was afoot. All week, agents of the Company had tacked up playbills about *The Winter's Tale*. From the hut, shortly after noon, I observed a dark stream of humankind flowing up Shoreditch Road. "Full house, fat purse," remarked Harry Smithton, scanning the sky for clouds. He penned up the two cannonballs so they would not get loose before it was time for the thunderstorm, gave an affectionate pat to the cannon, which he would have no chance to fire this performance, and ordered me out of the hut.

I slowly climbed down to the tiring room with apprehension lying like a rock in my stomach. Even now, I was never so easy about going on the stage as Robin or some of the others appeared to be, and Perdita handed me my greatest challenge yet. Sweet-tempered maidens are more difficult to play than strong-minded women such as Constance, for it is harder to charm than it is to command.

But what made me even more uneasy was *The Winter's Tale* itself. In the three months since I copied it, the play threatened to rearrange me, setting deep roots that pushed up the settled soil and disturbed old longings. Henry Condell met me at the bottom of the stairs. "Dost know thy part?" he asked. I nodded, puzzled, for he himself had drilled me on it. Then he added, "See that you play only that."

This was the only instruction he had ever given that concerned somewhat other than posture and voice. The whole Company was feeling their customary apprehension about a new play. Master Will had admitted he was not quite satisfied with it, and when the playmaker doubted his own work, how could the players launch upon it with confidence? All summed, it was a tense company belting and lacing themselves for the public, none more tightly strung than me.

The third horn blew as the dresser set a wig upon my head. Robin and Dick were trading tales in a corner, cracking and eating nuts as they were often warned not to do before a performance. Young Lawrence Bates, a child borrowed from St. Paul's Chapel to play Mamillius, sat on the edge of the tiring-room loft, swinging his legs and humming a monotonous tune. Kit had already descended and now paced the length of the downstairs rooms with a majestic sweep of train, picking at the chapped skin of his lips. His fingernails were stubs. I backed down the steep stairway as the noise of the audience faded to murmurs, then whispers, then dropped to that quivering, expectant silence I had come to know well. The musicians in the gallery struck up a brief and lively version of "Nutmegs and Ginger," at the end of which John Heminges and Augustine Phillips strolled out upon stage as courtiers of the two kings, engaged in a conversation that would serve as introduction to our story.

Most actors can recall performances in which the play becomes so real, in speech and deed, that they could be acting their own lives. This is a hazard of the profession, not a benefit, and any player who values his sanity will put some distance between himself and his part, even if that distance is no wider than a hair. Still it happens: the edge dissolves; the player and character drift into one skin and become so joined they cannot tell each other apart.

This happened to me, though not all at once. In the second act

I appeared as a nameless lady of the court, and my only work was to look dismayed at the accusations heaped upon Hermione by her husband. Even a doorpost could have done this, in the heat of Kit's portrayal. His back remained straight as a rod throughout; it was the set of his shoulders that betrayed the inner turmoil—disbelief, outrage, grief. As always, his hands spoke as eloquently as voice or face, whether pointing in accusation, laid upon a fevered brow, or entreating heaven with palms up and fingers spread. He and Master Burbage as Leontes formed an axis between them, a wave of feeling that caught the players up with it and crested at Hermione's trial.

By then I was not acting. As Leontes brought lie after lie upon his wife's character, I ached with the lady. Hermione made her defense with a calm fury and utter conviction, appealing at last to heaven for the verdict: "Apollo be my judge!" Then the two courtiers appeared straight from the Temple at Delphi, bringing the words of the Oracle which would vindicate or condemn her. In a booming, breathless silence a courtier read them out: "Hermione is chaste, Polixenes blameless . . . and the king shall live without an heir if that which is lost be not found."

"Ah," sighed our audience, and I jumped. I had forgotten them.

"Hast thou read truth?" demanded Leontes of the courtier.

"Aye, my lord, even so as it is here set down."

A pause drew out, longer and longer until the very air seemed heavy enough to crack. Then Leontes said, "There is no truth at all in the Oracle. The sessions shall proceed. This is mere falsehood."

Cries of "No! No!" broke out from the surrounding galleries. They were still protesting when a servant arrived, bearing news of the death of Mamillius. Hermione swooned at this ill word and Leontes, shocked into reason, repented his destructive folly. He swore to repair the damage, but it was too late. Paulina rushed into his presence half-crazed with grief, heaping damnation more harsh than his own: "Thy tyranny, together working with thy jealousies—O, think what they have done, and then run mad indeed, stark mad!" To this she added a sorrow to top them all. "The queen, the queen, the sweetest, dearest creature's dead, and vengeance for it not dropped down yet!"

A moan ran through the Theater. Paulina's news and the lamentation that followed seemed to release pent-up remembrances of past sorrows. Women wept; men shook their heads. Some small part of me noticed that Robin was overplaying Paulina, that sweat was plastering the corset to my chest, that Richard Burbage had dropped a passage from his repentance speech. But none of it mattered; a family was ripped apart before my eyes, the bond between man and wife broken, and I myself bore the consequences. The family was mine.

In the tiring room I shed my court gown with no sense of relief—the performance was only half done, my part not even begun, and already I was exhausted. On stage Master Will, as the unfortunate Antigonus, observed the weather—"The skies look grimly, and threaten present blusters"—this said in the face of a clear October sun. Then he sadly abandoned his wrapped bundle, the "poor babe," to the will of heaven. The threatened storm approached on a roll of thunder pealing ominously from the hut above, and Antigonus made his hasty exit—pursued by the bear, which emerged so suddenly from the curtained space at the back of the stage that ladies in the gallery shrieked aloud. Close upon this horror arrived the simple shepherd who took up the infant, and with her, the story.

Starling found me behind stage in costume for Perdita, a country gown with a soft collar, laced up with a flutter of colored ribbons. No ruff or farthingale, but the dresser had insisted upon filling out the bodice in front. Gregory and Dick were stuffed likewise, all three of us enduring the sly remarks of the stage boys. On stage, the wily Autolycus was cozening the shepherd's son out of his money while pretending to be a traveler in distress; the audience loved this rogue, laughing with delight. As for me, I felt bruised all over with an excess of feeling, and Starling's news did nothing to calm me.

"That medal," she began breathlessly. "The one that belonged to your father, that you carried the image of in your wallet, and—"

"What?" My mind, moving slowly, suddenly caught up with her meaning. "Yes! What of it?"

"What were the words on it? *'Bibite ex—'*"

"*'Bibite ex hoc omnes,'*" I finished impatiently. "What of it?"

"Richard—keep still—I just saw it."

I felt the back of my neck prickle under Perdita's flowing locks. "Where?"

"A gentleman in the second gallery, a little left of center—he called me to him to buy a piece of gingerbread. He carries a wallet beneath his cloak, and when he reached in to get it, I saw the medal on a chain around his neck."

"Are you sure?" I could scarcely breathe, in the heat and crush of the changing scene.

"Look up, Richard," Edmund Shakespeare remarked in passing. "Next is our cue."

"I am sure. He's wearing a tall black hat with a purple ostrich plume—"

"Richard! Our cue!"

"I'll watch him," she promised, and darted away, leaving me in a worse condition than before. But I stood up somehow and moved to the curtained doorway, where Edmund took my hand and drew me out upon the stage.

❖

Gliding over the boards in my short, smooth-gaited walk, I felt a tremor of misgiving that Perdita's lines would fly away, as Nerissa's had done on that first occasion last May. But I had changed since then. The stage itself had tempered me, and all the steps taken on it seemed now to lead to this lost child, soon to be found. I walked into Perdita, and the proof is this: throughout the following scenes, through the extravagant praise of the lady's beauty and grace, no one laughed.

In her first scene she is being wooed by the young prince Florizel. She knows he is a prince, but allows herself to be drawn into his fantasy of their coming marriage, all the while knowing that it cannot happen. When she meets the disguised King Polixenes at the festival, she admits it to him in veiled terms, while welcoming him with flowers.

The flower speech had terrified me while I was learning it. Perdita goes on far too long (to my mind) about flower seasons and properties; I had fancied the audience would all be asleep by the end of it, or else tossing nutshells upon the stage, as they often did when bored. But miraculously, they listened and caught the point of the speech: that flowers should not be crossbred, princes should not marry with commoners, and shepherd maids should not aspire to be queens.

Henry Condell, as Polixenes, contradicted me, protesting that mixing a purebred stock with a wild one can result in a hardier plant. The groundlings nudged each other, for they saw how Polixenes had set himself up. Sure enough, the king failed to apply the wisdom of nature to the case of his own son. When Florizel announced his intention to marry Perdita, his father threw off his disguise to let the young man know beyond doubt that there would be no crossbreeding with shepherds in *this* royal house. He departed in a rage, leaving Florizel no less wroth, and Perdita sad and sorry: "I told you what would come of this. . . ."

I turned away from Edmund Shakespeare, as though giving him up forever, and boldly gazed over the lifted heads of the audience. In the second gallery, a purple ostrich plume appeared to bow in my direction. With proud resignation I continued: "This dream of mine—being now awake, I'll queen it no inch farther, but milk my ewes and weep." A face took shape under the narrow brim of a tall black hat, a face of noble lines and dark piercing eyes and a dark beard, neatly trimmed. A stranger's face, yet he seemed to know me. His look was so intent, it almost spoke: You do well. Play on.

I did play on, and played better than ever in my brief time on stage—missed no cues, lost no lines, breathed a fullness into that part that was life itself. Perdita grew into what she truly was; layer by layer, the secret of her royal birth revealed itself and she was finally reconciled with her father, to loud cheers from the house. By then much was resolved: Perdita and Florizel pledged to marry, the two kings made friends again.

But there remained the matter of Hermione, never known nor properly grieved by her daughter. When the curtain of the discovery space was swept aside to reveal Hermione's statue, a murmur rippled through the theater. Our audience had followed us into the heart of the story and gazed equally enthralled at this likeness of the lamented queen in royal robes, a crown upon her noble head and a stillness and serenity wonderful to behold.

"Masterly done!" exclaimed Polixenes. "The very life seems warm upon her lip."

"The stillness of her eye has motion in it," Leontes mused, "as we are mocked with art."

A melancholy tune spiraled down from the musicians' gallery. I moved toward the statue as though drawn by it, my hands out. The words leapt so readily to the tongue, I did not have to think about them: "And give me leave—and do not say 'tis superstition, that I kneel and ask her blessing." I knelt and reached for that hand, which, in the reaching, became my mother's hand. I forgot everything then—the man with the plume in his hat, the players, the audience, even my part, which I had become. Paulina, the sorceress of this conjuring, hastened to forbid my touching the statue, and likewise held back Leontes from kissing those lips that seemed so warm: "You'll mar it if you kiss it, stain your lips with oily painting. Shall I draw the curtain?"

"No!" commanded Leontes. "Not these twenty years."

"So long," said I, near tears, "so long could I stand by, a looker on."

And so I could have sold myself a slave for twenty years to see my mother again, fresh and calm and finally at peace. I knelt with a heart full of all I had never said to her, all I longed to ask. I, the lost one, begging to be found. Her head was turning toward me, so slowly the movement could scarcely be seen; unblinking, the ice-gray eyes tracked an invisible curve to the point where I waited with hands outstretched.

Then Kit fixed his eyes upon me, and solemnly broke wind.

This, needless to say, was the last thing I expected. It popped my illusion and set me back firmly on the boards, a youth in a dress put down by another youth in a dress—my mother still cold in her grave and my head reeling, for a moment, with pure absurdity. Few in the audience heard Kit's reply to me, but a gust of tittering rose from the side galleries and I felt my face flame up. Robin, also red-faced, but with suppressed laughter, commanded the statue: "'Tis time; descend; be stone no more."

To the vast pleasure of our public, Kit stepped down from the pedestal, a paragon of grace and dignity. The apprentices, laborers, and gentlefolk who made up our audience shouted and stamped their approval, silencing quickly as Kit pronounced a blessing over me in lovely, melting tones which, to my ears at least, were tinged with mockery. I'll *pay* you sometime for this, was my thought. Then my glance went to the second gallery, where a purple plume quivered with the force of its wearer's applause. I stared at him without pretense and saw him nod at me, unmistakably.

Behind the stage, Robin doubled over with laughter while John Heminges took Kit aside for a stern talk. Stern talks occurred often these days; Kit was becoming difficult to handle. Many of the players—even Richard Burbage—complimented me on my work, but in a reserved manner that let me know it was not wise to get lost in a part. Master Will told me as much in so many words, but I scarcely minded him. I was stripping off Perdita without ceremony, right in the path of the stage boys and players, and when Starling found me I was half-naked.

"Richard," she panted. "First—you were a wonder. You had us weeping." Her reddened eyes showed it, but I was in no frame to be moved.

"Well, stop," I replied roughly. "'Tis only a silly play."

I dropped Perdita's gown upon the tiring master, ignoring his protests, and climbed to the upper level to retrieve my clothes. Starling brazenly followed; her head popped above the landing just as Dick was pulling up his breeches. With a squeal he turned his back, demanding, "What's this, you bold-faced wench?"

"Possess yourself, Dick, or find another trade," she retorted. "Actors can do without modesty."

"They'd better, with prying females about." Gathering up his doublet, shoes, and netherstocks, he scurried down the stairs with an indignant snort.

"Don't detain me, Star," I said, scrubbing the paint off my face with a towel. "Let me dress and then let me out."

"Where are you going?"

"To catch a purple ostrich plume."

"Richard—on no account must you follow that man."

I paused in the midst of tucking in my shirt. "And why is that?"

"Because he wants you to. Listen. He called me over again to buy an apple and went through the exact same practice as before. I saw the medal."

"What's your meaning?"

"He wanted me to see it. Why me, you ask? I'm only a penny gatherer and apple seller. He must have known our connection and that I'd tell you. Stay away from him, Richard. It's a trap."

I sat down on a trunk to tie the strap on my shoes. "That's all a surmise."

"I thought we decided to pursue this no further."

"It's something else I'm after now."

"What?" She was as wrought up as I by now, her lips actually trembling and tears spouting in her eyes again.

I merely shook my head. She knew nothing of Owen Mercer and his sad end, and even if I'd wanted to tell her, now was not the time.

"I should never have told you of that man!" she cried.

"Too late; you did." Taking up my cap and cloak, I descended the stair with her woebegone face hanging over me like a lantern, and dropped the last few steps to the floor. I then skirted round the edges of the tiring room so stealthily that no one noticed my exit.

The crowd was still pouring out of the Theater when I joined them, to all appearances just another apprentice on holiday. I sighted my prey easily, for purple was not a common color for plumes. He dressed soberly otherwise, in black with silver piping and a silver chain draped across the shoulders, a gold-hilted sword in a scabbard with silver clasps. He strolled along in conversation with another gentleman, at such a leisurely pace I was at no pains to keep him in view. He was well set up and agreeably tall, with broad shoulders and an easy manner, walking along with his thumbs tucked in his belt, elbows out. Once or twice he laughed with his companion, and I wondered if something in the play had amused them.

I was surrounded by talk about the play, for it had pleased, and the folk were eager to speak of their favorite bits. Some even commended me. I felt as if I were two people, public and private: one occupied the minds of citizens going home to supper while the other skulked alongside listening to descriptions of himself that sounded like no one he knew. It was a strange experience, truly.

Just outside Bishopsgate my quarry paused, nodded a farewell to his companion, and set off briskly down a narrow street known as Wall Lane. The other man continued toward the gate. I turned the corner at Wall, a squalid haunt of ale houses and rented lodgings and businesses barely respectable, and pretended to dig a pebble out of my shoe while the man in black exchanged words with an elderly matron as she swept her front step. Then he set off again, at a pace that made me trot to keep up with him. By now it was near five o'clock and the October sun, fat and golden as an egg yolk, rested on the cluttered horizon behind me. I pulled my cloak a little tighter against the chill. Wall Lane was sparsely populated at this hour—to my advantage, else I might not have seen the purple plume turn an abrupt corner and disappear down an alley. It struck me as curious for a gentleman to slink along mean byways like this.

I loped to the same corner, but waited until I saw his dark form stride the length of the alley and turn to the right. Then I darted after him, intending to close the gap between us. I emerged on a twisted lane so narrow that the upper storeys of opposite buildings nearly touched, and saw him walk to the last house on the row, an abandoned, tumble-down shop with boarded windows. Then he ducked through a low doorway and disappeared.

I glanced around me. The lane, which was boxed off at this end by the city wall, seemed almost deserted—pinpricks of light burned through cracks in the shutters, occasional coughs and murmurs came through the doors, but the only soul in sight was a ragged fellow wrapped in a blanket and stretched out upon a narrow bench. I edged closer to the doorway that had swallowed up the man in black, and began to distinguish the sound of two voices within. Squeezing into the space between houses, I laid a hand upon the wall and put my ear to a place where the plaster had fallen, revealing a crack. I could make out no words at first, and closed my eyes to hear better.

Then I felt a change in the air, a tiny gust of wind. Something seized my elbow and pulled me out of my hiding place, then secured both hands behind my back in a tight, painful grip. Next I knew, my head was pushed down to clear the low doorway and I was bundled into a small room with one tiny window that admitted little light. My eyes adjusted slowly to the gloom; the first thing they saw was a tall black hat with an ostrich plume, sitting on a rickety table.

"Now, boy," came a voice. "I am not disposed to dally with you. Release him, Bartlemy." The grip on my wrists loosened. My heart beat faster as a man approached the table, slowly peeled off his fawn-colored gloves, and laid them on the rough surface. His hands were pale and appeared to glow in the waning light. Suddenly, his right hand flickered like a sword tip as he pointed an accusing finger. "Why did you follow me?"

I was still trying to catch my breath after this sudden shift in fortunes; the air in that miserable room crowded thick and close. "If—if you please, sir. When I saw you at the Theater, I th-thought you wished to talk to me. You singled me out most particular."

"I beg to differ. It was you who singled me. Last week you appeared at my chambers and made certain threats. Why?"

"What! Are you—are you Master Feather, then?"

"Who else would I be? How do you know me? Has anyone pointed me out to you?"

"No, sir."

"What is your name?"

My mind was racing, but to my surprise the fear was less. I was almost relieved to meet him at last, in spite of repeated warnings, and determined to make the most of the opportunity. "My name," I said slowly, "is Richard. Richard Malory."

I watched him very closely, but the light was so dim I could hardly make out his face, much less any small flicker on it that might indicate this name meant anything to him.

"Malory," the bearded man repeated, with no inflection of surprise or dismay. His companion turned to him with an unspoken query, and I recognized the fellow who had been walking down the Shoreditch Road with Master Feather. He must have doubled back and circled around to make this rendezvous: a trap, as Starling had feared.

"Move closer, boy. Bartlemy, a light." The fellow behind me stepped forward, fetched a candle from his pouch, and set it on the table. Then he opened a tinderbox and took out the flint, allowing me a few blessed moments to think. Now that the shock had worn off, I was becoming aware that something seemed amiss. The whole means of conducting me here smelled of—as I should know—the theater. He knew where I worked. If Master Feather wished to talk to me, why not just send a message, instead of this elaborate set-up and capture? I wondered if they had staged it all to frighten me, as they had done with the street riot.

Snap, snap, went the flint. Master Feather said, "When you appeared at my chambers you claimed to have a case for me. You said you had lost something. What was it?" A spark leapt from the flint and lodged in the tinderbox, whereupon the one called Bartlemy quickly bent down and blew it to a little flame. He then lit the candle, and in its small golden glow I recognized the sharp eyes and pimply chin of Martin Feather's new scrivener. He was dressed in rags, and I knew I had last seen him stretched out on the narrow bench across the lane. That banished any doubt: this was a staged encounter.

Well. Both sides could play that game, and I had not spent a season on the boards for nothing. Quickly, I decided my part and assumed a bold stance.

"I have lost something, and I know who took it—your clerk!"

He blinked at this. "My clerk? Matthew Merry?"

"Aye, sir. He jumped me and robbed me. He took a whole shilling!"

"What are you saying? Do you expect me to believe that a man of his character and profession spends his off-hours robbing boys?"

If my response was not what he expected, neither did I expect this. I could draw only two conclusions: he was playing ignorant to throw me off my guard, or else his clerk had acted alone.

"I know what I know," was my stubborn reply.

"How do you know it, then?" he asked.

"Because of that pewter ring he wears. I saw it close up, when he attacked me, and later I saw it on his hand, when I was at Middle Temple."

"You're an actor. What were you doing at Middle Temple?"

"The theater was closed that day because of the weather. I was passing the time with a friend of mine, the sausage vendor, across from your chambers—you've seen him." Master Feather passed a look to Bartlemy, who merely pursed his lips in reply. "While I was there, I saw Merry leave the chambers and recognized him. The vendor says you're an honest man—I thought you might want to know your clerk is a thief!"

I feared what he would say next: then explain the other time you appeared at my chambers, asking questions about another clerk. A shilling figured in that tale, too, did it not? I was feverishly working out a reply, but to my surprise he changed tack completely. Undoing the three top buttons of his doublet, he reached under his white ruff to unclasp a narrow chain. "Have you ever seen a device like this?"

He held it out to me: a bronze medallion showing a hand holding a cup. It might have been the very original of my copy, so perfect was the resemblance. Fortunately, I was waiting for such a confrontation sooner or later, and betrayed nothing but thoughtful study. "I have."

"Where?"

"At Lord Hurleigh's funeral last summer. It was on the grave cloth, I think."

"And why were you at that funeral?"

"As a paid mourner, sir."

"Is that respectable work for a member of the Lord Chamberlain's Men?"

"The Company was touring, sir. I could use the money. Especially after your clerk took that shilling—"

"Enough!" Abruptly, he turned away, swerving out of the candlelight, and took three paces to the window. There he stood, gazing out at the blank wall of the next house. The other two watched me as intently as cats watching a mouse, Bartlemy in particular.

"Have you ever met a man named Peter Kenton?" Master Feather asked, with his back turned.

"Please, sir. I'm just an apprentice. I know hardly anyone outside the profession—"

"Have you ever met him or heard of him?"

"No, sir."

"John Beauchamp? Or Beecham, as he is sometimes known—have you ever heard that name?"

By now I was sure of it: whatever Matthew Merry had done or knew, he was keeping much of it from his master. If the attorney was unaware that I had carried an image of his medallion, or that it was taken from me, or that I had met John Beecham, then I would not be the one to enlighten him.

"I know him not, sir. I wish to go. If you will not give me justice against your clerk—"

"*Enough,* I said!" He turned back to the table, bent swiftly, and picked up an object from the floor. Then he was at my right shoulder, a presence suddenly as tall and forbidding as the Tower. I smelled a dusty scent, felt a rough texture scratching my face. "I'll tell you this, Richard Malory." I felt a sudden chill at his pronouncing that name, as though a cold breeze had blown off Finsbury Fields, where long ago two men met with drawn swords. "I perceive you have a fair imagination," he went on. "Pray you, imagine this grain sack pulled over your head, and bound up tight, and then dropped in the middle of the Thames with you in it. My counsel to you is, lay off. I cannot vouch for your safety, should you wind yourself further in this coil. Canst follow me?"

"Aye, sir." My voice felt tight as a bowstring; the two words were all I could manage, for I was no longer acting.

He left my side. "Then I'll leave you to find your way home. Remember I was merciful, and breathe not a word of this to anyone . . . or you may find my mercy extinguished." I saw his pale hand glow behind the candle flame and then abruptly close upon it. In the darkness a curl of sulfurous smoke met my nose, like the beckoning of hell. I heard the three gather up their few implements and leave, almost as quietly as ghosts blown upon the chilly October breeze. A line spoken by King Leontes came to me: "I am a feather for every wind that blows." True, but now a Feather was doing the blowing, and I the thing blown, light and uncertain, drifting this way and that over the ever-changing earth. The words we spoke to each other might have been a play of sorts, but I knew that the threat was as real as the scratch of coarse sacking against my face. God help me, thought I, alone in that featureless, nameless room. God catch me.

"Not a word to anyone," he had said—but Starling was not "anyone." And for certain there was no avoiding her; she pounced when I came through the Condell's gate, with the hungry zeal of a tiger. "Oh, thank God! I thought . . . but never mind what I thought. Who *was* that man? You must tell me—for the past two hours I have died a thousand deaths!"

This last I put to her tendency to exaggerate. We found a place on a window seat far from the hearth fire, where we could talk privately. I had feared that Master Condell, who was enjoying a rare night at home, would upbraid me for skipping a rehearsal. But he merely paused, in the middle of a conversation with his wife and son, to fine me the amount set by Company rules. Lady Alice, whom I had not thought inclined to sympathy, grabbed Ned and Cole when they galloped toward me and bore them off to plague Robin instead.

When we were settled I told Star, "The man was Martin Feather."

"Ah!" she burst out, then tempered her lively face so as not to draw attention. "I knew it."

"So did I, somehow. That part was not surprising. But other

things were. . . ." I went over the interview, with its curious turns and missed cues, then voiced my conclusion: "From all I could tell, there seems to be much he doesn't know."

She thought this over. "But that cannot be. Why would he have made himself so scarce? And why would you be warned away from him by two different men if he were innocent of any plot?"

"I didn't say he was innocent—he had that medallion, after all, and set some store by it. But he was not scarce today. He put himself in the middle of the gallery, where he was certain to be seen."

"And it was as I said—he lured you into a trap."

"He did. But it was odd how they went about it. As though it were all a play." I paused and swallowed. "Except at the end."

"Why? What happened at the end?"

"There is something I haven't told you. Something I learned about Martin Feather. . . . He . . . he killed my father."

"What?"

I related the story I had from Ben Jonson and watched her eyes grow wider. "Oh, Richard," was all she said.

I was rubbing my hand against my thigh, thinking out loud. "Now. He seemed not to remember the name Malory, but that was pretense. Of course he knew it—he sent us money under that name. Whether he associates me with Robert Malory is another matter. He made no sign of it, in the presence of his henchmen. But his last words to me were a threat."

"So . . . will you heed him? Will you let it alone?"

"They did not sound like idle words to me. Would you like to fish my body out of the Thames when I disappear?"

She shook her head.

"Then I must let it alone." I watched my hand on my thigh, rubbing the rough woolen hose as if the dark stench of Wall Lane still clung to it—harder and harder, the flesh warming, then burning. Finally, I gripped so tightly, I could feel a bruise forming under each finger. "The question is, Will it leave me alone?" I turned to the window, where night had laid its cold palm, leaned my forehead against it, and admitted to myself that I was truly afraid.

Starling raised a hand and rested it lightly on my knee. Then she let it fall. A moment later I heard her slide off the window seat and leave me alone with my fear, but the peculiar warmth of her touch remained. A small, light touch that spoke more clearly than words ever could. A simple touch that told me she cared for me, as more than a friend.

The warmth spread from my knee to my face. It was like a gift delivered into my hands—an awkward, unmanageable gift, squirming like a puppy. What might I do with this? Did I even want it? Starling's affection weighted me like another burden. Yet I found myself wondering, in spite of everything, what it would be like to kiss her. . . .

✧

The Winter's Tale played for two more perfomances.
I walked through them with appropriate voice and
gesture, keeping a good arm's length between Perdita
and myself. On the third performance our patron
appeared in the gallery—Lord Hunsdon. Though less
than three months had passed since I saw him at the
funeral, he appeared much older, and the players
confirmed his health was poor. "He'll not be with us
much longer," Will Sly confided to me, and that was a
measure of some distress on his part, for he seldom
spoke to me at all. Lord Hunsdon had been the
Company's staunch friend since its beginning, but who
could predict the temper of our next patron? Masters
Burbage, Heminges, and Shakespeare returned from
an interview with gloomy looks that belied their good
news—Lord Hunsdon had extended his usual invitation

to perform at Whitehall over Christmastide. The Company's status was thus affirmed and even exalted, but none could say for how long.

As October went on, more and more of our performances were given under blustery skies to a house only half-filled with hardy souls. Once a northern gust blew over our scene of a May frolic and dropped a light mantle of snow upon the god Pan and his attendants. As one of those attendants, robed in summer draperies and strewn with silk flowers, I came very close to quitting the theater then. "We grow too old for this," remarked Will Kempe to his comrades, after suffering the part of Pan. "From now on we must perform only winter's tales in the fall so we might dress in furs. Or battle tales so we might hop around nimbly enough to keep warm."

"Or no tales at all," Master Cowley laughed. "Merely battles. Have at thee!" He jabbed with a poking stick, which Kempe parried with a wooden sword, and then the two gentlemen were cavorting like boys, making havoc in spite of the tiring master's protest.

As for me, I felt as old as the year. "Solid," was the way Master Condell put it. "You're settling, Richard. Though you've much yet to learn, I see you as a solid performer now, and the better part of the Company agrees with me." This was the best word I had received from anyone about my future, but it failed to satisfy. "Solid" meant that I learned my part, remembered actions, manipulated my voice to fit the words, adjusted my movements to show feeling. If Master Smithton in the hut were ingenious enough to construct a mechanical figure of such talents, it would have done as well. "Solid" was not the mastery of Richard Burbage or the brilliant promise of Kit Glover. Only once had I entered fully into a part—and frightened everybody, including myself. It seemed I must give too much to the stage or too little; I had struck the right balance with Constance, but that was long ago. At the end of the season I might solidly walk off the boards never to return, and in a month all recollection of me would be gone. I confided this to Starling one Sunday after church.

"But why should that trouble you?" she asked. We were walking home from St. Mary's on a blustery, chilly day, near the end of a long procession of Condells. An armada of gray-bottomed clouds plowed across the sky, white tops unfurled like sails. "Why should you care?" Starling asked again. "You never liked the stage. You've not been happy since you came."

This was not entirely true. I'd known happiness in my master's house, and it wasn't that I disliked Lady Theater so much, but feared she disliked me.

"Who says I care?" I hiked up my cloak against the chill.

"No need to say it. It shows in your look, your walk, your whining voice."

"I do not whine." I was regretting that I had opened my mouth, as I often did with her. "But there is this in me, that wants me to do my best. As St. Paul says, 'Whatsoever your hand finds to do, do it heartily.'"

"I think there is *this* in you, that hates to be bested by anything."

I stopped and turned to her in exasperation, but could think of no reply. Jacob and Tobias stepped around us with identical grins that said, At it again? They hurried to cross the street in front of a drayage cart, leaving the two of us alone on the corner.

"Ha," she said. "I am right."

"You are presumptuous. You are quick to size and speak a thing you know nothing of." Further, you are right, I thought—but did not say. And at that moment she might not have heard, for all her attention seemed taken by some movement on the far side of the street. I followed her gaze to the row of hawthorn trees now half-stripped of their red leaves, and a pair of scholars passing behind them, black robes billowing in the wind. The sight seemed unremarkable and not worth the scrutiny she gave it. "Star?"

"Ask me anon." With no more farewell she charged into the street and crossed with a quick, determined step, leaving me suspended in mid-argument. Starling could be seized and carried away by an idea while slower mortals choked on her dust. I sighed mightily and walked home at my own deliberate pace.

Betty drew me aside when I entered the house, her manner sly. "Richard," she said, "I've a message for you, delivered but an hour ago." She took from her bodice a small, folded paper crumpled about the edges. The seal remained whole—Betty would not be tempted to break it, for she could not read.

But what made my breath come shorter were the initials on the seal: JB. He had written my full name below it, in a spiky hand.

"Did anyone see this?" I demanded. "Who brought it?"

"None, sir. I've kept it safe. 'Twas a ragged little urchin brought it." She smiled coyly. "By a fine lady's hand?"

Covert messages could mean only one thing to her—and it was not unusual for ladies, fine or not, to carry on dalliances with boys in the theater. During the season Robin received giggly love notes as a matter of course. So I shrugged, allowing her to think what she would, and folded the message over once. "Thank you, Betty. We will keep this between ourselves, won't we?"

She agreed, tittering, while I turned and galloped up the two sets of narrow stairs to the attic room. Once alone, I studied the seal, but could think of only one person with those initials. Scarcely breathing, I lifted it and read these words:

> *My eyes are upon you yet.*
> *You have done well, and I expect great things from you. From me, expect nothing, fear nothing, be surprised at nothing. You owe me a great debt, and I may be forced to call it in.*
> *Watch and wait.*

A great debt. Called in. Watch and wait. My heart flew up into my throat. I tore the paper in half, then put the two halves together and tore them again, and again and again, until the message was reduced to scraps. Then I scooped them up in my hand and rushed back down the stairs, through the great room and kitchen, and out the door of the buttery, making for the servants' privy in one corner of the yard. Once safely inside, I tossed all the fluttering pieces of paper, with the seal, into the muck below. I stood in the near-darkness, one hand against the rough board wall. But the sensation of relief lasted only a moment. The burden of the message could not be made to disappear.

Starling was waiting for me when I opened the privy door—not a welcome sight.

"What?" I nearly shouted. "Is this where fashionable ladies and gentlemen meet now? Is there no place I can be at peace?"

"I have somewhat to show you," she replied, quite calmly. "Come with me." Without another word she turned and led the way past the garden and around the house, where the Condells were gathering for dinner. It crossed my mind that they would miss us and exchange glances when we came in late together, but Starling had no regard for the looks of the thing—or any other thing, else she would have marked my state, observant as she was. I followed her to the street and down to the corner, where moments earlier she had so abruptly left me. Here she turned and pointed to the row of hawthorns.

"Look at it. Four months ago the trees were all in leaf and from here you could see little behind them. True?" I nodded. "You remember Ned's tale of the bear?"

"I remember."

"Now suppose—" I could see she hoped to present the calm face of a master of logic, but the ferment of her thoughts bubbled through. "Suppose you are Ned, standing here. You see a gentleman walking toward us on the street—a gentleman with a golden beard and orange cape, crowned in a dark velvet cap with a partridge feather sticking out the side of it."

"Star. I told you to let it alone—"

"This is only a surmise. You may do as you will with it. Mind the partridge feather; the eye goes at once to that, and marks not so much the rest of him, especially his face. Therefore, the feather goes first." She trotted several paces away, then turned and started toward me slowly, reaching up her right hand to pull an imaginary ornament from an imaginary cap. "He can hide it away in his doublet. What is left is a plain black or brown cap, squarish like a lawyer might wear. By now he is at the corner, where he may pause a moment to make sure no one is passing. With his way clear, he steps behind the trees and reaches around his back"—she imitated this action—"where, under the cloak, is room to hide a barrister's gown. He pulls it forth, which he can do still walking, and throws the gown over cloak, sword, doublet, all. The beard may come off. I wager it does, and he can pull up his cowl to cover any redness it leaves on his jaw. In any event, he goes in as a fop and emerges as a lawyer. A changed man—or we may say, a changed beast."

I passed a hand over my face. "Such as a bear."

"Now mark, a child of Ned's fanciful turn of mind could see a black robe appear where somewhat else was expected, and call it a black bear, could he not?"

"Especially after being exposed to your fanciful turn of mind."

She waved that aside. "Follow you now what this might mean?"

"I follow, but like it not."

"Meaning?"

"Peter Kenton was John Beecham in disguise." She clapped her hands with a crow of triumph, a delighted response I could not share.

"Or," she proposed, "John was Peter in disguise. *Or*—" Her expression heightened, as though struck by a new thought: "John and Peter are both manifestations of someone we've not even met."

I stared at her, then convulsively shook my head and started back across the street. She fell in beside me, obviously disappointed in my lackluster response to her brilliance. "It was clever of you to work it out," I said, by way of compensation.

She made a modest shrug. "I only thought you should know. It is for you to act upon. I do wish the man would appear again, now that I know what to ask him—but be assured, I won't seek him out."

I could only nod in reply. I knew the man might well appear again, for I had just heard from him to that effect. But all my questions for him now boiled down to one: *What do you want from me?*

All Hallow's Eve blew gustily and raw, from mid-morning all the way through a performance of *The Spanish Tragedy*. While an audience filling less than a third of the Theater milled about and shivered, we of the Company held on to our hats and fought to keep our voices steady. Afterward we walked—or ran, more like—through a tavern scene that would be played the next day should winds and rain permit, then the Lord Chamberlain's Men broke rehearsal early and gathered in the tiring room to discuss a business matter. As the days were growing ever shorter, Jacob and Watt, the Heminges' footman, had arrived with torches to light us home.

"Fearful stirrings in the city," I heard Jacob say to Robin.

"Why not?" was the reply. "'Tis All Hallow's Eve." Robin had already confided to me his intention to "slip out" this night.

Jacob shook his head. "More than that. There's real trouble on the boil. They say the papists are rising again. The master needs come quickly so we can get safe home, lest you fancy your head broke."

The master was still in conference over a matter of lease and rents. Vital as the question was, our immediate peril seemed greater. I approached Master Condell to break it to him.

"How's that? Trouble?" he said to me, with an irritated frown. "Nothing out of common for All Hallow's Eve. Still, 'tis certain there's no untangling this coil tonight. John, shall we be off?"

Master Heminges agreed, and the party broke up with mutual mutterings and head shakings. We formed our usual procession, with the torch bearers in front and Robin, Kit, and me bringing up the rear. The air nipped as we started down Shoreditch Road; the setting sun spread a lurid glow of purple and scarlet over the scattered huts of Finsbury Fields. A quarter-moon hung over Bishopsgate like a strung bow, and bonfires pulsed across the landscape, built to discourage the demons abroad this night, or perhaps welcome them. Whether they believed in demons or not, laborers and peasants in the country had used All Hallow's Eve as an excuse to get drunk and break all the commandments, and I suspected city folk did the same. Kit's first words bore this out.

"Are you for tonight?" he asked Robin, artfully shading his words just under our masters' conversation.

"Doubt not. I'll slip out on the second watch and meet thee on Cheapside. Buckler's Tavern?"

"No, the Wheel and Distaff. I know some lads there."

"Content. And what say you to Richard here, as one of our party? Tomorrow is my birthday—we can make a proper celebration."

Kit's pale eyes went to me, a flash in the gloaming. "What says he?"

I saw mockery in that glance, which pricked more than it should. "I say, if you mean to throw yourself in a brawl and get your noble face hacked, I had best stay home and learn your part for tomorrow."

"No, Richard," Rob put in. "That's not the way of it. He's a madcap, true, but I keep him out of trouble." I heard a short, ironic grunt from the madcap and Robin went on more earnestly. "Credit us with more sense than to run a risk. Will you come?"

"Will our master player permit me?"

"I am not your master," Kit said, his voice quite level and without any hidden meaning that I could catch. "You may come or no, as you will."

"Will you?" Robin asked eagerly.

We were approaching Bishopsgate, where another bonfire blazed up against the city wall and the cavorting figures around it cast weird shadows. Too late I recognized that I had put myself in a bind: to refuse, now that I had been invited, would look like cowardice or ingratitude.

"I may," was my answer—but we all knew that I would.

The Wheel and Distaff was roaring at half past eleven. Robin and I walked in upon a crowd of patrons engaged in a game of snapdragons: attempting to sip raisins out of a dish of flaming brandy without singeing their beards. Kit was seated below a smoky window surrounded by his "lads." There were three of these, all common apprentices by their looks, and all armed. Rare is the Londoner who does not carry a weapon of some sort, though apprentices are limited to daggers no more than eight inches in length. As one of these weapons was employed in paring an apple, I could see that the boys were pushing that limit. Play lovers all, they fawned upon Kit and welcomed Robin and me as extensions of his glory. "Well met," Robin giggled, sliding onto the bench beside Kit and drawing back almost at once. "Oho! Might this be a length of steel I perceive under thy nighted cloak?"

"It may," came the reply, "but you'll hold your tongue about it."

"What?" I hissed, well under the current of tavern noise. "You have a sword?" He nodded coolly. Rob had told me he went armed for some of these midnight excursions, but I thought he meant daggers. By law, only gentlemen could carry swords. This promised more excitement than I wished. "If you bring on a fight, Kit, by this hand I swear I'll not stay to see it or lend you any aid."

"I'll want no aid from you," he replied, in his carrying voice as smooth and supple as a snake's body. "Go now, if you please, and may the sniveling goddess of the fainthearted speed your path." His little crew cheered at this. I saw now why he put up with them: they were his protection, in case he got himself in too deep.

"Come around, the both of you," complained Robin. "Mend your quarrel and be at peace for one night." He stood to fetch two tankards from the shelf above his head and poured for himself and me from a flagon of ale. "What's afoot?"

Kit replenished his own cup. "More than mischief. We may stand in the way of doing our country some good this night."

"The bloody Catholics are on the rise again," one of his henchmen put in. (Kit had introduced them as Nat, Hal, and Jamie, but I never learned who was which.) "That's all the talk abroad."

"That's always the talk," said I. Suddenly thirsty, I drank down half the ale in my cup. There must have been a touch of scorn in my voice, for when I looked at them again, their stares were hostile. "Well, isn't it? I've been in London scarce seven months and all I hear about is the bloody Catholics."

"We must be always on our guard," one of the boys piped up. I shrugged and knocked back the rest of the ale. It seemed stronger than usual, or perhaps only affected me that way, as I had little else on my stomach.

"True," said Kit. "We must be on our guard, for in the wide world there is no creature as subtle and conniving as a papist." He turned on me a look of perfect composure tinged with mockery. I abruptly recalled another time he had looked at me thus: on the stage, breaking my heartfelt portrayal of Perdita with an elegant fart.

I felt myself waxing hot. "Aye, there is no creature so cunning as a papist, unless it be an actor. But what would we do without them, else we would have no excuse to cry havoc or raise hell in the streets?"

"Why, you talk like a papist yourself," snarled one of the boys.

"No fear, no fear," Robin said nervously. "Richard is as true a Protestant as any of us—you should see how he dotes on Foxe."

"Does he?" Kit murmured. "Does he read for his own edification, or is he making notes?"

I scowled. "Notes for what?"

"Why, for gutting, burning, and otherwise torturing Protestants, when your faction comes to power again."

His lads guffawed at this, and I flushed with anger. The anger, a long time building, went so deep it made me speechless; I could only glare and sputter until my mind closed upon some words not my own. Words from a play: "D-do you bite your thumb at me, sir?"

The three apprentices let out a collective breath, sharp with ale fumes. They recognized this line from *Romeo and Juliet* and knew what came after: a fight. A fight between actors was as good as any other, to their minds—perhaps better, for the novelty of it. Kit's reply showed he was willing to oblige them. "I d-do bite my thumb, sir."

"But do you bite your thumb at *me*? Sir."

"Heaven defend us!" Robin rose and grabbed the nearest dagger from Nat, Hal, or Jamie, then leaned over the board with an arm twisted behind his back and the blade pointed up. "If the two of you are so bent to carve up actor's flesh, then take mine! Only take it off the bum, where it won't be missed!"

After a very brief, stunned pause, the boys laughed. Kit smiled with one side of his mouth only and whacked the part of Rob's anatomy thus exposed. Somewhat deflated, I settled back on the bench and rubbed a hand over my face. Robin straightened up, with an anxious look that belied his merry words. "Is that sacrifice enough to make you friends?"

"Friends?" repeated Kit. "No." (Friends? thought I. *Never*.) "But we may be allies, if only for tonight."

Robin settled for that and poured another cup of ale all around. "Content. But you've yet to say what adventure we're allies for."

Nat, Hal, and Jamie then contributed their notions, mostly having to do with vandalizing or otherwise tormenting suspected Catholics. Robin seemed willing, but I had already descended to this particular hell and had no desire to go back to it. Kit merely drew apart in his peculiar manner and implied, when asked, that such infantile tricks were not to his taste.

"What then?" asked the boys, in whining tones. "What to do?"

"Leave it to the moment," said he. "Let fortune guide us. We'll venture out after this round and see for ourselves what's afoot." This put them in a better humor, as if aimless mischief in Kit's company were better than mischief by design with anyone else. In tribute to their devotion he raised his cup. *"Bibete ex omnia—"*

I cannot explain what happened to me then. I was stretched like a wire, weighted at both ends with fears and worries and enemies known and unknown. One of them was this boy, whom I could have admired so easily, yet who despised me for no reason and mocked me with words that had become a nightmare. I knew he was ignorant of their meaning to me, but my last thread snapped; I popped up and threw my remaining ale in his face.

A stunned pause followed, then Kit was on his feet. He fetched me a backhanded slap across the jaw that dealt far more insult than injury. Under its sting I realized I could take him, for though he was taller and older than me, we weighed near the same. What's more, I *longed* to take him—my fist ached to make solid contact with that proud nose, that disdainful eye, but Robin caught hold of it. I heard him babbling, "For God's sake, Richard, remember thyself! Kit, sit down and take his measure. Play the man, Kit, whatever he meant—"

Kit's own words thrust at me under Robin's parries: "—Sniveling puppy—been asking for this since we met—Lay off!" Through a haze I saw him toss back his cloak and lay a hand on his sword hilt as his comrades ducked. I threw my empty tankard, having no other weapon at hand, and enjoyed the brief satisfaction of seeing it bounce off his head. A cry rose from all sides as his blade flickered in a half-circle over the board, then I felt it glide across my left arm near the shoulder, slicing doublet and shirt and drawing a little freshet of blood in its wake. Furious, I lunged for his sword hand and caught it around the wrist, squeezing hard while I punched him in the ribs with my other fist. Robin was shouting, the boys cheering; the next moment strong arms wrapped around us as one body and hustled us into the chilly night. The voices of grown men scolded: "None of this, you young hotheads—take your quarrel to the streets!"

Then we were alone, the six of us, a little circle of quicksilver under a sky glittering with stars. Kit and I panted like runners and eyed each other with a pure hatred. "I'm not done," said he.

"Nor I."

"Then let us find cover, where we won't be disturbed."

"Kit!" Robin wailed. "Richard! What are you about?"

I heard myself say, "Follow me. I know a place." Then I turned before anyone could challenge me on it, quickly leading the way to Gracechurch Street. They fell in behind me, their steps ringing on the cobblestones. Robin stuck to Kit at first, pleading with little effect. My arm had begun to sting, though the cut was not deep— he had only meant to score me like a sausage. I shook out a handkerchief and bound it on the move. We turned south on Gracechurch, where we almost ran head-on into a company of the watch. With one accord we pulled up our cloaks, but they had more urgent concerns this night than curfew breakers and passed us by with scarcely a look.

Robin left Kit's side and darted to me as we approached the Bridge. "Where are we bound?"

"Southwark."

"That's good. We can drop this mad scheme and make for the Bear Garden. There should be enough savagery there to let your bloodlust."

"I have another place in mind."

"Richard, listen to reason. He could kill you with that sword."

"He won't use that sword if I've none." I snorted. "He's too much the prince."

"With his fists, then. He's angry enough."

"Well, what am I? Prankish?"

"Refrain for me then—tomorrow's my birthday."

"Oh. And the world must stop because you turn thirteen."

"Well, if I mean nothing to you, think what the Company will say." Clearly, Robin's taste for adventure faltered when it broke the boundaries he had set for it. No disaster, for him, equaled that of losing his position in the Company, and he predicted dire consequences for all of us if Kit or I did any lasting harm to each other. He made the point over and over, and I stopped listening as we crossed the Bridge. Traffic seemed undiminished, even as the midnight chimes tolled down upon us. Many of the foot travelers and all the ladies were masked, turning black, egg-smooth faces in our direction, faces in which only the eyes lived. Laughter rang out on every side—a sharp, rasping laughter that sawed the nerves. From the riverbank came a sudden barrage of short, popping noises, followed by a scream.

I spoke up loudly enough for all to hear. "We'll need torches, where we're going."

Until then our way was light enough, but this would not be so in east Southwark. Nat, Hal, and Jamie appointed themselves light bearers; one grabbed a torch from a bracket beside a door, another from the Bridge tower, another picked up a discarded club half-trampled in the river muck that, when dried, managed to hold a fitful flame. Thus, our lights hissing and sputtering like our tempers, we passed the noisy sailors' taverns and the quiet bitter streets of the elderly poor, arriving at last at the gate of the house that used to belong to my aunt: now a ruin. I felt a stab of remorse owing to the last time I was here at night. It made me pause, but then I pushed open the gate and stalked up the flagstone path as the boys behind me fell silent. At the doorway I hesitated again. The cut on my arm was throbbing. Behind me a voice spoke, so bleached and flat I could not tell whose it was: "What is this place?"

The front hall, damp and black, closed around us like a mouth. I listened intently but heard no sign of the beggar who had made his home upstairs. The others crowded in, light from their torches leaping up the stained walls. "There was a pile of rubbish in the great hall," I said, my voice huddling close. "If it's still there, we can light it to see by."

The charred pile was well picked over. Working silently, we raked pieces together and threw some broken timbers on top, then one of the boys put his torch to it and held it there until a wave of flame rippled along a horizontal board. We watched, as though charmed, while the flames spread, licking at half-burned sticks, pieces of furniture, shutters, blackened books, shards of glass. Kit shook himself free of the spell first. He unbuckled his sword belt and let it clang on the floor, then threw off his cloak and began to unlace his doublet.

"Let us not drag this out," he said. "We must draw up terms."

Robin hastened to take charge, as though by commanding the action he might control the damage. "Do you agree to no inter-ference?"

"Just so. This matter is between the two of us only."

"Then take heed," Robin insisted. "Whatever you do, no blows above the neck. If you deal a split lip or black eye I'll run home straight and swear I never saw you this night. And don't cripple each other, or the Company will have your heads. Whoever is down for five counts loses the match. And if—"

"God save us!" one of the boys gasped. He was staring fixedly at a point beyond Robin's head, and all of us followed his gaze toward the rough oval burned in the ceiling. At the far end of this opening our eyes caught a movement, and a sound—a lonely creaking sound, the protest of old timbers groaning under an unaccustomed weight. The draft created by our fire had caused the motion of an object hung from the rafter of an upstairs room.

It was a long shape, ill-defined at first until its slow rotation revealed a pair of slipper-shod feet. Casting upward, my eyes took in a long gown, such as a scholar or clerk might wear, stiff arms, spread fingers, a belted waist . . . the face remained in shadow.

"Richard," Robin whispered. "What *is* this place?"

I grabbed the nearest torch and bounded up the stairs. With all five pairs of eyes on me, I crept along the edge of the charred floor and stopped near the body, torch aloft. And waited, my heart pounding violently, for the revolving form to reveal itself.

He turned toward my light as though irresistibly drawn: the jutting cheek bone, the high-bridged nose, the skewed mouth, the bulging, light-colored eyes of Matthew Merry.

I threw the torch on the bonfire below, bolted for a window— mangling the beggar's canvas bed once again—and threw up the pint of ale that had set so uneasily on my stomach.

Nat, Hal, and Jamie bolted. Kit and Robin stayed to see me home. Robin was almost undone, but Kit pulled together quickly and by the time we crossed the Bridge, he seemed in complete possession of himself. As for me, though I felt somewhat steadier after losing the ale, a solid core of dread remained.

Of course I had to tell them something, and what I said was mostly truth: that the house belonged to my aunt, a secret papist who had fled during the unrest of that summer, and I had made one visit since to see what remained of it. But I claimed ignorance of the hanging man, or of anything that might have transpired there after the house was looted. After a few questions, they pressed for no more and seemed convinced that I was as ignorant as they. It might have been the finest acting work of my life thus far.

We all agreed the man had died recently, like that very day. "He's stiff, that's why," Kit explained. "This should be reported."

Robin quaked at the thought, though to say true he had not stopped quaking since we left Anne Billings' house. "Not by us!"

"Who then, pray?"

"What does it matter? The Company will hang us up by the thumbs if we tangle ourselves in a murder."

"Who said murder? Why not a suicide?"

I did not think so. I had seen many criminals hang and knew how they struggled. Even a suicide would struggle at the last, and I had seen no signs of that—no clawing, no mark of fingernails at the neck, no clenching of the jaw. Merry's face looked almost serene, as though he had submitted peacefully. My guess, after thinking it over in the clear night air, was that he was knocked senseless and then strung up. But I said nothing.

"Murder or suicide matters not," Robin whined. "It's a coil that we are best out of."

"Calm yourself," Kit reassured him scornfully. "I can drop a word where it will never come back to us."

"Where is that?"

"Do you want to know, truly?" Robin emphatically shook his head. "Thought not. Leave it to me."

At the corner of Coleman Street Kit parted from us, turning south rather than north, and I understood he was on his way to "drop a word." Obviously, his world extended past the bounds of the theater, but at that moment my curiosity was dead. I watched him go, then turned homeward with Robin, who couldn't leave his worries alone, and couldn't keep them quiet.

The next day, news was all over London: the Queen's agents had uncovered the fountainhead of a deadly plot against Her Majesty, and by quick work had taken him into custody. This man had long been suspected, and the discovery of the body of one Matthew Merry, fellow conspirator (who had apparently hanged himself in remorse), furnished all the evidence needed to capture and convict him. On the body of Master Merry were papers confirming the guilt of Martin Feather, a respected attorney of Middle Temple. Three conspirators were arrested along with Master Feather, but others remained at large, and citizens were requested to step forward with what they knew of Peter Kenton, Anne Billings, John Beecham. . . .

A trial followed swiftly, wherein the guilt of all was confirmed. And thus Martin Feather was condemned to die on 12 November, the year of our Lord 1597.

THE ORNAMENT OF DECEPTION

❖

"God was merciful to him," Starling said for the fifth time at least, speaking of Matthew Merry.

For the fifth time I agreed, my "aye" a dense puff of steam upon the cold air as I stamped my feet in the crust of snow covering Tower Hill. Far better for the law clerk to be killed outright than suffer the state punishment for traitors: to be hanged until the life was near choked out of them, then cut down, disemboweled, and quartered while still living. Three other conspirators had already come to this miserable end: the poor steward at the Lion and Lamb, a boatman who ran messages, and a servant of the late Lord Hurleigh, who had been hiding Martin Feather on the nobleman's estate. Feather himself was a gentleman, and entitled to a gentleman's execution. A well-aimed stroke of the axe would finish him, and afterward his head would ornament the Bridge tower in the shameful place reserved for traitors.

Tower Hill is a grim and barren knob, ornamented only by the gallows' table and block, all set upon a wooden platform somewhat smaller than the stage at Burbage's Theater. This was a stage of a different sort, though with much the same purpose: to amuse and instruct the public. I was here because I had to be, and Starling because I asked her. God seemed to decree it as well, for a drop in the temperature and a light fall of snow convinced the Company to cancel that day's performance, leaving me free. Executions were never my choice of amusement, even as a boy in Alford, but my fears could not be put to rest until this man was dead, and I had to see it done.

We stood on the nether side of the gallows, well back, where the crowd did not press in so closely. When the drums began, a steady rumbling that filled us like water, I felt Starling's hand steal into mine. Her hand felt warm this bitter day.

Executions have their own gloomy pageantry, but still I wish more dignity might attend them. A stirring passed through the assembly as we waited; heads turned and a cry went up from the Tower gate, where a cart containing the condemned man had emerged. A band of miscreants accompanied it, shiftless boys not so far from the gallows themselves, who jeered and made obscene signs and threw dirt clods until constables pushed them aside with their pikes. The crowd pressed together and blocked my view of the cart. "Can you see? Can you see?" Starling asked, while I shook my head impatiently. The noise increased until it packed solid all around us, then quickly died away as a short, springy gentleman bounced up the five steps to the platform. He wore a few pieces of ceremonial armor, sported two plumes in his helmet, and carried a scroll under his arm. When all was quiet, he unrolled the document and proceeded to read the charges against the prisoner.

Everyone knew them by now. "Father Martin" had confessed to forming the Holy Restoration Society, a crew of fanatics dedicated to placing a Catholic successor on the throne after our Queen's death. Philip Shackleford, Lord Hurleigh, was their chief candidate, being kin to Elizabeth, a covert Catholic, and open to their schemes. If the Queen took too long to die, Master Feather confessed he would have hastened her end by poison or some convenient disease. But divine providence had intervened instead, striking down Hurleigh in the prime of life. This dealt a severe blow to the Society, but did not kill it. Certain conspirators were still in communication with the courts of Spain and France, and there was evidence that their recruitment continued. The Society's downfall was rumored to be the work of an informer.

We heard the court's version of all this, which stated that Martin Feather, Esquire, stood guilty before God and men of high crimes against his Queen and countrymen, and was therefore justly condemned. More followed, but Starling and I were not well placed to hear it. When he came to an end of the charges, our official rolled up his paper and stepped to one corner of the platform.

The prisoner then came forth, dressed in the black robe of the Jesuit order. At the sight of him the crowd blazed up again. At this distance he looked shorter than when I had seen him only a few weeks before. His time on the rack had bent his back cruelly, but even so there seemed less of him than suffering alone might account for. He turned to the main body of the crowd, away from us, and began his speech before their jeers had ceased. This quickly silenced them, for everyone desires to hear the last words of a famous criminal. The moment his voice reached me, I knew something was wrong.

"Come," I said to Starling, and still holding hands we worked our way among the throng. Master Feather's last words departed from the usual form of execution address: rather than express sorrow for his sins and appeal to heaven for mercy, he assured us that his conscience was clear and God would so judge him. Brave words, but misguided, and the people were not taking kindly to them. Angry mutters were beginning when I at last pulled up before the platform, not ten yards from the condemned man. I looked directly into his face and a little cry escaped me. "Richard," Star whispered, staring too. "Richard!"

This was not Martin Feather. Or at least, he was not the man I knew as Martin Feather.

He concluded his speech, turned abruptly to the executioner. Drummers began a swift, steady beat as the customary exchange passed between them. From the executioner: Do you forgive me for the act I am bound to perform? From the condemned man: I do. A black bandage tied about the eyes, and a cry went up around us: "Long live our Queen!" "God bless Elizabeth!" Calmly, the prisoner knelt and placed his head upon the block. The drums rolled, louder and faster, the shouts rose in a kind of ecstasy as the headsman's axe made a swoop in the air. The first blow mercifully severed the spine; thus the traitor was beyond knowing when the second struck off his head.

I turned abruptly and pushed through the crowd, Starling close behind. "Who—?" she began, but I shook my head with a look that cut her question short.

We plodded toward East Cheap as a roar went up behind us—a cry of approval at the display of the traitor's head. A few paces before us a boy about my age stumped along on a wooden crutch, his left leg bent at the knee and bound up with linen. We caught up with him easily, and in passing I happened to look his way. Something in his sullen glance made me turn and stare.

I knew this boy, even though his rosy face looked thinner and paler now, and the eagerness had dimmed from the eyes I had last seen peering over Master Feather's copy desk. "You once worked for him, didn't you? Samuel?"

Sullenness flashed to terror on his face. "They've already questioned me. I know nothing about it. Leave me alone."

"But I saw you at his chambers. Did he dismiss you?"

He looked down resentfully. It was then I noticed that his right hand was bound up, resting in a sling. "This hand dismissed me. And I know who crippled it—the one who took my place as scrivener."

"Do you mean you were disabled on purpose?"

"It was not meant to look that way." The boy had no use for me, but like most people when they are wronged, he burned to tell about it. "I was going home one night after dark, when a band of three or four ruffians rolled me over in the street. One of them was the fellow who took my place. I would swear to it."

"But how could you know that, in the dark?"

"Because I pulled out a hank of his hair with my left hand before he knocked me down and stamped on my right. And later, while my hand was being bound up, I was still holding it. His hair was sooted black, but under the black it's bright red—red as new copper. The very next day he had taken my job. I saw him there after I was dismissed. But I lost my proof."

A strange tale, this; street brawlers were not generally qualified to take over scrivener's duties. But Master Feather's last scrivener was clearly something other than a scribe.

"Do you need a position?" Starling asked, her voice betraying pity.

"I have a position," he growled. "I sell ballads at St. Paul's for a hack printer. His next work will be about the just end of my late master, whose shoes he isn't fit to clean—" The boy broke off, suddenly remembering that Martin Feather's was a most dangerous name to praise. He drew back into himself and let us walk ahead. By the pinched looks of him, the ballad-monger he worked for now was not nearly so generous as the late attorney.

So the true Martin Feather was truly dead, but that left the false one—the tall gentleman who bore himself like a king and threatened like a highwayman. Plus his redheaded henchman, Bartlemy, who apparently did more than threaten.

"Set in the attorney's chambers as a spy," Starling decided as we tried to make sense of it later that day. "By the gentleman of the purple plume, no doubt."

"To what end?" I asked. "Who are they working for?"

"Why, the Queen, we must hope, else England is in a sorry state with two rival bands of conspirators. They are rough players, whatever side they may be on, to trample that poor boy's hand all because they wanted him out of the way."

Rough players indeed, who had threatened me with drowning, and I did not wish to believe they were the eyes and hands of our most gracious Queen. But that was not what troubled me most. "Master Beecham—or Beauchamp—is still unaccounted for."

"Aye," she said, frowning. "He is the piece that doesn't fit."

"What do you mean?"

"Look at it: here is Martin Feather, Matthew Merry, your aunt, and who knows else in the plot, all either dead or fled. On the other side are the man with the purple ostrich plume and his lad, Bartlemy."

"We know not what 'side' they are on."

"Whatever it is, they must not be part of the Holy Restoration

Society, or Bartlemy would have been taken. But Peter/John seems to have his own plot going. He has been wanted by the Queen's agents since July, but still manages to elude them. He has been closely associated with Martin Feather, but warned you against the man twice. And that's another thing: his particular interest in you."

This was not "another thing." It was *the* thing, as far as I was concerned. The death of Master Feather, sad as it was for him, had settled nothing for me. I was still waiting for John Beecham to call in his "debt," and the apprehension of it hung over me like a headsman's axe. Yet what did I owe him? A shilling, a job on the docks, a firm push along the chain of events that led me into the theater—what was all that worth?

"You haven't heard any more from him, have you?" Starling asked, with a searching look.

I shook my head. The less she knew about this aspect of the plot, the better for her.

Three weeks passed with no word from Beecham and no Yeomen of the Guard come to arrest me for conspiracy. The heaviness in me lifted, though only a little. Our performances were fewer and the audience diminishing; on some days the groundlings even brought their own wood to build little fires in the pit. Late in November we performed Part One of *Henry VI*, my first play. I had come a long way from the ignorant lad who had to be cued by a kick in the shins; now I could cue myself and elbow my way in for a look at the plot with the best of them. As if in tribute to my progress, my old friend Zachary appeared amongst the hired players. It was the first time our paths had crossed since Lord Hurleigh's funeral in July.

"And what a stew that gentleman cooked for himself, eh?" Zachary remarked to me. We were perched on the edge of the tiring-room loft, moments before the performance was to begin, while members of the Company rushed to and fro below us. I was shivering under my cloak, but weather seemed to have no effect on my companion. "Just as well for him to die when he did, or he'd never have got that pretty funeral we gave him. Which reminds me, lad. Something came of that I've been meaning to tell thee."

"What is it?"

"What's it worth to you?" he countered.

I was low on coin, as always, but then remembered the chunk of gingerbread Starling had given me. I took it out of a fold in my cloak and broke it in half.

After making short work of it, Zachary went on. "You disappeared that day, recall? No sooner had we left the Abbey than you ducked out of your robe so fast it was still standing. Next minute a gentleman showed himself and demanded of me who you were, how I knew you, and other nosing queries of that kind."

"What did you tell him?" I asked, more than curious.

"That I knew not thy name, nor thy place, nor thine honorable kin. That I met thee on the street only the day before and broke with thee over the mourner's job and made a penny off thee withal—meaning my recruitment fee, mind, and not any other

255

money that might have passed between us. Of that which I told him, part was true and part less so, and no business of mine which he believed."

"Did he give his name or office?"

"Nay, lad, but as he was flanked by Yeomen Guards I guessed he served the Queen, somehow."

"Did he have bright red hair?" I asked quickly. Zachary shook his head. "Then, was he a tall man with a good build, a dark beard, and eyes that seem to look through you?"

Zachary's jaw dropped almost to his chest and his eyes rounded to shilling size. "Saints defend us, thou hast the long sight!" So saying, he performed various complicated signs over me intended to ward off mystic powers. I had to smile, though the news was not comforting. So the counterfeit Martin Feather was an agent of the Queen, as Starling surmised. He could easily have stationed himself amongst the mourners without my noticing him, or perhaps even donned a black robe and carried an ash pot—though my sense was that the deep-hooded robe had shrouded Bartlemy.

"So," I said. "He got little out of you. How did he take it?"

"With right poor grace. He took my slate with all the names on it. Though it was little use to him, I warrant."

I agreed silently, wondering what a time they must have had with Ned Cut-Nose and Flat-Faced Francis. The third trumpet sounded and the players began assembling below. I stood up carefully, set aside the cloak, and adjusted the folds of my gown. "I am obliged to you, Zachary. It's late news, but worth knowing. You won't pass it on, will you?"

"What do I know to pass on?" He held up one fist with the thumb bent out. After a moment I caught on to the gesture and crooked my thumb around his to show that we were agreed. "And you are not obliged to me, little brother," he added, with a sweet smile. We climbed down to join the opening scene—a funeral, as it happened—and I did not understand what his last statement meant until the performance was over and Zachary long gone: he had taken the other half of my gingerbread.

Early in December the Company closed the Theater to make ready for the season at Whitehall, a great undertaking. To my surprise I was included. Robin was at great pains to impress on me what an honor this was. We would perform five plays throughout the fortnight, presenting each to the servants during the day and to the court at night: *The Merchant of Venice*, *King John*, and three others. There was some disagreement over *The Winter's Tale*, but Master Will prevailed on the "nay" side, claiming he wished to revise it.

The Lord Chamberlain himself requested *King John*, perhaps as a gentle reminder to Her Majesty that she had narrowly missed being poisoned by a Jesuit, as the unfortunate John was poisoned by a monk. It was in this play that a change of casting occurred: the part of Constance was given to me, and Queen Eleanor assigned to Kit. It was only sensible, Master Heminges said;

257

Eleanor was older than Constance, and Kit older than me. Content? Kit was not content and made no attempt to hide it. The quarrel we had tried to settle on All Hallow's was unsettled yet, and the scenes between Constance and Eleanor now had a bite to them that seemed to please the Company.

Between ordinary vexations like Kit and extraordinary worries like John Beecham and the Queen's men, I could not summon much anticipation for playing before the Queen. But one bright, cold December morn a huge white-and-gold swan glided down-river on twenty fluttering oars, paused long enough at bankside to board the Company, and swept off again with its cargo, cleaving the silvery water to the cadence of the boatmaster's chant. Thus the royal barge captured me and bore me away to the pomp and pageantry of Whitehall, a place that made our staged pageants look like child's play.

Our first court performance took place on the second night after our arrival. It was a masque, not a play—an elaborate costume dance in which many of the lords and ladies took part. The Company draped my naked chest in cloth of gold and stuck me shivering on a pedestal to portray Cupid, the god of love, with a golden bow in one hand. Across from me, Dick shivered likewise as a silver-clad Apollo, clutching a pearled harp. My only duty was posing, and if that sounds easy, then everyone should try it once: try to maintain some sense of what you are about while impersonating a god, perched above all the nobility of England, all dressed to outglitter each other in a clash of gold and jewels. How can I describe the light? It was as if the sun had broken up and scattered itself in thousands of pulsing points: there were lanterns strung from one side of the Hall to the other, stained-glass windows high above giving back the candle flames in tints of red, blue, and green; tall braziers set on either side of the stage, bouncing glints from polished armor, buckles, and blades. After only a short time of it, I had to turn my stunned gaze to the ceiling, where gilded arches disappeared in pearly smoke.

That was my introduction to the Royal Court—a total immersion into light, after which I was tempered, and better fit for duty. Our court performances occurred every other night. In our first week, the masque fell on Tuesday, *Romeo and Juliet* on Thursday, *Tambourlaine* on Saturday. Alternate nights we had to ourselves, and during days we rehearsed, performed our plays before the servants, and acted as ceremonial footmen between times. In this office I discovered that nobles are no more dainty in their manners than respectable people of the lower classes, and their table-talk is no more exalted—in fact, most of it somewhat less. The ladies and gentlemen within my hearing were consumed with court gossip: who was seeing too much of whom, and who was in or out of the Queen's favor, and who had silenced Lord Fatback or Lady Simper with devastating wit.

All four apprentices lodged in one large room, which soon proved too small. Dick and Robin insisted on bringing home the gossip, chattering on about Lord This and Lady That as though they were on intimate terms. As for Kit and me, we were at each other's throats within hours, in word if not deed, holding shouting matches over trifles. At the end of our first week it came as a relief to all of us when Kit struck up a romance with a chambermaid, who took up more of his free time (and more pleasantly) than I.

Within eight days I had come un-dazzled. Court life made my head ache, and after our performance of *The Greek Warrior* on Monday night, I could not go back to our drafty chamber and listen to Robin and Dick compare the ladies and gentlemen to various animals. So I stepped out, under a sky as clean-cut as a colander turned upside down and punched with starlight. My head slowly cleared in the cold as I circled a frosted garden and followed the flagstone path into a service courtyard.

Two guards passed as I entered, without so much as a nod to me. A whiff of starch and blast of steam pelted me from the open laundry door, but otherwise the place seemed still and empty. The hour was drawing on toward midnight. Distant conversations hummed, from this direction or that, peaceful as roosting birds in the still, cold air. I had nearly reached the center of the courtyard when two sharp cries met my ears, one of anger and the other of pain. A little scream followed, of the kind made by girls when they can't help screaming but don't want to be heard. Before I could fit all this together, steps were racing toward me; and then my arms were full of girl.

The extraordinary week had jumbled my senses so that this did not at first seem over-strange. Despite the cold, she was warm, a soft yet springy armful that made me think of Starling. Her palms pressed against my chest as though pushing back, even as her fingers twined in my cloak. I could not make out her face, but felt everything else—she flowed toward me, a spill of unbound hair and unlaced clothing.

"Stop them," she gasped, panting, though she could not have run far. "They'll kill each other!"

"Who?" I said, my heart thudding to match hers. "Where?"

"In the stable yard yonder. I'll fetch the guard. Stop them!"

She pushed away and ran on. I stood for a moment, absurdly wishing I could have held on to her a little longer. Then the noises at the far end of the yard penetrated my brain, and I followed them, passing below a stone arch into a smaller enclosure with a row of stables along each side. All was very dim, but two figures dark as shadows in the starlight wove a pattern in the open space. From an occasional dull glint I could see that both had drawn daggers. One slender form was clearly on the defensive, dodging with the grace and skill of a dancer. The other moved more slowly and seemed exasperated by the chase.

"I'll teach you to poach on my preserve," he puffed. "Stand still!"

"So you can stick me? I think not," said the other, and though it was thin with effort I would have known that voice if it spoke from six leagues underground. It belonged to Kit.

Well, thought I: he's finally stepped in too deep, with his "lads" nowhere about to pull him free. He had carelessly (or, given his reckless bent, deliberately) chosen to court a lady already attached, and here was the piper demanding to be paid.

I cannot say I rushed to his side. No, I thought about it first. He had it coming—but if he were killed, that would mean more work for the rest of us. Besides, no Christian could stand by while his fellow man was in trouble, even if the fellow man loathed his very guts. With some trepidation, then, I darted behind Kit's opponent, awaited my moment, and dived upon him. Wrapping an arm around his neck, I delivered a hard blow to the kidney with my right fist. He was stouter and taller, so I depended upon surprise and could expect to make only the first punch good. I heard the youth wheeze in pain and shouted to Kit, "Put up your knife! Knock him once, and let's be off!"

Kit rushed forward and punched the lad in the stomach. I could feel my grip loosening, and knew it could not hold much longer, but Kit had to stay to deliver another blow, and another. Our adversary choked out, "Help! Murder!" and there came a sound at my back that chilled my blood. It was a low chuckle, which let me know the stable yard was not empty.

"Turned out to be a mouthful you've bit off, hey, Jeremy?" the voice said. Then I felt strong hands on my shoulders, breaking my grip and pulling me off. I ducked the blow I felt coming. Next minute Kit and I were back to back, squared out against three assailants. "Have you a dagger?" he gasped at me.

"No!" I snapped back. "I don't go for walks *expecting* to save your backside."

"You should have stayed out of it, then." He parried with his knife, adding, "I was holding my own. There's a hayfork against the wall behind you. Follow me." We lunged for the wall and I seized the hayfork. Kit turned and nicked one fellow on the shoulder, crying, "Back away and let us by, or I'll serve up more of the same!"

Two of them went for Kit and one for me, but before I could bring up my weapon, a fist slammed against my jaw and spun me back against the stones. I tried to gather my strength to hit back before he could come at me again, but he was already coming, a force of destruction older and larger than I. Faster too—he ducked easily when I swung at him again, and twisted the fork out of my hands. I flung up my arms to protect my head and waited for the worst.

But instead of a blow came running steps, a swoop of steel, and a moan from my assailant. Someone new had joined the fray, and he seemed to be on our side. In the confusion I reclaimed my hayfork but found no chance to use it. By the clang of steel our unknown ally showed he was well armed. A determined swordsman, if not a graceful one, he beat back two of our foes while Kit dealt with Jeremy. The clatter of a dagger on stone, followed by a high scream, told me that someone had been bloodily disarmed. Then I heard footsteps approaching at a run.

"Someone's coming!" I panted. "The guard—"

"Run," said a strange voice at my side, directed at Kit. Then I felt a hand closing on my sleeve.

The next few moments were tumbled together—shouts, a laugh, Kit's sweet voice cursing as he slipped on a heap of dung; that hand on my sleeve, pulling me across the stable yard and around a corner; a screech of rusty iron hinges, stone steps slick with ice and a wrenching pain to my knee as I slipped on one of them; finally a little alcove between two battlements, where a fire in a small iron brazier burned cheerily. My teeth were chattering and my jaw throbbed.

"Sit here," commanded the voice, and the hand pushed me down on a hassock covered with sheepskin. I looked around at the stone walls on three sides and the open sky above—a guard station, I reckoned, empty now except for my companion and me. He dropped down on a saddle chair with the fire between us and pulled a cap from his head. Even in the weak light, his bright hair gleamed.

"Bartlemy!" The name slipped out of my mouth. "What makes you here?"

He glared. "Have we been introduced? I think not. I'm here to ask questions of you, not explain myself."

He was winded and put out—rescuing me from a brawl had probably not been a part of his plan for the night. But that related to my original question: "Am I under watch?"

"I said I would do the asking." With an exasperated sigh, he brought an apple from under his cloak and took a huge bite of it, talking around the mouthful as he chewed. "We are still looking for two men—Peter Kenton and John Beecham. What do you know of them?"

"Nothing."

"That is a bold-faced lie, my lad; may God strike you dead for it." He paused, as though waiting for me to fall lifeless at his feet. When it did not happen, he took another bite of the apple and let a thread of juice run down his long pimply chin. "Not long ago I talked with a Thomas Southern, formerly of the wine trade. Does the name mean anything to you?"

"Of course," I said, thinking fast. "I used to work for him."

"Very good. And he said that when you applied, you told them you were sent by a man named Peter Kenton."

"It was only a name I picked up on the docks. I thought it might help to recommend me. I was almost starving—"

"When did you see him last?"

"I've never seen him."

"Think, now. A fellow that tall would be hard to forget."

Hah, thought I. I may be sore and bewildered, but you'll not catch me up so easy as that. "So would a fellow with carrot-red hair and nasty table manners."

That roused him. "You've missed me all week then!"

So I *had* been under watch. This was useful to know, but not cheering; Bartlemy was no gentle knight sworn to my protection. He got hold of himself, and his tone sounded almost careless when he asked, "Have you noticed any beggars about St. Mary's Parish?"

"No—" I began, a thoughtless denial cut short. For the word "beggar" made me think of the poor leper who had moved into

Anne Billings' house and apparently abandoned it.

"No?" Bartlemy repeated, catching my hesitation.

"I mean, of course. Beggars are everywhere about London."

"Ah, but not all of them carry clappers to warn people away."

"Not all of them are lepers."

He fixed me with a hard stare. "Do you not have the wit to know that sheltering traitors amounts to treason?"

I was barely treading the murky waters of this exchange that threatened to pull me under. "I'm sheltering nobody! Why ply me with all these questions? Go ask the beggars themselves—you may find Master Beecham has fallen on hard times."

"We are not talking about Master Beech—" He interrupted himself, paused, and popped the rest of the apple into his mouth, core and all. Then he eyed me with a ruminative look, as though chewing me along with it. "That's a fetching thought."

At first I knew not what he meant. Then I did.

I had meant to say Kenton, and it was only a chance remark about falling on hard times, but now we both saw that the reason neither man could be found was likely because he was going about in another guise. Such as a nameless beggar. My heart plunged; unaccountably, I felt like a betrayer. But as it would not do to show dismay, I played ignorant.

"*What's* a fetching thought?" I wailed. "Why can't you just leave me alone?" He held up a hand to silence me. Firm steps and weary voices met our ears—the guards returning from patrol. We jumped up together.

"Quick," Bartlemy said. "I'll see you to your room. And then you'll see me no more."

My jaw swelled, but not too badly, and Kit hid the deep cut on his hand with a glove. He didn't seem in the least grateful to me. In fact, the scenes between Constance and Eleanor were even more inspired—we could have struck sparks off each other during the court performance of *King John*. The lords and ladies enjoyed it greatly, picking their favorites and cheering us on. True to his word, Bartlemy remained out of sight, though I looked for him. For a youth so hard to mistake, it was uncanny how he could make himself disappear at will.

The Merchant of Venice brought our court season to a close— and brought me to a revelation of sorts. I stood upon the makeshift stage in Nerissa's gown as Bassanio mused aloud over the three caskets. Sweet music from the gallery accompanied his choice: whether glittering gold or showy silver, "the seeming truth which cunning times put on to entrap the wisest." A complex blend of perfumes from our audience washed over the stage, and a veil of smoke blurred every light. Standing in the midst of the "seeming truth" which was our play, I finally understood the meaning of "cunning times."

All the grandeur of the court flowed upward to a platform at the middle of the Great Hall, covered in rich green velvet: on that dais a throne, and on the throne a Queen. The poets praise her as "Gloriana," England's pride. I remember her sitting very still, though they say she laughed and commented through our performances as freely as the members of her court. To me she was a white face in a gilded ruff—a pearl in a setting of gold.

But by now I had heard the faint creakings of the bulky, oily machinery needed to hold up this show. It was the noise of plots and counterplots, of people murdered and displaced, of hands and lives broken, ugly incidents encouraged to achieve a desired end. Under the pageant of royalty lay dozens of feverish, calculating men and women doing any act necessary to prop it up or bring it down. The white-faced figure on the dais across from me played her part no less than I played mine, except that she never came off stage. It was her business to "deceive the world with ornament." A necessary business, for she held the pride and fortunes of a nation in those fine white hands, and those artful poses she struck. But I knew, if only by desperate whispers, what it took to hold her up.

On our return to London I kept silent about my meeting with Bartlemy, but supplied Starling with details of the court and of my adventure with Kit, which failed to improve our relations. "'Tis certain he hates me, but I would like to know why."

"Oh, that's simple," she airily explained. "You're the only one who stands to rival him." I snorted at this, and she continued in better earnest. "It's true. Not even Robin can come near you when you are at your best. That isn't often, I'll grant, but Kit takes time to notice anything that threatens his standing. You can't expect him to warm to you."

I was not inclined to believe this. Starling had never liked young Christopher Glover, and I knew her feelings for me. Still, I won't deny that she had hit me with a powerful thought.

The Company allowed an interval of rest after our court season and the weather obliged, blowing in a chill that held the city fast for a week. The river froze from bank to bank and skaters thronged both sides, using poles to push themselves along. Robin got up a party of apprentices, servants, and Condell children and herded us all down to the Thames for an afternoon blessedly free of plot and play matters. Tramping home late in the day, with the winter sun bleeding over the horizon, our mood was partly dampened by the sight of a lame beggar shuffling up Aldermanbury Street. Knowing Bartlemy's interest in beggars, I now gave them a close look when they appeared in the neighborhood, but this one was taller than the man I had in mind. Some yards beyond him, we missed Ned, our special charge; Starling turned to find him talking with the lame man. "Ned!" she called sharply, and we saw him shake his head before running to join us. "What was he telling you?" Starling asked him.

"Nothing. I thought it was my school beggar, but 'tis not."

"Who's that?" I asked.

"I see him sometimes about the school when I get out. He tells me stories. The merriest beggar I've ever met with, though his face is all scabby." The boy dashed on ahead of us, and I gave little thought to what he said. Until later.

During the next week a southerly wind blew off the coast and the sun decided to show its face. Whenever this happened, all the acting companies hastened to their theaters to put together a performance or two, or as many as the weather would permit. Winter plays are always well attended, no matter the temperature, for by this time Londoners are heartily sick of confinement; they wrap up as best they can and pack in. On Tuesday the Lord Chamberlain's Men performed *Tambourlaine,* a rousing story of military conquest, and very popular—the groundlings thronged so thick that their combined breath made a little fog over the stage.

Wednesday's offering was to be *The Winter's Tale,* as Master Will had rewritten some bits that he wished to try out. Perdita's part suffered little change, but I was stale on it. Once home from the Theater I made directly for the attic, as it was the only spot in the house where I might have some quiet for study.

Young Ned passed me on his way down, with a giggle and a sidelong look. This did not bode well, for he liked to leave surprises for me, Robin, or his brothers under our bedclothes or in our shoes. For my own peace of mind I scouted the room before getting to work.

The prank revealed itself early. I merely turned over my pillow and there it was: a sealed paper and a small leather pouch tied with a drawstring. The seal with its "JB" had been lifted and clumsily stuck down again. Unlike Betty, Ned could read. The paper felt heavy in my hands, and I thought of Bassanio in *The Merchant,* pondering the lead casket with its ominous inscription: *Who chooseth me must risk and hazard all.* The temperature had plunged with the onset of night, but the air was quite still, a clear ether in which street noises rang like bells. From the corner of Aldermanbury and Cattle streets, a watchman cried five o'clock. The piece that did not fit, as Starling had called him, slowly fell into place.

Ned had mentioned a "school beggar" who told him tales, a man unaccountably merry despite his disfigured face. A man liked by children, who could gain a child's confidence and enlist him to deliver a message.

A man who dared not approach me directly, for he knew I was being watched.

A man to whom I owed a great debt, which he seemed confident I would repay.

My hands shook as I opened the message, with good reason. It was a risk and a hazard, but perhaps I was a bit of a gambler, too, like my father.

> *The time draws near. If you would know my*
> *secret wounds and hidden hurts, meet me at the*
> *west side of the Bear Garden tomorrow, at two*
> *hours past noon. I will find you even if you mark*
> *me not. Come as Perdita, or her sister, and*
> *whatever else you may do, come alone.*
> *The sign that accompanies this message is*
> *my pledge.*

I opened and upended the leather pouch, and into my hand spilled a string of wooden beads, painted white and blue with the pearly luster that had caught my eye on my first day in London.

The Masker Unmasked

❖

If fevers could be brought about by will, my task would have been simpler. As it was I had to slip into the kitchen and palm a measure of dock root from the apothecary cabinet while Nell's back was turned. An hour before bedtime I mixed the powder with a little milk and drank it down, and in very short order I was in the same condition as Kit the previous spring after he had eaten the spoiled meat. Mistress Condell dosed me with a raspberry infusion, but dock root held the upper hand in my inwards for most of the night. At daybreak the master shook his head and asked why I could not have managed to get the pukes during an off-theater day, then sent Jacob to Richard Cowley's house, where Dick Worthing boarded, with Perdita's part for him to learn.

My body was wrung out and weak by morning. When Master Condell left with Rob for the Theater, I indulged in the great luxury of having the bed to myself—though sleep eluded me, as it had for most of the night. The mistress was down with one of her headaches; otherwise she would have tried to coax me downstairs by the fire. Starling came up just before her departure for Shoreditch with a dose of tea and a bit of dry toast. She suspected something, but I pretended to be so dozy, she gave up trying to get it out of me.

During the dinner hour I rose and dressed in my second-best doublet with a small schoolboy's ruff, then bundled up my cap and cloak and squeezed through the attic window. The next few moments called for utmost care, for though the window could not be seen from the street, part of the roof was visible, and someone might be watching. To my knowledge no one had ever crossed the roof in daylight, but I accomplished it without raising an alarm. Once grounded, I took the alley to March Lane, passing from one side street to another all the way to the Bridge.

The air felt almost warm, but that was an illusion—the shadows retained all the chill of winter, and I could with justice wrap my face up to the nose in my cloak. A meat pastry bought from a vendor at Bankside helped restore my strength, and when the Bear Garden came in view only my heart felt queasy.

A hard-faced, long-jawed young woman guarded the west gate. Chestnuts popped savagely on the grill beside her as vagrants loitering nearby stamped their feet with sharp emphasis to keep warm. I scanned their ranks, then turned to the penny gatherer. "Has a beggar passed through?"

She rolled her eyes. "Is that the sun in yon sky? Beggars pass through all day. They turn over their next-to-last penny and wager the very last on a match. More beggars come out than go in, I promise you. Will you be going in?"

It was my last penny I turned over to her, on a wager of my own.

Tobacco smoke stung my eyes as I pushed through the aisle standers. The Bear Garden is built almost exactly like the London theaters: a round structure lined with galleries. But instead of a stage for pretended conflicts, there is an open ring filled with sawdust, where beast battles beast in a conflict all too real. The galleries were full of roaring men and not a few women, while groundlings ranged around the pit two or three deep. My past experience with bear-baiting was limited to exhibition matches in tavern yards, where the dogs were usually drawn off early. But this was a battle to the death—I could hear it, almost smell it. The bear was Ajax, a hulking brown creature in the prime of life, surrounded by no less than four snarling mastiffs. The number had been five, but one of them was down. In fact, the conqueror was using him as a footstool, his huge ivory claws slowly digging into a bloody hide as the dog writhed and whined. Ajax took all apparent delight in his victim's suffering and was loathe to move his foot even while his keeper prodded him with a hook. Two mastiffs had circled around to the bear's back; as I watched, one sprang and landed square upon the spine, digging in with his claws and teeth to find purchase. Ajax roared—a cry echoed by every soul with money riding on him—and with a twist of his massive shoulders flipped the dog in the air, whirled about, and swiped him on the way down, laying open his back. A howl went up from the unfortunate beast, and blood in a hot, red spray.

I turned my head away, and in that moment heard the laugh. The noise of the crowd throbbed in my ears, but that sound reached them nonetheless. The laugh was higher in pitch than I remembered, though still bold, strong, infectious. He stood some three paces ahead of me: a slight figure in peasant's garb holding a staff, his head covered by a hood. His shoulders, under a patched blanket, shook with the vigor of his laugh. I gathered my strength and butted through the packed crowd, earning evil looks from dislodged spectators as I pressed toward him. When at last I stood with scarcely a stay-pole's width between us, I raised a hand and tried my voice. My lips moved, my tongue worked, but nothing came out at first. Then after a swift inbreathed prayer I let my hand fall, with one word:

"Father."

He turned, with an open, delighted face that seemed to leap out from under his hood—a face neither old nor young, with round blue eyes and a wide mouth and smooth cheeks. "Richard! I knew you would . . ." Abruptly, his smile flattened. "You've disobeyed me, boy. This is not how you were told to appear."

I expected him to accuse me thus and had an answer ready.

But my voice failed. The moment was stretched in all directions and warred with its own extremes: hot blood under a cold sky, a warm smile and a chilly rebuke, the unceasing noise and the stubborn knot of silence within my throat. And, stretching back as long as I could remember, my own longing for and revulsion toward this man. My distress must have showed, for his expression changed yet again. He took my arm and cleaved a path for us through the spectators. As we neared the entrance, a great shout arose and the inhabitants of the galleries jumped to their feet—whether it was because Ajax had downed another mastiff, or because one of them had finally clamped its jaws upon his neck, I never knew.

Once we were outside I drew in mouthfuls of fresh air, for the bear pit had come near to suffocating me. Speech remained impossible. My companion pointed me in a southeasterly direction and let go my arm. For some time we walked in silence, though I could feel the probing looks he sent my way. We passed the Rose Theater (prompting guilty recollections of where I was supposed to be at this hour) and turned east. A row of gambling dens and brothels stretched before us, upper windows open to catch the last of the winter sun as lightly clad women rained down bawdy greetings on passers-by. My companion hesitated, then decided against this particular route. Instead we proceeded a little further south and turned into an alley, stinking with sewer refuse but empty except for cats. After a time he asked, "Does this speechlessness oft affect you?"

"N-n-no," I said, with some effort. "That is—not oft."

"A strange impediment for an actor, hey?"

"I . . . I can speak words . . . that are n-not mine."

"Ah. Well, that makes perfect sense. You have found your place, and I congratulate you on it. Would I had found mine so young!"

Much could be said to this—that I had by no means settled into acting, that he had made a "place" for himself once, and abandoned it—but I could lay tongue to none of it. I shrugged angrily, and he went on: "So—how did you determine who I was?"

"By—" I cleared my throat. "By your last message."

"And . . . ? Must I pry everything out of you?"

"By the words from the sonnet."

"Very good! It was a careful message, all the more since I don't come by paper so easily these days. Or anything else, as your own eyes may witness."

"Are you as poor as you look?"

"Nay, poorer. All I can lay claim to at the moment is this stick."

"But how—how came you to such a pass?"

There was a world implied in the question, and he seemed to know it, for he took my arm again and pointed me toward a little grotto built into a stone wall. It was the home of a former spring, long since played out; a climbing rose vine in want of pruning tumbled over the stone arch, a few dry brown roses still clinging stubbornly to its branches. He sat on the top step of the grotto in a patch of watery sunlight and motioned me to do the same. Not until my bottom touched the cold stone did I recognize how weak

I felt—all a-tremble with the lingering effects of dock root and a meeting engorged with too much feeling. Robert Malory pushed back his hood.

His face was thinner than when I had first met him in Abbot Lane, and paler, too, with a wan look about the eyes. We did not resemble each other overmuch, though I had inherited his build. Probably his voice also, for I heard a resonance in it as strong as his laugh. But it was with my mother's face that I looked at him, and if he had the conscience to feel abashed by my hurt-fawn gaze, he did not show it.

"The debt I owe you . . . ," I ventured, slowly, "is life. I suppose."

"There is no 'suppose'; I was there when you were got."

"What do you want?"

"Just this. I am to make my escape this night and need your help. A skiff from France is tied up east of the Bridge, and at the turning of the tide a lady was to step aboard this little vessel and cast off for the Channel. Perhaps a schoolboy would do, but I doubt the searcher at the port in Deptford would take me for a schoolboy after a close look at this weathered mug, don't you?"

"You assumed too much," said I, sullenly, "if you thought I would change clothes with you without qualm."

"I assumed on our shared blood. Is that too much?"

"If you wanted women's clothes, I could have brought them—stolen them, more like. But I won't pretend to be what I am not. I may steal for you, but I will not lie."

"Why, Richard," he said, with his winning smile. "You grow

suddenly eloquent. But think about it—I could not spell out my plan in the message, lest it fall into the wrong hands and bring wrath upon your head. I have tried to be careful of you."

"Have you? Was that 'care' that jumped me in the street last spring and took all that was dearest to me?"

"Ah. 'Tis well you reminded me." He fumbled in the rags and laces that covered his chest and eventually came out with my old leather wallet. It felt warm when he delivered it into my hands. "Nothing left inside but the sonnet and the Rector's letter of commendation, which I judge to be completely truthful. The shilling is long gone, I fear, my need of it being greater than yours. The rubbing is ashes—my faith, what a blow to find your mother had made that! Had you not been carrying such a dangerous token, we would have let you be."

"I wouldn't have shown it."

"You showed it readily enough to my sister. And did I not warn you to stay clear of Martin Feather? You are not easily led, my boy. How were we to know what you would do?"

My head felt crowded with too much coming too fast. I shook it, and shivered, and closed my eyes. "Who are 'we'?"

"Now that," said he, "is a vexed question. 'We' no longer exist. With the stroke of the headsman's axe, our union fell apart. Or well before that, to say truth."

"Who are you, then?"

"Who am I? Oh, Richard. Our time is too short—"

"Are you a Catholic?"

"No."

"A traitor?"

"Only in the eyes of the government."

I might have replied that the government's were the only eyes interested in judging such things, but let it go. My voice had come back with a vengeance, and questions tumbled over each other. "If you cared not for the faith, how came you to be so deep in this plot?"

He raised a hand and let it fall. "How to answer? I was at a point in my life of longing to be part of some great thing, to tinker with the machinery that moved kings and queens and shifted fortunes. And if we had succeeded, well—you could now be looking at the next Lord Chamberlain. My sister was in it, and though I never liked her, I have always admired her in some way. She can give her all to a cause greater than herself. For a time I thought I could do the same."

"Why would you think that? You could not even give your all to a cause your own size."

He thought this over, then said, "I feel your venom, lad, and cannot fault you for it. But I have my life to live, and you have yours."

True, I thought, but mine is a life you brought into being, and should have held in more regard. I bit my lip, then asked, "What can you tell me of Owen Mercer?"

He threw back his head with a laugh and I could see that many of his once-fine teeth had fallen out, a sign of ill care, bad food, hard times. But his laugh belied it, and he swore with a good-natured heartiness. "You've not been idle in knowledge-gathering, have you? I could tell you much of him, but it would all be bad, and it's unlucky to speak ill of the dead."

"How did he come to be dead?"

"By a most wondrous pretense, the greatest of my career, though it was a pity there were so few to watch it. We all agreed it would be best for Owen Mercer to shuffle off. He had become a nuisance, and nobody liked him much, not even me. Our duel would be a good pretense for Father Martin, too: if he was known to have killed a man for love of a lady, who would suppose he was really a priest? So we met on the Green at Finsbury and went four rounds with the steel before he scored me in the heart, where the sheep's bladder was. He was a good swordsman, like many a Jesuit; he made me work for my end. I went down in a wonderful welter of blood, and some hours later the pious Anne of Southwark declared me dead."

He went on to tell of his year in France, forging both a new identity and a ring of connections who would be useful to the Society. When he returned to England, it was in the person of smooth-shaven, bespectacled John Beauchamp, a noted scholar of the law and sometime associate of Martin Feather. As he talked, I could almost forget the deadly implications of what he said, for it was a wonderful story of clever devices and narrow escapes, told with relish. From his manner, one might think it had been little more than an elaborate game with him. Intrigued in spite of myself, I asked, "What part did you play as Peter Kenton?"

He gasped in amazement. "What say you? Only one person knew I was both Kenton and Beauchamp, and that was my sister. No, truly," he added, to my expression of disbelief. "It's always wise to conceal something, even from your friends. Not even the steward at the Lion and Lamb knew, though he dealt with both of me. By what sorcery did you come by it?"

I pressed my lips together, unwilling to say more. But then he laughed again, as though pleased to have sired such a clever son. "No matter. I warrant that girl had somewhat to do with it. When Tom Southern told me there was a housemaid claiming I had wronged her, I guessed who it must be. We knew where you lived by then, on account of your barging into the chambers demanding to see John Beecham, and I decided it was worth another warning to you. That was Kenton's last appearance."

"Did they know what I was to you? Feather and Merry?"

"Aye. My sister would have told them, if I didn't. Merry was almost beside himself when you burst upon him that day—he thought he'd thrown a lasting scare into you. Failed to reckon on the Malory stubbornness, hey?"

I did not return his smile. "And you killed him?"

He looked down, the smile quickly fading, and plucked a loose thread from the hem of his jerkin. "Alas, I did. It was not planned. The man was somewhat of a son to me—if you'll excuse the term, Richard. 'Twas I who brought him into the Society when he was a seminary student in France. But everything changed when Lord Hurleigh died. They had begun to suspect me of double-dealing even before, but it wasn't true." (With a start, I noticed how "we" had become "they.") "Shackleford's death spelled an end to their plan, but they would not give it up. Both were good men and true, but schemes had twisted their minds out of shape. They threatened to expose me. Once my sister had fled to France, I was without an ally. We met at the foundling hospital, Merry and I, and I could feel which way the wind blew. The matter came down to his life or mine, and so . . ." He trailed off, leaving the particulars of what followed to my imagination. "I meant to wait one day, then take what I knew to the Queen's agents, and bring down the whole rotten structure. The papers left on Merry's body were to prove what I said. I did not expect the body to be found so soon—that scotched my plan. Once he was discovered, who would believe me?"

So he did not know who had made the discovery. That was well, for I felt an odd twist of guilt over it. It made no sense. If he spoke true, this man was a traitor, a schemer, a murderer, and a would-be informer—why should *I* be the one to feel guilty? "Were those the papers you took from Master Feather's lodging?"

"Just so. I have marveled how it was you came upon me at that very moment, but such are the mysterious ways of God. When I took them, the papers were to insure my safety, nothing more. Even then they had begun to doubt my full devotion, and 'twas necessary to let them know that if I went down, I would not go alone."

"So you stored them away in a secret place."

"Aye; with sweet Margery, who knows blessed little—of anything."

"Who is Margery?"

"A friend." The sudden firmness in his tone told me that this avenue was closed. Nothing daunted, I chose another.

"What of your sister? Did she get away safe?"

"Aye, thank God, though after she was gone our circle fell apart. Her house was the conduit for our messages. But she lives on, in Burgundy. 'Tis she arranged for my escape." He fell silent, as though awaiting further questions, but what he had told me already possessed my mind. I sat on the cold stone step, shivering as the shadows crept across the alley into our laps and rubbing one thigh with an unthinking hand, harder and harder. After a moment he went on quietly, "So Peter Kenton has disappeared, and John Beauchamp is in hiding, since both are wanted men. This pitiful beggar you see before you is my only guise now. And if I wish to become even more obscure, I paste some very hideous scabs on my face and take out my clapper, and most are glad to hold clear of me."

"The Queen's agents are looking for someone like that."

"And how do you know . . . but never mind. No more lepers. I hoped to make my exit as Henrietta Marceau, but Henri will have to do."

My shoulders twitched, as though to throw off an absurd sense of blame. "Why . . ."

"Why what, Richard?"

"Why did you leave us?"

Though it was the question I had longed to ask from the

beginning, I was amazed to hear myself asking it. He sat very still as the sun slipped behind the stone wall on the opposite side of the alley. The play at the Rose had ended; I could tell by the distant chirp of boat whistles from the bank, where wealthy patrons called for their personal watermen to ferry them over the river.

At last he said, "No answer I could give would satisfy thee. Would it?"

I made no reply, recalling my childhood fancy that he was away on some important mission: true, as it turned out, though vilely distorted.

"We had best be off. The tide turns in an hour, and we must take the long way."

A rising wind flattened the cloaks against our backs as we turned east on a miserable twisting lane. Ragged children and vagabonds stared at my merchant-class garb as we passed. For as long as we stuck to the back streets, my father regaled me with his adventures as Mercer-Kenton-Beauchamp, relating this incident or that as if it had happened only yesterday. If he lived to tell it, tonight's escape would be another tale for the books, all of a piece with the fantastic fabric he had made of his life.

As we approached the Bridge and the streets became more populated, he pulled his hood forward and slowed his walk to the halting shuffle of a beggar. We passed Winchester Palace in this manner, and St. Savior's, and on to Southwark Street. Here he turned north toward the Bridge and motioned me a few paces ahead of him. The roadway was fairly quiet at this hour, and over the wind

I could hear his flat-footed steps behind me, and the tapping stick of a blind man. As we passed under the central tower, I glanced up to where the remains of Martin Feather's head stared down with empty eye sockets. The shuffling steps behind me continued without a pause. A gentleman passed, and the next moment I heard a clink of metal on wood, and the beggar's whining thanks. He was an excellent actor, I thought, torn between shame and a twisted sort of pride. "Turn to the right," he called, softly, as we neared the end of the Bridge. "We go to thy first place of employment, hey?"

I turned without a word, and once clear of Thames Street he joined me again, tucking a wooden bowl into the bosom of his rough jerkin and tying up the coin in his pouch. "A token for my journey—it bodes well." Then he fell silent as we tramped down the rough plank walkway over the marsh. The wind set up a desolate wailing as we approached the former warehouse of Motheby and Southern, of which little remained but the pier. Those two had dissolved their partnership, as I had it from Ralph Downing. Motheby attempted to open a tavern on the South Bank, while Southern returned to his home in Kent and threw himself upon the mercy of relatives: two more lives ruined, or at least disrupted, by the intrigues of Martin Feather and the man beside me.

The river was at its height, lapping over the wharf. Two galleasses were tied up at the end of the pier beside Roger Coverdale's fish warehouse—long ships from the Continent, of a kind that used to drop anchor before Motheby and Southern almost daily. My companion moved quickly from my side, stepped off the walkway, and advanced toward the ships. What he saw between them appeared to satisfy him; he took a stone from his pouch and skimmed it over the water in the direction of the current. This must have been a signal, for he came back to me straightaway and said, "The skiff is here. Now we must find a place to change."

He strode up the pier toward a boat shed, confident that I would follow. But I hesitated. What he asked me to do was a crime against Queen and country, yet his life was at stake. He was my father; how could I let him be taken and executed? On the other hand, how could I knowingly lend aid to a traitor? At the end of the pier he turned; the wind caught his voice and made it sound very far away. ". . . Richard?"

You chose it, I told myself savagely. You chose to risk and hazard all. Now finish it. I hurried after him.

In the boat shed, out of the wind, he traded his rags for my respectable garb and in so doing put on yet another identity. "Henrietta's name is on the papers, but I can rub it out," he explained cheerfully—at least he bore me no grudge for spoiling that plan. "This will bend my sister's wit; she has no doubt been telling everybody to expect a lady. Well, I shall be Henrietta's twin. And that reminds me, how does Susanna?"

I told him what I knew, very mindful that after more than two hours together he had only now come around to inquiring of her. Nor had he inquired of me. True, he and his comrades had been watching me for the last many months and knew, in general terms, how I did. Still, it would have meant something if he had asked,

"And what of you, Richard? How is it with you?" We stood uneasily in the boat shed after changing. My doublet, handed down from Harry Condell, hung loose on him, for though he was slightly taller than me, the hardship of the last months had carved several pounds from his slender frame. I had already begun to itch; his clothes were lousy and I suspected the first thing to do on reaching home was burn them. Or chuck them in the alley and climb the roof to my room stark-naked. The wind had blown in a freezing rain that spattered like birdshot on the flimsy wooden walls of the shed. I thought of making my way home in it, and felt altogether as miserable as ever in my life. "I would know one thing more from you," I said then.

"And what is that?"

"When you left us—what you told my aunt . . . She said you left because you were m-maddened by jealousy, and I must know . . . I must know if there was anything in it—"

"No, Richard." His voice fell gently. "But your aunt is a woman who must have reasons, and I gave her one she would understand."

"'Twas a vile slander, then."

"I won't deny it, but where's the harm? I knew it would not get back to the lady in question, and never meant it to get to thee. Know, then, that thy mother was honest and true. And much too good for me."

I wanted to ask how he could allow that good woman to waste away in the provinces and never let her know his whereabouts or whether he lived or died. And how he could put the children of his body so out of mind as to make up a world in which they had no part—as though his imaginings meant more to him than anything real.

But the words crowded my throat and would not emerge. What finally came out, after a struggle that left me feeling hot and ashamed, was a line from *The Winter's Tale:* "Then we need no grave to bury honesty; there's not a grain of it left upon the earth."

He was silent for some time, and though it was too dark to see anything but shadows, I could feel his eyes upon me. "You are too young for bitterness, boy. I am sorry the scene ends this way. Still, you are at the beginning of your own play, and free to make of it what you will. As for me—"

Over the steel-gray water darted two tones of a whistle, a signal from the waiting boatman.

"The tide turns. I must be off." My father picked up my cloak to wrap himself in, then hesitated. "Why, Richard," he said. "Would you take the beggar's cloak from him, his only covering? Here, give it back to me. 'Tis a bitter night—I must have some solace." I felt him pluck his old patched cloak out of my hands and throw my good, warm, and whole one about my own shoulders. He accomplished this with fair grace and light spirit, disguising the fact that he had just sentenced himself to a long river passage with only a threadbare covering. "Come with me a ways before we part."

The squall of frozen rain had passed while we were in the shed, and the wind blew a rift in the clouds. A near-full moon, now on the rise, beamed an alien brightness. "A blessing or a curse?" he mused. "For by it I may see thee, but I dare not be seen. Well, lad—" He halted suddenly on the pier, as did I. The glancing moon silvered the water and revealed a little skiff looking small and anxious between the two galleys, its square stern tugged seaward by the tide. I felt his hand touch my arm lightly. "Who knows if we shall meet again? I must say, there is much in thee to be proud of, and I—"

His last words twisted off in a kind of sob. I turned to him and felt his cold hands on my face. My own hands moved, as though of their own will, and gripped his shoulders—those same shoulders I had perched upon as a child, that proved too unsteady to support me for long. The rain had stopped, so the wetness he felt on my face must be tears; I could not begrudge him those. It was a lifetime of longing he gathered up in his hands, he who could not hold it.

Thus he was. The lost had been found, and yet a greater part lost again. He had told me truth, but made his whole life a lie, a trick. I had searched for Leontes and found Autolycus instead.

"Ah, Richard . . . ," he began, and I heard great feeling in his voice but knew not what kind, or how true. I was never to know, for at that moment we heard thudding steps upon the pier and sprang apart. A fluttering figure blew at us like a full-rigged ship in a gale and plowed into my father, knocking him off-balance.

"Richard!" it cried. "Thank God I found you—I've searched everywhere—"

"What demon from hell is this!" he sputtered as I hissed at her, "Star! What is it?"

She was well-nigh undone, and the sound of my voice coming out of the beggar's clothes sent her reeling back, staring at the figure she had supposed, by the cap he was wearing, to be me. But she recovered quickly, took stock, and asked no foolish questions. "You must be off. All of us—must disappear at once. The Queen's Yeomen are searching the bank and will be here soon."

"By the bloody nails!" my father swore. "They must have tracked me to my lodging at last, and Margery has opened her mouth and spilled the little she knew."

"Who is Margery?" I shouted, all my wistful feeling quite gone. "Another 'fine woman' you've taken up with?"

"Please you, Richard," Starling begged. "Let it go!"

"Aye, Richard, let it go," said my father, "as I go. God be with thee." He backed away a few steps, then raised his hand. "One thing more—stick to acting. You are quite as good as me." His triangular smile flitted by like a ghost in the moonlight, then he turned and strode down the long pier, the ragged cloak snapping. He walked with a smooth confidence, and never looked back—the playmaker of my life, who had created and moved me from afar and now left me again. Yet in spite of all I found myself admiring his self-possession. Starling tugged at my arm.

"Now *come,* you must. There's no time. I hear them."

And indeed, over the quay came scattered shouts, cries, a splash of torchlight on the water. There was no outrunning them.

Starling appeared to have thought it out already, for, never slacking her grip on my arm, she skimmed over the pier and around to the back side of Roger Coverdale's warehouse. I cast one glance toward the river and caught the shadow of a little skiff riding the gray current, outlined by the moon. The sight stayed with me as we ducked under the boardwalk and skirted the brick foundation of the warehouse, bending low. Starling discovered an alcove in the foundation and darted in, pulling me after her. The narrow space was filled with barrels of salt fish, but we wedged between two of them, dislodging a family of rats. The briny smell burned in my nose as I leaned my head against a barrel. Broken clouds were scudding overhead, and perhaps the boat escaped detection. I wished so, and didn't wish, and was overtaken with violent shudders not entirely due to cold.

Starling told me what had happened at the Theater: how, at the beginning of the fourth act, she was accosted in the second gallery by a thin, loose-jointed young man with bright red hair sticking out from under his cap. He demanded to know why I was not playing Perdita. She refused to say anything unless he identified himself (though of course she guessed), and Bartlemy lost his temper. "He was furious to miss you, and I think it made him careless. He told me you seemed to have a special attachment to an enemy of the Queen's, and that he and I would hang together until he found you. He seized my arm and when I pulled away, he snatched me back, and so I screamed that he meant to take advantage of me. It stopped the play for an instant. He turned as red as St. George's cross, and let me pull away from him, and everybody laughed."

The shouting voices were very near—directly overhead. Footsteps trampled the boards one way and then another, and Starling paused in her story. We shrank against each other as though to make ourselves small, and suffered a bad moment when someone jumped off the wharf and ran along the mudflats just outside our hiding place. But the opening in the bricks is near-impossible to see at night, and the steps faded away. Starling went on. "I slipped back to the tiring rooms just long enough to tell Robin to cover for you, if you weren't in bed when he got home."

"Lie for me, you mean." The sound of my own voice, after lying silent for so long, surprised us both.

"I suppose. What would you have me do? He disappointed me, though—said he wouldn't get into trouble for you. Little rabbit!"

"Why should he risk his position with the Company?"

She paused, then whispered, "I would."

"You are not Robin." I felt drained of all emotion, including gratitude. "What else?"

"Oh, a nightmare. I ran home straightaway and of course you weren't there. I got out of Neddie what he'd read in that message to you. He dropped some hints this morning—you know how he can't keep anything to himself. But all he could say was that you were to meet somebody at the Bear Garden, so I went there, and had such a time trying to find you, with the taunts of the men and all and—oh, leave it. So I tried to think of all the places connected with this business, and went next to your aunt's house, but found nothing—even the beggar's things were gone. So I came back across the Bridge, and on the other side I saw a party of the Yeomen marching toward me, headed east. That made me think of the warehouse, so I outran them and reached the wharf, and saw someone I thought was you, only—"

The anguish and strain of the last hours had caught up with her, and she was sobbing, unable to continue. The novelty of Starling rendered speechless bumped me out of my own misery. I felt her shaking, as I was, and opened my arm to spread my cloak around us both. She burrowed into the scratchy fabric of my father's jerkin; soon I felt the warmth of her tears through it, and the beat of her good, loyal heart. I took her hand, grateful after all.

She should not have come. I was now accessory to a crime, and she had made herself accessory to me. But I was not strong enough to bear this burden alone.

"Star," I said. "Let us not lie anymore."

"Of—of course not, Richard. Have I ever lied to you?"

"That fellow you took for me . . . was the man we knew as John Beecham. But don't ask me who it was really."

"I think I know—" she began.

"Then don't say it. It would put you at risk, and I could tell you neither yea or nay. I don't want to lie. I cannot—"

Then I had to stop, for I was crying, too.

The Bear's Grin

❖

Next day the weather held, and we performed *Romeo and Juliet*. That was good for me, as I carried only a small speaking part at the beginning and merely stood about (or leapt about, in some semblance of fencing) for the rest of the play. It was all I could do. The night before, Starling and I had reached home just before supper—a fortunate time, because the household was gathering around the table. I shed the beggar's clothes and climbed the roof to my attic room wrapped only in my cloak, while she scouted Master Condell's disposition. By God's good providence, no one had missed me that afternoon, with Thomas and Ned in school most of the day and the mistress down with a headache. Of course Ned knew I had been summoned to the Bear Garden, but he was a flighty child, easily distracted. Besides, Starling had threatened to strangle him if he said anything. Rob knew I was not in bed when he got home, because he couldn't help looking, but he spoke not a word, either for or against me.

Or *to* me—he remained oddly silent throughout the night and the next morning. Since our discovery of the hanging man, his manner toward me was never entirely easy, and now he appeared to think I might be marked out for the Tower or the scaffold. I could have used another friend, but loyalty is a mature virtue. Robin, for all his worldliness borrowed from the stage, was still just a boy— a frightened boy. So was I.

Directly after the performance of *Romeo and Juliet* as Robin and I made for the stairs behind stage, an unseen hand reached out of nowhere, clapped over my mouth, and pulled me into the farthest corner of the tiring room. It was that quick. One moment I was a weary performer making to change out of costume; next moment I was a prisoner in my own place of refuge, face to face with a gentleman in black. We were in the keeping room, a sort of closet where the tiring master stores costumes that want mending or cleaning before another performance. The cold sun, low on the narrow windowsill, cut a beam of brightness across the silver chain on the man's shoulder. He had taken the plume out of his hat, but otherwise looked exactly as he had appeared on the day I followed him from the Theater.

"My name is John Clement," he began abruptly. "The young man beside you is Bartholomew Finch, my very able assistant. We serve the Lord Chamberlain in defense of Her Majesty." I glanced to my right, but already knew it was Bartlemy who had abducted my person so ably I doubted if Robin knew it even yet. The surprise was that they worked for our patron, but I had no time to ponder it as the man continued. "We have told you the truth, and from you we expect no less. Where were you yesterday at eventide?"

"I was . . ." I cleared my throat, but could not stop the dreaded hand closing around it, choking off not only words but wind. To my horror I recognized what happened: my father had made it impossible for me to lie. The barest suggestion of becoming like him in that way caused my tongue to swell, my mouth to dry up. No cat and mouse now, with Master John Clement; I was caught by the tail.

"What is your association with the man known as John Beauchamp?"

But how could I tell the truth? Telling the truth would seal not only my doom, but Robert Malory's, and my aunt's, and put Starling in danger also. Plain fear waved me off that path.

"It is no use pretending there is no association," Master Clement went on. "We know that a man so named set out for the Port of Deptford yesterday around five o'clock. We also know that you did not appear in yesterday's performance. Another boy played your part."

"Badly too," put in Bartlemy—not only kidnapper and mauler but theater critic as well. He leaned against the wall, arms folded, regarding me with his sharp eyes.

"Well?" said his master. "Where were you yesterday at eventide?"

"So please you, sir . . ." My voice came out as the barest whisper—both of them had to lean close to hear it. "I was sick—"

"All day? Can anyone swear that you were in your bed around the first watch?"

Starling would, but she was now in her own bed with a nasty cough picked up from yesterday's adventure. Besides, I could not let her lie for me.

"Let me acquaint you with what we know, lest you try to dodge us again with some lame tale about losing your wallet. We have had an eye on you since you appeared at the chambers of Martin Feather. Since Bartlemy recognized you from the funeral, we marked you for questioning, but you appeared to be innocent when I confronted you. So we set you aside. But then last November a body was found in an abandoned house in Southwark. Know you the house I mean?"

I managed a nod.

"We got word of that body through one connected with this Company. Was it you?"

"N-n-no, sir. It was not me."

"Would you swear to that?"

"I would, sir."

"Have a care. We have caught you in one lie already. You claimed to know nothing of one Peter Kenton, yet Bartlemy discovered that you used that name to get a job on the wharf. Redeem yourself now with the truth. Where were you last eventide?"

I said nothing. My father must have got away, else they would not be so desperate for information. And I had enough information now to hang me. The relief I felt at Robert Malory's escape was far outweighed by a sense of certain doom.

"We are in no haste," Master Clement said, his words grinding. "We can keep you here all night, if need be. Where were you last eventide?"

I held my silence, which seemed to double and multiply until it filled the tiny room, pressing down upon me with inconceivable weight.

"*Where were you—*"

"Well, I'll tell you, since he can't," came a voice from the curtained doorway, and my questioner started in surprise. It was Kit, half-changed into street clothes with his doublet unlaced, standing with one hand on his hip and the other grasping the door frame as though he had just leaned in to drop an indifferent word. Then he dropped it, and stunned us all. "He was in the play."

John Clement glanced from him to me, and back again. "We have reason to believe he was not. Why did Master Finch not recognize him?"

"'Tis unlikely anyone could have recognized him, covered head to foot in yon coat of fur." Kit nodded to the opposite wall, where a huge ghostly form, hung upon two hooks, loomed out of the dim light.

"You're saying he was the *bear?*" The man's tone clearly implied disbelief.

"Just so. He was sick yesterday morning, and still sick when he arrived late. The Company thought it best not to let him on stage in a costume he could puke over. Puking within a costume matters not—the skin is due for cleaning anyway."

Master Clement released a short breath through his nose, then turned to his able assistant. "Well?"

"What can I say to that?" Bartlemy exclaimed. "Anybody looks like anybody else in a bear skin."

"I can set you right on the other thing," Kit continued smoothly. "'Twas I got word to you about the body in that old house, though it wasn't supposed to come back to me."

John Clement—reluctantly, it seemed—shifted the focus of his questioning. I heard, as through a fog, Kit explaining our fracas on All Hallow's Eve, making it sound like nothing more than a boy's adventure that turned grim. He told it mostly as it happened, and so plausibly even the false elements made perfect sense. A long pause followed the tale before Master Clement spoke again, returning to the matter at hand. "So you still claim it was this boy in the bear skin yesterday."

"Aye. It was to be me, but I get out of playing the bear anytime I can."

The man turned abruptly to me. "Why did you not say so at once?"

I opened my mouth and tried again, but still could not force a single word.

"What ails you, that you can't speak for yourself?" young Finch demanded.

"He frights easy," Kit explained, with the hint of a sneer. "He used to freeze like this even during a performance. If he weren't his own worst enemy, I would have choked him myself, long ago."

"What suits him for the stage, then?" Master Clement challenged.

"Come and see for yourself, sometime," Kit replied, his voice cold. "If you doubt me otherwise I pray you ask Master Condell, or any of the others."

The Queen's agents were not convinced, but they were out-faced. I recognized their dilemma: Lord Hunsdon, their master, was also our patron, with a long habit of protecting the Lord Chamberlain's Men. Unless John Clement possessed hard evidence to convict me, he could not lay a hand on my person, nor confront a respectable member of the Company with suspicions that might be groundless. So there the matter lay, at an awkward angle: he could get nothing out of me and could open no cracks in Kit's tale.

After a few more questions, mere stabs in the dark, the two of them had no choice but to pack up their doubts and leave with as fair a grace as could be managed—though Bartholomew Finch sent me a look on his way out that clearly expressed his opinion: *Guilty*.

I followed them to the doorway, and found myself trembling violently. Mixed with the relief was a strong tincture of guilt, for I had deceived them. Or allowed them to be deceived. A lie con-sented to was no different than one spoken, to my mind. But honesty was not so simple a proposition as I once had thought.

Nor was friendship. Once the Queen's men were out of sight, a rustling sounded among the costume racks and a disheveled figure emerged—Robin, still in Juliet's white shroud, who had eavesdropped on the interview and made no bones about it. All came clear to me then: it was he who sized my peril when I disappeared and decided he could not let me sink after all, but fetched Kit to my rescue. Not entirely the scared rabbit. "Rob—" I began, my voice catching.

He flung up a hand and backed away. "Say no more. If you are off the hook you were dangling from, 'tis well, but pray you have a care for my virgin ears." With that, he scampered off to change.

I turned to Kit, who had, against all expectation, saved my backside. He spoke before I could: "Someday, we may talk. You interest me; I'll not deny it. There is more to you than can be seen in a sixmonth, and curiosity has the better of me. For now we consider all debts canceled. Content?"

"Content." They were calling for us from the stage. I put out my hand, which he pretended not to see, but turned away with his straight back and gliding walk, ever a figure to inspire and provoke.

That left only me and the bear.

By now, he was little more than a shadow on the wall, but the fading sunlight brushed a gleam upon his glass eye and ivory tooth. He seemed alive and breathing, a broody presence haunting the edges of my life—not just now, but always. He was the unexpected element in the play that reared itself so suddenly the audience gasped aloud; that changed everything, then disappeared. Slowly I crossed the little distance that separated us, raised an unsteady hand, and placed it on his foreleg, high up where the shoulder would be. A powerful muscle had once inhabited that skin, the living flesh of a Brutus or Benjamin or Ajax, that could rip me open with a single swipe. Or, in another mood, fold me to himself and keep me warm. With a long sigh, I leaned my head upon the empty chest.

I might never see my father again. Or he could reappear suddenly, years hence, and change everything. I could expect no more from such a gad-about soul. He had given me, perhaps, all he could: a chance at life, a rousing tale, and a word of advice. "Stick to acting"—another inheritance from him. But if I do, I resolved, the acting remains on stage. When I walk off, it will be as myself.

Master Condell was calling my name. I stroked the rough fur, then let my hand fall and backed away from the beast, taking a last look into his open jaws—which, at that angle, appeared to grin.

As we were locking up the Theater that evening, Ben Jonson arrived with a fair copy of his latest play, which the company had agreed to perform, tucked under one arm. "This is still a comedy, I hope?" Master Will inquired, taking it from him. "You've not delivered to us a changeling child in comic bands?"

"Aye," growled Master Jonson. "'Tis *Every Man in His Humor,* as agreed. I remind you that my tragedies are highly regarded at Oxford—unlike, may we admit, this most lamentable tale of Romeo and Juliet which you trot out every time you need to stuff a house."

"Success is a telling argument, Ben," Shakespeare replied. He and his sparring partner fell in behind me as I trailed Kit and Robin, Condell and Heminges, Watt and Jacob with their torches. I was exhausted, after a day that sorely tried both body and spirit, but by now was daring to hope that the nightmare was over.

"Time will vindicate me," Jonson stubbornly affirmed, and he went on to relate exactly what it was that troubled him about Romeo and Juliet. This seemed to be an old argument—I saw Kit glance back at them with a sardonic grin—but it was new to me. Master Jonson's chief complaint was that the story skipped around too much, and certain other Shakespeare plays were even worse. He believed in something called "the unities," which meant that the action in a play should occur in one time and place, with each scene unfolding directly from the previous one. This was how the Greeks did it.

"But life is not like that," Master Will insisted. "Life cannot be tied in a package. It sprawls and tumbles."

"Oh, life!" Ben Jonson snorted. "Art should exalt life, not reflect it."

"Illuminate it, rather . . ."

True enough, I thought. Life was not theater, where stories come to an end and all is understood. I might never understand Kit, who walked ahead of me now, turning a negligent ear to Robin's

304

ramblings. I might never fulfill Starling's hopes, never satisfy all my mother's aspirations, or my own. The theater could not answer all my questions. But it could, perhaps, illuminate them.

I looked back at it—a worn, somewhat shabby building packed with shadows—and for the first time felt a pure, unmixed affection. I had been driven to it by circumstance, but knew I would stay—for now, at least—by choice. Facing forward again, I caught Master Will's preoccupied smile, as he listened to his companion's weighty judgments.

"Time discloses the truth, and the merit . . . ," Ben Jonson said.

". . . and did you see that gull in the side gallery, with the white sleeves?" Robin cried indignantly. "He blew a tobacco ring right in my face during the ball scene!"

"Receipts down, and the rent due in a month," John Heminges complained. "If Master Giles raises it again we may be playing in the street. . . ."

Bishopsgate loomed out of the darkness, pricked with torch-light. I had a part to learn, a dance to practice, then sleep—the dreamless, unhaunted sleep of an honest laborer whose debts are canceled. Content?

Content.

All the characters named as principal players of the Lord Chamberlain's Men are historical figures, as is the Lord Chamberlain himself. However, Henry Carey (Lord Hunsdon) actually died in 1596, a year before this story takes place. I extended his life a little longer because his sympathetic presence was needed. Lord Cobham, the next Lord Chamberlain, was no theater fan, and London's acting companies went through several anxious months before Cobham himself passed away and the office went to Henry Carey's son, the second Lord Hunsdon.

Lord Hurleigh, Martin Feather, and all the members of the Holy Restoration Society are fictional, though their aims were not. Throughout her long reign, Elizabeth survived several attempts to replace her with a Catholic monarch. The most famous was the Babington plot, which centered around Mary Queen of Scots. Another was the Throckmorton conspiracy of 1583, in which a Catholic nobleman negotiated with agents of Spain and France to invade England and restore the "true church." Just before and immediately after Elizabeth's death in 1603, rumors of plots swirled around Arabella Stuart, a distant cousin of the Queen. The king of all plots was discovered in 1605, when Guy Fawkes attempted to blow up Elizabeth's successor, King James, together with Parliament, making a clean sweep of the Protestant government. Needless to say, he did not succeed.

Readers may wonder why the Globe Theater is not mentioned in this story. The answer is, it wasn't built yet. The Theater, where the Lord Chamberlain's Men performed most of their plays at this time, was owned by Richard and Cuthbert Burbage. Unfortunately, the Burbages did not own the land their structure was built on, and disputes over the rent would soon lead them to seek other options. The result was the Globe—but that's another story.

Shakespeare scholars agree that *The Winter's Tale* was one of his last plays, not an earlier one as it's represented here. But undoubtedly he borrowed the plot from a book by Robert Greene, which had been published in 1588. Suppose Shakespeare wrote the play, shelved it for several years, then came out with a rewrite? It's possible. A historical novelist, like a playwright, might step outside the facts for the sake of a story, but should never step outside the realm of possibility.

Don't miss
THE AWARD-WINNING SALLY LOCKHART BOOKS
by Philip Pullman

The Ruby in the Smoke

Sally Lockhart enters the seamy underworld of Victorian London in search of clues to her father's mysterious death. Pursued by villains and cutthroats at every turn, the daring sixteen-year-old heroine learns that she is the key to two dark mysteries—and it's worth her very life to find out why.

An ALA Best Book for Young Adults • A *Horn Book* Fanfare Honor Book • A *Booklist* Editors' Choice • A *School Library Journal* Best Book of the Year

The Shadow in the North

The year is 1878, and Sally Lockhart has gone into business for herself. When one of her clients loses a large sum of money in the collapse of a shipping firm, Sally seeks out the identity of an elusive industrialist—only to uncover a diabolical plot that could subvert the entire civilized world.

An ALA Best Book for Young Adults • A *Booklist* Editors' Choice Nominated for the Edgar Allan Poe Award for Best Mystery

The Tiger in the Well

Sally Lockhart, trying to put her troubled past behind her, has settled into a comfortable life with her daughter, Harriet, her career, and her London friends. But her world comes crashing down around her when a complete stranger claims to be both her husband and Harriet's father.

An ALA Best Book for Young Adults

The Tin Princess
featuring characters from the Sally Lockhart trilogy

Three young Londoners—Adelaide, Becky, and Jim—journey to a tiny country high in the mountains of Central Europe. They're an unlikely trio to lead a nation, but before long, Adelaide and her friends are forced to fight for the crown—and their very lives!

"A swashbuckling adventure story."—*Booklist*